After six months deeply in love with each other, childhood best friends Logan and Christian are excited for their first summer away from home. With one year of college under their belts, they're ready to grow up and see what the rest of their lives will be like together by strengthening their relationship over the next few months. But fate has never followed their neat plans.

Christian receives an opportunity to pursue one of his greatest unfulfilled passions: acting. It's a chance to explore a talent his parents crushed before he could dream of spending his life studying it—but is he up to the challenge? Is it worth taking the risk, knowing his family won't support him?

Logan struggles with his attachment to Christian and his fears of being left behind. If Christian's career on the stage takes off, will he abandon Logan and replace him with far better lovers? And how can Logan be so hypocritical when another man has caught his eye? Or has that man perhaps captured Christian's attention as well?

Their relationship will be tested far beyond their imagination—but love always has room to grow, even in the face of fear.

PLAYING HOUSE

Rough Play, Book Two

Suzanne Clay

A NineStar Press Publication

Published by NineStar Press
P.O. Box 91792,
Albuquerque, New Mexico, 87199 USA.
www.ninestarpress.com

Playing House

Copyright © 2020 by Suzanne Clay
Edited by Elizabetta McKay
Cover Art by Natasha Snow Copyright © 2020

Printed in the USA
First Edition
March, 2020

Print ISBN: 978-1-951880-76-7

Also available in eBook, ISBN: 978-1-951880-75-0

Warning: This book contains sexually explicit content, which may only be suitable for mature readers, homophobic language from a minor character, and an attempted assault of a trans and a bi character.

To my wonderful spouse, for celebrating every little change in our lives.

Chapter One

Logan's muscles ached like hell. It probably had something to do with the mountain of opened boxes sitting in the corner of the small bedroom. With the massive bed taking up the lion's share of the sunshine-lit room, his empty moving boxes cluttered up the rest. Everything still wasn't in its place, but he couldn't be mad about it right now. This was home for the summer—away from Fulton State University.

Words couldn't express how grateful he was not to be going back to the little town of Greenbarrow. God knew he'd have finer company here than there with his family.

The sound of footsteps crumpling plastic bags on the floor behind Logan made him speak. "You haven't changed a bit."

"Don't need to change when you're perfect." Christian's familiar drawl had the same effect on Logan that it always did: a slow series of tingles drifted down his spine. "Don't be roasting me on how I pack shit."

"You make it so easy." Logan turned around and pointed at the equally messy pile of empty bags. "That. Look at that. I'll buy you suitcases, duffel bags, anything you want—just stop putting everything in a goddamn *trash bag*."

Christian slung an arm around his shoulder and kissed his cheek. "How much does it cost to get you to stop running your mouth?"

Difficult to think of a price, really, when goose bumps were still skittering over his arms. He turned his head and found Christian's mouth less than an inch away. "...half an hour of making out."

"Done."

With a solid shove to his back, Logan landed facedown on the bed, then grunted when Christian's weight crashed down on him. Instincts kicked in—he dug his elbow into Christian's side and shoved him away, then rolled away to get a better position for wrestling.

Six months of dating, and they still acted like they had every day of their thirteen years of friendship. It wasn't an easy habit to break. For every kiss they shared, there was Christian pinning Logan down until he said *uncle* and swore he'd do the dishes that night. Each evening they snuggled in one of the tiny bunk beds in their dorm, and they couldn't keep from shit-talking each other until their eyelids were heavy.

Weirdly, Logan thought being out of college for the summer would make their relationship a little more like a movie—soft, sweet, and romantic—but as he lunged for Christian and pinned an arm to his chest, he realized things might never change. And he was okay with that.

"I said making out," Logan gritted out as he batted one of Christian's massive hands away before it could grab his hair. "Not me kicking your ass again."

Christian laughed breathlessly. He snagged the back of Logan's neck. "This is just foreplay, baby, don't be silly."

Baby. He still wasn't used to that either. The air caught in Logan's chest long enough for Christian to put him on his back. With the sight of his stunning boyfriend rising above him, all dark skin and dangerous eyes and smirking lips, he didn't much feel like fighting anymore.

Whatever energy was overflowing in Christian seemed to dissipate. He trailed the back of his fingers down Logan's cheek, leaving a path of fire behind them. One finger snagged in the neckline of Logan's T-shirt as Christian bit his bottom lip and sighed.

The mood changed fast with Christian, and Logan never knew how to keep up. Not even after all this time. All he could do was watch him with a sense of wonder and see what he was going to do.

"I was gonna ask if you wanted to grab some food now that we're done unpacking," Christian murmured. He tugged at Logan's shirt, and the hook in his belly yanked even harder. "Now I'm pretty sure I wanna eat *you.*"

Logan exhaled sharply. "You know you don't gotta ask."

Christian crashed down, their lips smashing together painfully, as he dug his fingers into Logan's thick curls. As he shoved Logan back on the mattress to try to get better leverage, something fell to the floor, and Christian lifted his head with a huff. "The fuck is that? Are you already breaking shit?"

"Me?" Logan shoved him with a laugh, then rolled over to reach for the fallen binder. "C'mon, this is gonna make you feel old as fuck. You ready?"

"Aw, hell." Christian lay on his side, head supported by his hand. "What's this?"

Logan opened the binder. Inside were a few memories that he wouldn't have shown anybody else for love or money—but Christian was different. He was the man he loved. And these little treasures included him too.

"Oh my God." When Logan held a photograph toward Christian, he took it with another rough chuckle. "You've gotta be kidding me."

"So cute," Logan teased, and Christian elbowed him.

It was an old, battered photo of Christian as a child in his first-ever church play. Some girl was trying to pull off her shoe in the background, and a boy was going completely off-script and pushing someone off the stage, but Christian stood very seriously at the front of the stage as he delivered some poorly written line or another.

"Jesus Christ," Christian breathed, shaking his head, and Logan threw an arm around his waist with a grin, snuggling closer to see better. Christian scoffed. "Damn. Probably a good thing I never went after that shit. I look stupid."

"You're a kid. You all looked stupid." Logan left a messy kiss on his cheek.

"Funny." Christian set the photo aside, then pulled something out from the other sleeve of the binder. "What's this?"

"Oh, that's…" Logan reached to take it away, but Christian was sitting up out of reach. "Hey, c'mon—"

"Ooh, I remember now! Baby's first monologue!"

Logan made another dive, driving Christian to his feet. "Don't! It's awful, man, give it."

"Not a chance in hell!" Christian turned his back to him and began to recite. "Family. Is there any deeper hell than family? Is there—"

Logan couldn't listen to a word. With strength he hadn't used since they'd started dating, he practically crawled up Christian's shoulders and snatched the paper away with such force that he ripped it free from the fingerhold of paper Christian had. "No, we're throwing this shit away right now." The mere memory of how enthralled he'd been by Christian performing it when they were teenagers was embarrassing.

"Hey, hey." Christian grabbed Logan's shoulders, but when he didn't reach for the paper again, Logan stayed still, tension in his chest. "Just 'cuz we were young and awful when we did that shit don't mean we shouldn't keep it. Remember where we came from. You know?"

Logan scoffed an unamused laugh. *Yeah, great to keep it around when we're never gonna get to follow those dreams again. Right.*

"Logan?"

"Just put it away, man." He offered the paper over his shoulder, then turned his head to watch and make sure Christian did as he asked instead of being an asshole.

The knock on the door drew Logan's attention back to the present. "Yeah?"

"Hey, it's me!"

"Just Noah," Christian said absently. "Who the fuck else would it be?"

"Shut up." Logan laughed, but moved to open the door.

"Hey!" Noah grinned up at him, flushed from his own exertions of unpacking. "Just wanted to let you know we've got cookies!"

"Cookies?"

"Yep! From Daiki." Noah gestured behind him, and Logan leaned until he could see a bouquet of sweets set up on the tiny, scratched dining room table. "He sent a note too. He says he wishes he could be here."

The bed creaked behind Logan as Christian spoke. "You're actually sharing your boyfriend's cookies with both of us? Now, that's friendship."

Noah chuckled. "It's not that big a sacrifice—I can't eat that many anyway." He blinked. "I wasn't interrupting anything, was I?"

"Nah," Christian drawled. "We were having a walk down memory lane. Then I thought I'd maybe fuck Logan's brains out. The usual."

Logan turned his head, cheeks flaming. "Shut up!"

"Just saying." Christian shrugged.

"Oh! Uh. Right. Right." Noah stepped back into the hallway, his hands raised. "You know what? I think I'm going to run to the grocery store, so, uh, if you guys need anything, just text me, I'll pick it up, no problem..." He was still talking as he grabbed his keys and walked straight out the front door.

Christian immediately burst out laughing, grabbing his bare stomach. "Did you see the look on his face?"

"Oh, you don't think he's entitled? Are you just gonna announce every time you wanna fuck me?" Logan shut the door and went for his belt with a roll of his eyes. Christian might be obnoxious sometimes, but it didn't stop the fact that his gut was stirred up, eager for a distraction from the binder Christian had tossed to the floor.

The look Christian gave him—dripping with heat and invitation—scalded Logan's skin. Christian licked his lips, his gaze drifting down, down, down, until it rested on Logan's hands. "Well, it's just damn polite, ain't it? Unless you don't want me to. You want him to be surprised when he sits there and hears us fuck every time?"

That was a bizarre thought, one that made Logan snort and roll his eyes and completely ignore the lift of carbonated bubbles in his chest, around his heart. No, instead of thinking about it, Logan kicked his pants off and crawled on top of Christian and got caught up in how goddamn lucky he was. He'd spent months thinking he'd never get to have this, but here they were, safe in their own bedroom, with a bed they could sleep in side by side and a roommate who wasn't going to throw a fit if they made love to each other in the middle of a weekend afternoon. As far as Logan was concerned, there was nothing ahead of them but hope and light.

He was lucky—too lucky—and he refused to think about what might happen if that luck ever ran out.

*

If there was anything that made Christian hungry, it was fucking Logan into the mattress—*their* mattress, he thought with a certain sense of pride. Noah might've donated the bed frame, but Christian had worked tooth and nail to buy them their actual mattress and the sheets that went on it, all so he could surprise Logan when they moved in. The look on his face had been worth every bead of sweat.

It could be a small thing, but after all those years of Logan giving him things, Christian being the reason they had a bed to share was huge. Poverty did that to a guy. He was damn happy Logan didn't have to know what it felt like. Even now, sitting across from him in their favorite restaurant, Christian knew Logan was going to pick up the tab for dinner, and he had to swallow his pride.

Soon he'd be able to do better.

"You there?"

Christian glanced up. "Yeah. Why?"

Logan grinned at him. "You were gone. Your eyes got all foggy. I've been staring at you for a whole minute, and you didn't even notice."

My loss. I could've been staring at you too. Even after all their time together, Christian didn't know how to say that without feeling like a fool—so he smirked. "I guess you liked what you saw."

"Shut up."

Cockiness was easier to put on than sweetness. He knew how to treat Logan like a bro, but anything more than that? They hadn't really had the chance— not in public.

Christian knew how lucky they were to be going to college in Fulton. It was only a hundred miles away from home, but so different from where they came from. Across the restaurant, he could already see another couple—two men—together, their hands joined over the surface of the table. While he and Logan stuck out like sore thumbs in the little diners in Greenbarrow, here, they blended in with the people of color both working and eating. Nobody even looked at the two of them.

Still, it was hard. Christian had spent so long ignoring everything about himself—his sexuality, his attachment to Logan, and his dreams for the future— that getting to express any of them had seemed impossible. He was probably bi. He was in love with

Logan. He couldn't watch a movie without his heart rising into his throat as he took in the elegance of the acting. So what? He was just supposed to ignore years of conditioning and embrace those parts of himself?

"You're about to be gone again."

"Hush." Christian forced himself to fixate on Logan's face. It swam into focus, every beautiful piece of him, and the crackling static in his mind began to fade away. "I'm here now. With you."

Logan's grin softened. "Yeah. Good. You'd better be." The utter adoration in his gaze was familiar, but it had the same searing effect on Christian as always.

Christian sipped his Coke. "When do you start work?"

"Tomorrow night." Logan pulled a face. "I've gotta be there at nine."

"At night?"

"Yep, night stockers typically work then—weird, huh?"

Christian reached out as if to smack him upside the head, and Logan leaned back with another laugh. "I swear to God." Christian kissed his teeth. "Noah too, right?"

"Yep. Same schedule so far. We'll see if they stick to it—I need him to be able to give me a ride there and back."

"They'd better. God. You and me only having one car thing is gonna suck. If I didn't have to use it for my job..."

"Yeah, well." Logan shrugged. "We signed up for it. We've both gotta work. Gotta pay rent, buy food, make sure utilities get paid... I'm not gonna leech off Noah. He's done enough for us. He doesn't need to carry us like we're kids."

"You know I'm with you. That's the whole reason I'm driving all over the city taking people where they've gotta go. Ugh. You learn a lot of things about people from where they want you to drive them, I swear to God."

Christian might've been a driver for the local ride-share service for a few months now, but he hadn't gotten used to it. It brought in enough for him to set money aside for the future—even buy that mattress for them—but not enough to keep Logan from having to work such a late job. "It'll pay the bills. I'm just gonna miss hanging out with you."

"Hey." Logan rested his hand on the middle of the table, voice soft. "I'm still gonna spend time with you. I don't care how tired I am or how fucked up my sleep schedule gets; I'm gonna be with you no matter what."

Christian glanced up. "Yeah?"

"Yeah. Who do you think I am?"

The man I love.

Christian's lips quirked. For once, the future seemed very bright indeed. They wouldn't have homework for a few months, he already had the money he needed to buy his books next semester, and he didn't have to report to soccer training for quite a while. All he had to do was work his ass off, spend time with his boyfriend, and make sure he hung out with Noah. Nothing else could go wrong.

Because of that, it didn't seem right for them to be sitting so far apart—across a table instead of a romantic booth, where he would've snuggled any girlfriend he had. And, as scary as it was, he slid out his fingers to meet Logan's hand in the center of their table.

As they touched, Logan's eyes widened, and he stared at their hands with a sense of wonder he couldn't hide from Christian. Logan turned his hand over, exposing the palm, and Christian covered it with his own.

"We're lucky sons of bitches, aren't we?" he whispered.

Logan nodded. "Yeah. I was thinking about that before we got here. It doesn't seem real. Doesn't feel as if I should get to have you like this."

"Well, you do. Get used to it."

Logan shot him a look, but he was already grinning, eyes sparkling as brightly as stars. "I could get real damn used to having you around all the time—in my bed, in my apartment, in my arms."

Something snaked up the back of Christian's throat—not quite fear, but certainly not bravery—and swallowing it was similar to pushing down a knot. It stuck there, right against his vocal cords, and ached. "...yeah." That was all he could say for now. But the way Logan watched him told him he wasn't upset by it at all.

Footsteps in the aisle made Christian jolt away before he realized what he was doing. He looked up at their server and blinked when he saw what he was holding.

"On the house. Compliments of the management." He set the piece of warm chocolate cake between them, vanilla ice cream starting to melt on top.

"What? We didn't order this," Logan pointed out.

"I know." The server, his name tag reading *Rey*, busied himself with piling their empty dinner plates on the tray he held, not quite hiding a smile. "We have too many slices, and my manager is letting us give one to a few tables." Rey glanced up. "I'm sorry if this is weird, but you guys look so happy. I couldn't resist."

Do we? Christian stared at Logan. *Can everybody really see how this guy makes me feel? How he makes the world light up?* When Logan didn't respond to Rey—only watched Christian back—Christian looked up before Rey could get away. "Thanks. Seriously. This...this isn't cool where we're from—us."

Rey nodded, expression serious and voice soft. "I understand. Trust me. But you're safe here. If you ever doubt it, hey, the next time you come here, ask for me, and I promise I'll take great care of you."

Something about this approachable man of color gave him a sense of safety he hadn't expected. *Are you like us?* The words were on the tip of his tongue, but Rey had already left, and Logan was picking up one of the two spoons on the dessert plate.

The dusky shade of pink on Logan's cheeks was all too apparent, even when he ducked his head.

Christian knew that color. Logan flushed as warmly every time Christian let himself say how he felt about him. It lit a spark of happiness right in his gut. "You're cute when you're happy, babe."

Logan opened his mouth and let out wordless stammering, then immediately started stuffing his face with the cake, and Christian chuckled as he picked up his own spoon. He understood. He didn't want to let Logan know when he was flustered either.

Still a damn pretty sight. Christian decided right then and there he'd do whatever it took to get that expression on his face more often. No more acting as if they were just friends. No more being too shy to hold hands or kiss him in public. They were safe here. They could be themselves.

Maybe their folks would find out about them someday, but not now. Not here. Not until they were ready. He truly believed that to the core of himself. All they had to worry about was getting ready for their second year at college.

As long as Logan was there, Christian knew he could do anything.

*

The second they got home, the sounds of Noah ripping a box open caught Logan's attention, and he pulled Christian inside by the hand. Sure enough, their roommate was sitting in the living room, unpacking the stacks of colorful, plastic dishes he'd brought into their suite almost a year before.

"Aw, you got started on all the fun in here without us," Logan said.

Noah snorted. "I figure one of us needed to. I wasn't sure if you guys were here. And...well, if you were busy, I didn't want to interrupt, uh..."

"Us fucking?" Christian asked with all of the subtlety of a stampeding wildebeest. "Nah, we were getting dinner, but you're right. You're probably gonna hear a lot of it. Might have to start charging you for the show in advance."

"Will you stop?" Logan slapped Christian's arm, then kicked his shoes off. "We're trying to live with Noah, not get kicked out."

"It's fine, seriously." Noah chuckled. "I just don't want to invade your privacy."

While Logan settled next to the box to help unpack, Christian swiped a stack of dishes and headed toward the kitchen, calling over his shoulder as he went. "You've already seen me in nothing but my boxers, dude. Trust me, I'm not worried about what else you might be seeing."

There it was again: the tug at Logan's gut when he thought about Noah's knock on their door earlier. Ordinarily, Logan felt that way when looking at Christian—beautiful and resplendent, laid out on the sheets, all six feet and four inches of him naked and begging for attention. But that couldn't be it. "Ignore him, Noah."

"I'm not very good at that yet."

"You'll get there." Logan smiled at him, and Noah answered with one of his own, his gaze lingering.

Christian came back with a cookie in each hand, working on one. "Damn, these are good."

"We literally just ate dessert."

"Yeah? I'm a growing boy." Christian sat on one of the dining room chairs and kicked his legs out, crossing them at the ankles. "Anyway, I'm not gonna disrespect Daiki by refusing to eat the food he so generously bought us."

Noah pushed the empty box aside. "He'll be happy to hear that." He sighed and sat back, looking at the ceiling. "I wonder if he's in rehearsal. I've been meaning to call him."

"You miss him, don't you?" Logan asked.

"More than I thought I would," Noah admitted. "I'm glad he's got this acting opportunity this summer, but I can't wait to have him back in August."

His phone rang, and Noah looked at it. "Wow, speak of the devil." He answered the call, but looked right at the phone screen—a FaceTime. Noah got to his feet and waved with a grin. "Hey!"

"Hello!" Daiki's familiar voice rang out. "I miss you! Did you get the cookies?"

"I sure did." Noah turned the phone around, and Christian waved where he sat, cheeks stuffed fuller than a chipmunk's. "They're being enjoyed right now."

"Perfect. Christian, don't eat all of them."

Christian swallowed, then sneered at the screen. "Fuck you."

"How's Logan?" Daiki asked.

Logan shifted into view of the phone and gave a quick wave at Daiki, who sat in a relatively dark room, lit only by a small bedside lamp. It had only been a couple of months, but he looked exactly like he had their whole freshman year. He'd been their second suitemate at the time, sharing a bedroom with Noah, and from what Logan understood, they'd jumped on each other just about as fast as Logan and Christian had.

"Hey Daiki, how's things?"

"Fine, fine. My folks are glad to have me back. They keep asking me how school is and talking about what subjects I'm taking next year." He rolled his eyes. "Don't exactly have time to talk about that when I'm rehearsing."

Logan grinned. "Are they nosy?"

"Nope. Just invested. Are you taking care of Noah all right?" Daiki smirked. "He's living with two handsome guys all summer...who knows what could happen?"

"Daiki!" Noah quickly turned the phone back to himself. "Don't be a dick." Even as he laughed, the sound was stilted, and he shot Logan and Christian an apologetic look as he headed for the hallway.

"We'll finish this chat in the bedroom so you stop weirding them out."

As the door shut, Christian looked at Logan. "You weirded out?"

"Nah." Logan shrugged. "Noah's just shy or whatever."

"Guess so."

Logan pulled another box of kitchen supplies close while Christian worked on the second cookie. Logan would give him another few minutes of being a lazy ass before he called him on his bullshit. "You'd think Noah would be used to Daiki's mouth by now."

"Guy's a force of nature." Christian popped the last bite into his mouth and brushed away the crumbs. "Guess he's kinda irrepressible. Must be how he aced his audition for the summer."

"You'd know that better than I would."

"Hey, I never did musical theater—that's a whole different breed of monster."

This was true. Logan's skills lent themselves to writing, but there was a reason he'd always written straight plays rather than libretto. Then again, he hadn't written in ages, and the last time he'd penned something was because he had the obsessive urge to see Christian perform it just for him...

Every single day, those old memories started making more and more sense: how Logan always wanted their futures to intertwine and how Christian was his greatest muse. It was just a shame that playtime was over. They were adults now. Christian might've been lucky enough to score a full-ride scholarship with his soccer skills, but Logan was chained to his family's expectations so they'd pay every penny of his education fees for him—and that meant pursuing a degree in education. They didn't need him to be wealthy, necessarily, just...safe. And playwriting wasn't safe. They'd made that clear.

Teaching literature was the kind of security his parents wanted him to have. At least he'd have the chance to talk to kids about the words that made him passionate. Better than Christian, who'd chosen accounting. How he kept his eyes on numbers instead of acting made no sense to Logan, but they both knew the impossibility of going against what their families demanded.

Even sitting here and talking about Daiki—lucky, fortunate Daiki, able to pursue musical theater even though his traditional grandparents were concerned for his future—brought a dull ache to his chest. "...how do you think he's doing?" Logan asked, barely aware he was speaking.

Christian hummed. He came down onto his knees next to Logan and helped him sort through the other kitchen supplies. "Fine. Probably already a star. Don't think it'll take too long before he scoops up that first Tony—it's gonna be easy for him, once he starts landing the roles. His local playhouse practically begged him to come home, remember? Bet they're hard up for legitimate talent since he ended up leaving."

Damn. The conversation wasn't making the pain any easier. Logan swallowed hard and nodded, then began carrying things into the kitchen to put away.

Grow up. This is your life now. You can see as many plays as you want once you can actually afford it. Right now, you've gotta finish your degree, get a job, and get out of Greenbarrow for good. Logan didn't have many dreams anymore, but the one thing he needed was a life with Christian. They'd stay in Fulton, where they were still learning that they weren't alone. He'd get a job at the local middle school while Christian snagged a starting position of his own, and they'd live in an apartment for a year or two while they saved up for a house before they got married.

Marriage. That had never come to mind before, but the thought of claiming Christian as his own for the rest of his life made Logan's soul sing.

A hand touched his back, and he looked up at the man he loved and blinked.

"You okay?" Christian wrinkled his brow.

Logan smiled. "Yeah, fine. Why?"

The way Christian looked at him, Logan could tell he wasn't accepting his words. Those eyes dragged over his expression, seeing the pain he held deep in his very pores. Logan could never hide from him, and he wasn't sure why he even tried, but Christian rarely pulled his secrets out by force. Instead, Christian kissed him—softly, barely a whisper of contact—before he took one of the big bowls from Logan's hands and reached high to store it above the sink.

"I love you," Logan murmured.

Christian's gaze jolted back to his own. "Where'd that come from?"

"I dunno. Just do." Logan squeezed him around the waist in a quick hug, then headed for the living room. He never made it. Christian snagged him with two strong arms and yanked him until Logan's back hit his lover's chest. Logan laughed, tipping his head back to welcome gentle kisses that took his breath away.

"You know I love you," Christian whispered when he finally broke the contact.

Perhaps one day, they'd be able to say that loudly—shout it from the rooftops, or proclaim it as law wherever they chose to tie the knot far away from their families. For now, he'd take the secret whispers in their kitchen, precious as diamonds.

Noah's bedroom door opened, and he came out, tucking his phone in his pocket. "Sorry about that."

"No problem." Christian let Logan go and turned toward the kitchen door, leaving Logan a little cold and missing his embrace. "We could've handled the unpacking ourselves—no need to apologize for that."

"Oh, no, um..." Noah rubbed the back of his neck. The auburn of his hair clashed with the pink of his cheeks. "I meant what Daiki said. Kind of embarrassing. He's such a kidder. I didn't want you to think he was serious. Please tell me you didn't hear anything else he said."

Logan hadn't heard a thing. He leaned against one of the counters and looked at Christian.

Christian shrugged.

"Pretty sure we didn't…" Logan trailed off as he took in Noah's appearance. Second by second, he was flushing a deeper shade. "Do I wanna ask why you look so red right now? Was it that bad?"

Christian grabbed one of the boxes and began breaking it down with a snort. "Probably just had phone sex is all."

"Hey!" Noah's voice cracked, and he covered his mouth as he stared at the floor. "…y-you know what? I think, uh, I might've left a box i-in the car; let me go check." And then he was gone, leaving the door wide open behind him.

Christian gave Logan a distinct look—*told you so*—then began making his way through another box.

"You're evil," Logan said, giving him a quick pat on the back of the head as he passed him.

Christian's response was a wordless spank that sent Logan reeling ahead two steps.

Chapter Two

Goddamn, I'm bored.

Logically, Christian knew jobs were made to be boring. They were like pulling teeth, each one, and the sooner he accepted that, the better—but, Jesus, something about being a glorified taxi was more annoying than he could have imagined.

He initially thought being a driver for a ride-share service would be a lot of him listening to his favorite music and getting paid to sit on his ass, but the reality of it almost put him to sleep every day. The money wasn't even all that good.

Better than a desk job.

With his future hovering right before him, Christian bit back his frustration and continued on his way to pick up his next ride.

They weren't far off. He pulled in front of the apartment building, and a guy already standing outside with a folder in hand quickly climbed into the back of his car.

"Hey," Christian said as he glanced at the app on his phone, reviewing the destination. "So we're going to the..." As the words entered his mind, his heart skipped a beat. "...Bay Playhouse, right?"

"Yeah." The ride buckled his seatbelt and got comfortable.

Christian looked through the rearview mirror at the guy studying the folder on his lap. It took him a second to remember what he was doing. He finally put the car in drive and pulled into traffic once more.

He didn't even know Fulton had a theater. The knowledge weighed on his mind, pressing down until it dug a dent into his brain. *Bay Playhouse.* Maybe he could take Logan there sometime. Maybe he could go check it out and see what productions they'd put on in the past.

Just to breathe the air for a few seconds.

Stop being fucking weird. Christian inhaled sharply and focused on the road, carefully following the directions given to him.

The rider was silent, and Christian often was too, but that folder was a beacon. It demanded his attention, and he couldn't deny it for long. "Have they got a performance going on this afternoon?"

"What, the playhouse?" The rider shook his head. "Auditions, actually, for the rest of the week."

Electricity jolted through Christian's chest.

"Open ones. Figured I'd give it a shot," the ride continued. "It's a new play and all, so there's nothing I have to live up to. It gives me a chance to make it my own, you know?"

"Yeah?" Christian's voice was thick. "Cool, cool."

Open auditions. Ones that people could just show up for. There was probably a line all the way out the door, heading a few blocks, filled with people eager for stardom. No way this guy would be seen today.

The playhouse wasn't far off. As Christian took the last turn, he expected to see people, but there was no one. Not a single person on the sidewalk or going inside the building. As he pulled up, the guy thanked him and climbed out.

No line. No wait. The man would walk inside and be seen immediately.

The car idled, shaking under him, and Christian took a long few moments to come back to the present. As he waited for the haze to clear, he switched off his app instead of looking for another ride, then let his feet drive him where they might. He went onward, heading nowhere in particular, but part of him was still stuck inside that damn theater.

Five years. Five goddamn years since he'd been on a stage. Perhaps that length of time wouldn't feel long for most people, but Christian was nineteen years old, and even just the past few months had changed his life. Anything longer was practically a lifetime. It connected him to a world he was no longer a part of—middle school, dreaming of being the star player on the soccer team, and rehearsing in his room as he ignored his homework.

Logan had always been right there with him in spirit. God, he could still remember the first time he realized how much Logan loved theater too. Middle school, he thought it'd been—eighth grade, over spring break—when he'd woken up to stones hitting his bedroom window. Christian had to drag Logan through his window before he fell and broke something. Dizzy and possessed by something, Logan's words had been slurred, and Christian had put him at the foot of his bed and told him to sleep there—no more sharing the bed how they had when they were kids, not when they were thirteen and almost grown. But Logan had been carrying something.

A play, hurriedly handwritten in sloppy ink. Nothing long or fully fleshed out, but just a long, amateur monologue.

It stuck to Christian as if it was a great work of art.

He hadn't meant to memorize it. He hadn't meant to quote it to Logan the second he saw his eyes open the next morning—but he couldn't help himself. Sleep hadn't been on his mind. All he knew was that Logan had opened a door for the both of them, where Logan would eventually write world-altering plays, and Christian would be his lead actor in every single one of them.

It was what would get them out of Greenbarrow—what would get them to California where they'd follow their dreams.

It hadn't happened, of course. Not a surprise. Two black boys from a tiny-ass town in Georgia becoming famous? Even now, the idea was laughable.

Then why aren't you driving home?

A horn blew, and Christian slammed his foot on the brakes a second before someone blew past him in an intersection. He'd almost run a stop sign. *What the fuck is wrong with me?*

He pulled forward, shaking, and parked on the edge of the sidewalk so he could rest his head on his steering wheel and force himself to breathe.

I don't care about any of this. This isn't me. I've moved on. That was fucking high school, all right? I'm in college now. I've gotta pay my bills and make sure I've got a future ahead of me. I can't be playing kid games anymore.

The thoughts didn't sound like him anymore, but he couldn't identify the voice.

He stayed there until the world began to melt away, searching diligently for the part of himself that would bury the old passion where it belonged. He didn't care how long it would take—he'd fucking do it.

*

Going without sleep had been easy for Logan during his freshman year of college. With how tests and projects kicked up late in the spring semester, sometimes the only way he and Christian would get alone time together was in the dead of night, where they could talk about their days and fall asleep in each other's arms just before dawn. A night job stocking a grocery store might not have made sense for most people, but it worked for Logan.

It was their first day out of training, and his body already ached all over, but at least he wasn't tired.

The job wasn't bad, anyway. Their responsibilities were clear-cut. The staff kept to themselves so they could get their work done before the store opened. Something told Logan he'd be happy to quit when he went back to school in August, but for now, the pay was worth it—and the company wasn't bad either.

He had Noah. Noah had gotten him the job when Logan began worrying how he and Christian were going to share their one car. Noah had saved both of their asses, and he probably didn't even know it.

At some point, Logan was going to change that. He'd give Noah anything to thank him for the opportunities he'd showered on Logan and Christian.

"Time for our first break," Noah announced, and Logan came out of his thoughts. Noah stood on his tiptoes to put the last can on the shelf of pasta sauce he'd been stocking, then grinned at Logan. "How're you feeling?"

Logan shrugged. "Fine. Not tired yet. Wish it was lunchtime though. I could eat a horse."

Noah laughed as he stepped away from his pallet. He went toward the end of the aisle, and Logan followed. "I'm still not used to calling it 'lunch.' It takes midnight snack to a whole new level."

"You're right." As they came out toward the registers, Logan caught sight of everyone else heading toward the break room for their fifteen minutes of rest. "I'm gonna buy a soda. You want one?"

"Sure." Noah beamed. "I'm just going to run to the restroom. I'll catch up with you in a minute."

"Cool." Logan watched Noah leave, wondering how the hell he could be so chipper at midnight, then headed for the break area with everyone else. He clocked out for his break on the way, then took the time to buy two small bottles of soda, taking care to pick out one he knew Noah loved.

As he propped himself against the wall outside the break room, waiting for Noah, he studied his fellow employees. For some reason, he hadn't expected the workforce to be so similar to a clique. They were all out of high school, and he thought they'd have dissolved quickly. But, sure enough, people were grouped together, laughing and gossiping about others he didn't know. The words floated through one of his ears and out the other. Eventually, he caught sight of a girl sitting by herself—young, her black hair sleek and straight, and her narrow, dark eyes focused on the book spread out on the table. She was the only person everyone seemed to be giving a wide berth to.

After a few seconds, she glanced up and met his eyes and gave him a smile, and he glanced away on instinct. *Man, don't just be staring at people, what's wrong with you?* A year out of high school and spending most of his time with only Christian had diminished his old habits, such as going over to ask her name and compliment her on how her vibrant green nail polish played against her tawny skin. It was as if he'd never been social in his life. He'd never thought about it before now, but the realization gave him pause.

Don't think too hard. You're probably just tired.

Realizing how time was quickly passing, Logan checked his watch. Several minutes had already gone by, and there wasn't much time left in their break. *So where the hell is Noah? Is he not feeling well?* Just in case he'd missed him somehow, Logan scanned the break room again, and when he came up empty, he decided to check the bathrooms.

The din of noise quieted behind him until there was nothing, his shoes quiet against the floor. Eventually, as he drew near, he heard a rough, muffled voice he didn't recognize, and he blinked, wondering who it might be. The bottles of soda were cool in his hands, sweating condensation over his fingers as he walked.

His blood went colder still when he turned the corner.

Noah shrank against the wall beneath a much larger man's shadow; he looked so small and afraid that Logan's heart kick-started into action. He put the sodas on a nearby display stand and had his hands curled into fists before he even knew what he was doing.

He and Christian had done this for years, finding someone being bullied and getting the asshole off their back. They'd never been able to throw punches first and ask questions later—they couldn't get away with that where they lived—but the threat had always been enough to de-escalate the situation. He swore he could feel Christian's energy right beside him, and he rode the wave straight to the trouble.

"How's it going?" Logan asked sharply.

The guy whipped his head around.

Huge, blond, looking as if he'd just walked off a football field—just the sight of him unsettled Logan. With no name tag, Logan couldn't even identify him.

The guy flicked his gaze over Logan. "What?"

"Just seeing what's going on." Logan thrust his chin in the air, sending the guy a heated gaze. He was aware of Noah staring at him, but he didn't move his eyes from the other man.

The man—*Blondie*, Logan decided—snorted, thumbing toward him as he looked down at Noah. "That your boyfriend?"

Before Noah could answer, Logan took two steps closer. "You wanna step away from him, pal?"

Blondie chuckled, a rotten and dark sound, then shook his head as he pulled away from Noah. "Whatever." He slammed his shoulder against Logan's as he walked past him, and by the grace of God alone did Logan manage to keep his footing.

He followed Blondie with his eyes for a few seconds, making sure he was going for good, then turned toward Noah. Noah stared at the floor, his hands pressed against the wall behind him, as though he was trying to blend in with the paint.

Logan hurried over. "Hey, you okay?"

Noah nodded jerkily. "Yeah."

"You sure?"

Noah hesitated. "I, uh. I have a history with that guy."

Logan looked over his shoulder. "What do you mean?"

"It's been a while. I never thought..." Noah shook his head. "I knew him when I was younger. We went to middle school together. And he, uh...remembered me." He spat a swear under his breath and raked a hand through his hair. "God, I never would've applied for a job here if..."

Understanding came. Just after Christmas, Noah had sat Logan down and explained what Christian had apparently known for months—that Noah was trans. It was a secret as vital and precious as Logan's own queerness, and he'd tucked it in his heart, promising never to breathe a word about it. That trust didn't come lightly, Logan knew. Receiving it made Noah's privacy and safety more important to Logan than any inconvenience it might give him.

Like right now. He'd rather be late coming back from break, as long as he made sure his friend was all right.

"What'd he say?"

Noah shook his head and answered, words clipped. "I'm not telling you. Don't ask me again."

"Okay." *What do I do here?*

Logan'd never been very touchy-feely with his friends, but maybe Noah needed a hug. Maybe he needed some secret comforting words that people like Logan didn't know. Not for the first time, Logan regretted being so *bad* at being queer. It seemed as if everybody online knew what to say to help somebody dealing with fuckheads, but he didn't have a damn thing ready. *Fuck.*

When Noah glanced at the bathroom again, Logan cleared his throat. "Listen, I'm not gonna leave you alone for the rest of the night, so you might as well pop in there and do what you've gotta do before we head back to work."

Noah didn't meet his eyes. "You don't have to do that."

"I know. Whatever. I'm just gonna hang out here and wait for you and sip my soda." He grabbed one of the bottles and cracked it open. "Cool?" *Nobody's gonna give you shit while I'm here. I don't give a fuck who it is.*

Though Noah took a visible deep breath, none of the tension left his face. "If you're sure it's not inconveniencing you."

"Nah. Go on."

Noah slipped inside the bathroom, and Logan took a long drink. Anger still burned inside him. He'd find that asshole, if he had to, and give him a piece of his mind, and beat the shit out of him—

And lose your job? Leave Noah here all alone to deal with him and whoever else might have something rude to say? And it's not as if you have proof Blondie did or said anything—who's gonna listen to what you have to say?

No. Cornering that guy wasn't the answer. There was safety in numbers. He'd just stick close to Noah and never let him out of his sight. They'd work every shift together. Logan would help him unload all of his pallets and stock each shelf. They'd become such a dream team that no manager would consider separating them.

Easy. Worth it to know Noah was safe and happy.

Noah came out, the sound of the hand dryer blowing behind him. He cleared his throat as he stared at his feet. "Okay, let's go."

"Yep." Logan kept pace beside him, offering the bottle of soda he'd bought him. "Here. Still cold."

"Thanks." Noah didn't say another word, but he gulped down the drink, white-knuckling the bottle. After a few seconds, he burped and quickly covered his mouth.

"You're excused." Logan bumped their shoulders together gently, but he didn't force him to talk. As far as he was concerned, they could work just fine in silence, and if Noah needed to vent, Logan would be there.

As they went back to work, he became Noah's shadow. He made sure that they kept pace with their quota. While all of their coworkers had earbuds in, silently doing their tasks without comment, eventually, Noah began to speak once more. He and Logan kept up a running commentary, discussing their relationships with their boyfriends and their classes for next semester.

It worked. Nobody even looked at them sideways—and that only confirmed Logan's determination to stick close by.

Lunch came in the wee hours of the morning, just a bit before sunrise, and Logan immediately found Noah sitting with his brown bag packed with a sandwich and chips. Logan sat beside him on the floor, where they could stare out into the night and see the sky starting to turn gray. *Let everybody else eat in the break room. That's fine. They don't need to know us.*

Logan held out one of the two tiny Snickers bars he'd brought, and Noah cracked a small smile as he took it.

There we go. That's what I wanna see.

Logan opened his own sandwich bag. "Y'know, now that we're the losers with shitty sleep schedules, we need to hang out a lot more."

Noah chuckled. "That's really how it's going to be, isn't it? God. Might as well say goodbye to seeing any of my other friends this summer. Even on my days off, I'm pretty sure all I'm going to want to do is sleep."

"Fine. Sleep. Sleep all you want—but I'm gonna be waking you up for something. Movies. Bingeing a show. Anything. Be ready."

Noah ducked his head, but he couldn't hide how his smile grew. "Video games?"

"Mm." Logan shifted closer, their shoulders touching. "You're on, man."

Color spread over Noah's pale cheeks, just beneath his few freckles.

He was a shy kind of guy, it seemed, blushing at every damn thing under the sun. Perhaps he wasn't used to people making a personal effort to hang out with him. Hell, maybe he was just thankful Logan was staying close by. Either way, Logan decided not to comment on that flush. Better he not embarrass the guy and make it worse.

Chapter Three

I don't know what to tell you.

Christian lay on his side next to Logan, watching him sleep in the sunbeams flooding their room. *It's nothing. It doesn't mean a damn thing, but...if anybody would understand, it'd be you.*

Just an hour ago, Logan and Noah had gotten home from their first night at work, and they hadn't done anything but brush their teeth and crash. Though all Christian wanted to do was bubble up about how he couldn't get the fucking audition out of his head, he had to let his lover sleep. They had to work again the next night. If Logan was exhausted and ended up dropping something and breaking it, Christian wouldn't forgive himself.

It meant Christian had to do this alone.

What *this* was, he still didn't know. It shouldn't be hard to get a damn audition out of his head—but it was clinging on, whispering to him that he might as well go check it out, just for old time's sake.

As if the second he got there, he wasn't going to fall in love with it.

He knew himself. He always tried keeping attachment at bay, but once something got in, he couldn't get away from it. Logan was a prime example. He'd been there since age six, and he'd be there until Christian died. Soccer was another—he lived, breathed, and ate it, and his body thanked him for it. A long time ago, acting had been one too. Something childish he could put down; it didn't matter nearly as much as other things. Acting couldn't make him a living, he'd been told, and he already had what he needed to get into a good college: soccer. Nothing else was important.

Who was he to tell his parents they were wrong? His mom wanted the best for him. His stepdad probably didn't give all that much of a shit, but since Christian didn't care about his opinions, it didn't matter anyway. And his dad... He didn't think much about him anymore, if he could help it—especially not since he'd begun a relationship with Logan. There was no safety there. Just danger.

Acting was one of those things his dad would consider *dangerous*. There was nothing masculine about it. It wasn't like working on a car or in the yard. It didn't do anything useful.

His dad had made it quite clear what he thought about "feminine" things, and what would happen to Christian if he stepped too close to the edge of one of them.

Logan might've started to undo the damage, but even as Christian climbed out of bed, he heard the whispers in the back of his mind. *"There's nothing natural about those two men living together next door. You make sure you raise yourself up right. You'll never be too old for me to whip you."*

The shadow it cast over him persisted as he dropped to his knees by the last of their unpacked boxes: the three containing their school supplies. He knew exactly which one to reach for, and how deep to slide his hand in before he found what he was looking for. A blue folder with his name and the year he was in ninth grade written on the front—the one and only acting class he'd taken. He'd signed up secretly, then dropped out of it the second his mom saw his first report card and demanded he stop wasting his time.

But it had been long enough to let his teacher give him something he could never bring himself to throw away. He took a deep breath and opened the folder.

His headshot from when he was fourteen. All the students had taken them in class, and his teacher had edited the photos herself. When she passed the pictures back a few days later, Christian had been astounded at the person he saw looking back at him. He'd tried to look tough when she turned the camera on him, but she'd reminded him that it was better to come across as *approachable*, and he'd done his best to smile for her. The boy captured on this piece of film had sparkling brown eyes, smooth dark skin, and teeth that gleamed. It was possibly the only picture he had of himself smiling.

Too young to use for an audition.

He wasn't going to go, of course. He just wanted to reminisce—wanted to remember the man he could've been if life had been different. Maybe if his family had a little more money, or he had more time, or his teacher had stopped him the day he turned in his notice to drop the course. But why would she? She had a whole class full of students to foster and teach.

There was no reason to keep him.

One more assignment lay hidden beneath the headshot: the résumé he'd typed up, listing all of his acting experience from childhood plays at church to those precious few experiences in middle school. Each role was immortalized on this piece of paper...and he couldn't use any of them for something professional.

The paper shook in his hands, and he set it down and dragged his legs to his chest.

Sometimes he wished he could go back to his younger self and tell him not to give up. So what if their dream colleges were fifty thousand dollars a year? So what if he hadn't gotten a full scholarship to any of them? Maybe it would've been worth it to take out loans. Hell, they might not have needed to go to college at all. He and Logan could've ended up in California making pennies, and they still might've been happier than the two sorry souls who'd graduated from high school without hope.

Sometimes, he wished he could change the path he was on.

Silence. Nothing but the sound of Logan breathing in his sleep. Nothing awake but Christian and the dreams deferred, until they were buried deeper than the center of the earth.

But through the quiet, he swore he could hear the faint rippling of the air around him, quivering and whispering and begging...

Fuck it.

Christian flew to his feet and lit his closet with his cell phone, his hands nearly ripping shirts off their hangers to see them better. All he needed was one shirt, just one that would make him look even slightly professional, like...like the pink button-down, the one he'd bought just because it made Logan look at him as though he was something delicious. The one that had made Logan sneak into the fitting room with him and blow him, where anyone could've heard them, because he looked so goddamn good in it.

He pulled it on and went to the bathroom, where he cast a critical eye over himself. He'd gotten his hair taken care of only a week before—the drop fade looked clean, and so did the short curls on top of his head. His skin was clear. When he put on the shirt, the lights in the bathroom brought out the warmth in his skin tone.

I can't be doing this, I just can't. But even as he thought it, he pulled out his cell phone and looked at himself through the lens. It wasn't perfect, but...if he turned this way, slightly, and held his arm just so, then...

Twenty pictures of variations of his head and shoulders filled his phone as though he was in a trance.

Noah had already set up Daiki's printer to his own laptop. Daiki was always printing out pictures and covering his walls in them—inspiration, he insisted, similar to mood boards, whatever the hell that meant. The printer was out in the open, on the desk pushed against the living room wall so they could all use it if needed.

It only took a few seconds of searching to find the photo paper, glossy and perfect.

Seconds more to plug his phone into the computer.

And then he was printing.

I'm a fucking fool. Look at this. Christian rubbed his face as he sat back in the chair and listened to the printer quietly chug along. *Anybody who's serious about this audition has actual professional experience. They're ready for shit like this. They don't take pictures on their phones and call that a headshot.*

No, he wasn't going anywhere today. He'd humiliate himself in front of people who lived in this very town. They'd never forget him.

The printer cut off, and he peeked, catching sight of his own face sitting in the tray. He plucked the photo up and examined the colors in the light.

It wasn't bad.

This is why I need you, Logan, to stop me when I do ridiculous shit. He was already opening up a word processor and downloading a template for acting résumés. In went his name, his number, and, embarrassingly, the last play he'd done in middle school.

They'd laugh him out of the theater. He couldn't bear to put anything older on there, but he printed it out anyway.

There it was. Christian Daniels and his résumé.

I don't even know what this play is about. He huffed and stood up. *I should go back to bed.* But he only took two steps before he returned to the laptop.

Research was vital, he remembered his teacher saying. He opened the browser and searched for Bay Playhouse, then the play they were currently auditioning for. Brief information. The woman who wrote it— Amanda Wagner—was a graduate of Fulton State, apparently, and her play, *Gunpowder*, was her first production since leaving school.

A love story. Two female nurses, falling in love while tending to soldiers during a war.

I can't be thinking about auditioning for this. It's about women falling in love. That's diverse enough. They're not gonna put a black man on stage in the middle of it. He closed the browser, shoved away from the desk, and started to pace. *They're not gonna be looking for somebody like me.*

But they were. He had the bare glimpse of it seared behind his eyelids: two male roles, ages eighteen to twenty-five.

And he was nineteen, wasn't he?

How far am I gonna let this go? Christian sank to the floor and dropped the headshot and résumé. *I can't dig this up. I can't. It took me too damn long to forget how much it hurt to let it go. I can't live through that again. I already lost my chance.*

Yet, he burned hotter than fire, scorching the carpet around him, threatening to take down the very walls.

He missed it. He admitted that much. He had never buried the desire to return to the stage. Every single time he watched a movie, he picked it apart and learned from it. No one knew. No one *needed* to know, not even Logan.

Somehow, he still remembered a monologue. He could recite it in his sleep. It was old now and not nearly as relevant as what others would use during an audition, but it was there.

Acting was in his blood. And if he didn't take this chance, he'd never forgive himself.

Just one audition. You'll go in there, be a fool, bomb it, and then that love will be killed for good. You'll never want it again.

Getting ready was a blur—washing his face, brushing his teeth, and forcing himself to eat a granola bar so he had food in his stomach. He had just enough time to regret it when his body began churning, and then he was looking at his watch and realizing that if he didn't do this now, he never would.

They might let me be part of the crew. I think that'd be good enough. All I need is to watch these people on the sidelines...

The thought carried him all the way to the car.

He remembered the way to the theater without even putting it in his phone. By the time he pulled up, he wasn't any more ready than he had been when he left.

But there were cars in the parking lot—the same ones that had been there the day before. People inside were waiting for him.

Let's fucking do this.

Entering a professional theater was so different from his performances in church and school. There weren't poster board signs everywhere telling him about the life of Jesus or the upcoming exam schedule. Instead, neatly framed photographs of every production this theater had put on lined the walls. The photos of the small stage showed lovingly crafted scenery behind the casts, with passion radiating off the page. Those actors, tired from a long week of performances, were still gleaming with love and life. They had no regrets, only dreams.

I want that. Christian's throat tightened as he took a shaky breath. *I want that so bad.*

"Excuse me."

Christian turned around, eyes widening. The second he saw the older white woman standing behind him, he opened his mouth, ready to apologize for trespassing.

"You must be here for the auditions." The woman smiled. "Is this your first time?"

Her cheerfulness threw Christian off his rhythm, and he took a moment before he nodded. "Yes, ma'am."

"I can walk you to where you need to be if you'd like?"

"Yes, ma'am, thank you." Christian dipped his head and followed her down the hall.

"I'm sure they'll be happy to see you, sweetheart." Her low heels clicked quietly on the floor as she led the way, gray hair gleaming from the overhead lights. "They've just set up. You're here early. I think you might be the first of the day."

He made a quiet sound and cleared his throat. "Dunno if that's such a good thing."

"Oh, they enjoy early risers, no mistake about it. Sends a good, clear message about your ability to be on time. I'm Dottie, by the way."

"Christian, ma'am. It's nice to meet you."

"Oh, no, the pleasure's all mine. Are you going to school at Fulton State?"

"Yes, ma'am."

"Do you very much like it there?"

His experiences at FSU were hard to put into words. The year before, he'd discovered a world unlike any he'd ever known—one he actually belonged in. Color filled the campus. One little sexual experiment with Logan and their girlfriends led him to explore the queer part of himself he'd always kept under wraps. Months of ethical nonmonogamy— dating both his girlfriend Charlotte and Logan—led all the way to Charlotte breaking things off with him so he could focus on a relationship with Logan, all without Christian's agreement that it was something he wanted. He was still bitter that Charlotte would make such a huge decision without discussing it with him. And then he'd almost ruined his relationship with Logan before it even really started, all from his own fear...

"It's all right," Christian finally said.

She hummed. "I hope it'll grow on you, Christian. And, if not, I hope you find what you're looking for."

Why are you being so kind to me? He clutched the folder to his chest, his heart racing beneath it.

Finally, she stopped beside a door and knocked on it. When a voice inside rang out to come in, she looked at Christian, beaming. "That's your cue, sweetheart. Just go on in there and do your thing. Good luck!"

He stepped back so she could pass around him. "Thank you, ma'am, I appreciate it."

"Happy to help!"

Dottie went back down the hallway, and Christian gave himself one more chance to take a deep breath before he opened the door.

The room was painted a brilliant shade of red he hadn't been expecting, and Christian lost a moment as he took in the rich tone around him. Three people sat behind a table, each with papers in front of them that they were still sorting out. One, the only man, sipped from a tumbler of coffee the size of an infant, and the woman in the middle of the three flashed Christian a smile.

"How're y'all doing?" The second the slow drawl slipped out, Christian wanted to shoot himself in the foot. Nervous though he was, he wished it worked in his favor—making him sharper and able to give these people what they wanted, not making him the good old southern idiot.

"Good! Good." The woman's grin only grew. She had startling green eyes, so vibrant he couldn't be sure if they were contacts. There was an easy way about her that he wanted to feed off so he could relax for two damn seconds. "You can come in further, if you want."

He was still standing in the doorway. He held back an impatient sigh at himself and pushed forward instead, letting the door shut quietly behind him. "My bad. I'm Christian."

"It's nice to meet you, Christian." The woman stood up and held out a hand.

Without thought, he opened his folder and put his headshot and résumé straight into her grip, and when she laughed he realized she'd intended to shake his hand. "I'm sorry."

"You're nervous." She set his headshot down without even looking at it but kept her eyes on his. "You can relax, I promise. I'm Amanda."

Amanda Wagner. The author of the play, then. No wonder she was right here in the center of the action. He shook her hand. With each second that he looked her in the eye, his muscles loosened up. "It's nice to meet you too, ma'am."

"Just Amanda, please. This is Sage, our director," she said as she gestured to the woman sitting on her left. "And Kumar, our producer."

Already wishing he'd printed out more copies of his headshot, Christian could only favor them both with a handshake the second their hands shot out toward him. "Good to meet you both, sir, ma'am."

"So polite." Sage's eyes sparkled as she picked up the résumé he'd set in front of Amanda. She skimmed it, then tossed it back to Amanda in less than a few seconds.

"Pretty short résumé," Amanda murmured once she picked it up.

Run. Get out. Run for the fucking hills, man. Though Christian's legs burned to escape, he fought not to hang his head. "Afraid I've...been out of practice for a little while."

Kumar made a sound as he set down his coffee cup. "So what brought you in today? Getting back into practice?"

"Well, I..." Christian had never been very good at finding the right things to say. He fucked things up constantly. Whatever pretty words they wanted, he'd never be able to find them, and he accepted that. The best he could do right now was be honest. "...I missed it, truth be told. Haven't done any work since...middle school, actually. But there isn't a day I don't think about it."

"Acting." Amanda rested her chin on her folded hands.

"Yes, ma'am. Sometimes I think I might've cut out a piece of myself when I stopped." He paused. "I'm, uh, getting ahead of myself though. Rambling. My bad."

"That's okay." Her smile widened again. "I'll cut you a deal, okay? It was rude of me to say that about your résumé, and I apologize. If you can forgive me for that, I'll forgive you for rambling."

There was a sweetness in her tone he wasn't expecting. Something told him auditions weren't this kind—that he didn't deserve the patience she'd given him. She wasn't really upset with his rambling, but she was giving him an escape. He could read it right there on her face. And the more he looked at her face, the more he wanted to give this entire meeting the respect it deserved, no matter how shaky he was.

"I believe I can do that." He made himself speak slowly, smoothing out the curve of his accent. He took a few steps backward so he could see all three of them easily. "Congratulations on completing your play. That sort of thing is a dream come true."

Amanda's smile softened. "It really is. Everyone dreams of producing their own work, but getting the opportunity to do it right here in town is excellent. Now I just need the right people to bring it to life." She inclined her head in his direction. "You have something prepared for us?"

"Yes, ma'am."

"Perfect." She sat forward in her seat. "If you don't mind looking at me as you deliver it?"

His own amateur nature embarrassed him again—he had no idea where else he might look—but he opened his mouth and let the words flow.

It was...easier than he remembered. Looking Amanda in the eye, he delivered phrases he shouldn't have recalled, but dripped like free-flowing water without hesitation. He painted a picture so vibrantly he couldn't help but live in it. Christian Daniels had no place here. His experiences could only shape so much of the world. They were small and tame. He lived within the lines: heteronormative, obedient to his family, and respectful to anybody who perceived themselves as his betters.

He was damn well sick of it. And perhaps that was why it was so easy to slip seamlessly into another role.

He tasted the tension in the air. A firecracker had lit inside his chest, the wick smoldering and his heart dangerously close to an explosion.

Unless he was with Logan or on the soccer field, Christian never got the chance to let go. With a ball at his feet, Christian could let himself spark and steal the eyes of the world. With Logan, he could tear his ribs open and show him his most intimate secrets.

But here, before Amanda and Sage and Kumar, he could light an entire block of TNT with one sparkler, and he was so very tempted to let it take him over.

But then the words ended. He came to the conclusion of the monologue, and for a moment, he couldn't find his mind again. Maybe he'd finally done it—found his escape.

The shuffling of paper shot him back to reality, and he took a sharp breath, zeroing in on the sound, then the people before him. Sage was writing on a legal pad, and Kumar sat with his eyes closed, hands tented. But Amanda watched him right back, just as she had his entire performance.

Fuck, he didn't know how to come back down. He might have one foot back in the room, but the rest of him still rippled nearly to the point of pain. He was straddling worlds, and he wasn't ready to be himself.

"That was lovely," Amanda murmured.

Christian gulped and gave a short half bow because he couldn't quite find the words yet.

"Thank you for your time, Christian. We'll be in touch if we'd like to have you here for a callback."

"Thank you, ma'am." He was half hoarse, but he couldn't leave the room without giving them one last impression. Christian came forward and shook their hands—Sage first, then Kumar cupping him between both of his palms as he gave a firm shake, then Amanda who gave him a squeeze.

He imagined he saw something encouraging in her gaze, and he rode it all the way into the hall.

He managed to take himself outside, but the second he reached his car, he realized he was too stirred up to drive. His whole body vibrated. If he put himself behind the wheel of a car right now, he'd cause at least half a dozen wrecks. No, he'd walk it off as best as he could.

What just happened in there? As he made his way down the unfamiliar sidewalk, he knitted his hands around the back of his neck. *You intense bastard. Probably scared them half to death. Professionals don't do that nonsense. They keep their heads. They stay in the moment and don't let it control them.*

It was almost a relief, really, knowing he was likely not what they were looking for—how could he be, if he acted like that? He wouldn't get a callback, and that was a blessing. If he did, he'd have to feel as if he was burning alive all the time.

He was going to be an accountant. He was going to have a safe, financially successful life, gray at the edges but pleasant enough. As long as Logan was there, Christian could handle the boring day job. He could let soccer fizzle into nothing once he was out of college.

And he could burn whatever part of his soul was so captivated by theater to the ground, bury the ashes, and make sure they never found a way to rise— no matter how effervescent he felt right here and now.

Chapter Four

For one foggy moment, Logan didn't expect to wake up alone. It took him a few seconds to remember that his sleep schedule no longer matched his lover's— that the light peeking through the blinds belonged to the afternoon, not the morning.

What time is it? He rolled over and squinted at his phone, looking past the two message alerts to see the clock instead. *Three? Jesus.* He'd already wasted most of the day. As he checked the alerts, he caught sight of his texts.

"Out for a walk. Be home soon." From Christian, and then the follow up. *"Don't tell me you're still asleep."*

Logan huffed out a quiet laugh and shot him a text back. *"Some of us didn't get in bed until 6am. So sue me."*

It was a shame. More than anything, he missed the feeling of waking up with Christian.

Up and at 'em. Might as well eat something. He crawled out of bed and pulled a pair of pajama pants over his boxers, foregoing a T-shirt—it wasn't anything the men here hadn't seen before. *Might as well throw some food together for Noah too.*

Bare feet padding across the carpet, Logan stretched his arms over his head and yawned. Noah's bedroom door was shut, and Logan slowed, considering it. Noah had worked his ass off at work. He deserved to sleep in, but he wasn't the kind of guy who liked wasting daylight either.

I can pack the food up and save it for him for later. The intimacy of the thought gave him pause. *Wait. What, am I packing his lunch box here? Chill out, Suzy Homemaker.* Logan shook the sleepy haze out of his head and continued to the kitchen.

They didn't have a ton of food. Noah had gone shopping, but Logan hadn't found his way to the store yet. While the general rule was that they could share food as long as they replaced it, he didn't want to deprive Noah of something he'd been planning to enjoy later.

Not as though you have much of a choice right now.

Sandwiches it was—something cheap and easy to replace. The wrapped bread on the counter wouldn't stay fresh for long anyway. The thick, crusty loaf made his mouth water as he worked, stacking meats and cheeses on top of slices smeared with condiments.

When Logan heard the front door open, he peeked over his shoulder with a smile. "Hey."

"Hey there." Christian kicked his shoes off, sending one flying across the room. "About time you woke your lazy ass up."

"Excuse me, who here was working all hours of the night trying to pay our rent?" Once Christian was in range, Logan snagged him by the front of his shirt, but stopped when he saw what he was wearing. "Nice. Does dressing fancy snag you more tips?"

Christian fingered the soft material of the pink button-down and cleared his throat. "Why do you say that?"

"I can't see you wearing it just for fun. Looks good though." *Real good.* His mouth was watering over more than the sandwiches. The familiar, pleasant warmth that always came in Christian's presence blossomed. "Something tells me you didn't wear it for me to check you out."

Christian chuckled and shook his head, kissing Logan's temple as he slid past him. "No, I, uh...I had some plans today."

Plans. Christian wanting to look that good for *plans* didn't seem as if it would work in Logan's favor. As Logan leaned against the counter, he pushed his initial suspicions away. "What'd you do?"

Christian cracked open a can of soda from the fridge and shrugged. "Just thought I'd take a chance on something, that's all. Is that for me?" he asked, nodding toward the sandwich.

"Oh. Sure." Logan pushed it toward him and started working on a second one. His stomach nervously flipped. "Are you gonna tell me what chance you took?"

"Yep. Just didn't know how you'd react." Christian picked up the plate, grabbed the big bag of Doritos from the pantry, and walked past him to sit at the dining room table. "I auditioned for a play today."

Logan dropped his knife. Out of all the things he'd been expecting to hear, that hadn't appeared anywhere on the radar. An image flashed before his eyes—watching the third straight performance of Christian's last play in middle school, memorizing every word so he could watch it in his head when he couldn't fall asleep. Then it was gone again, and he realized Christian was staring at him. "I didn't even know we had a theater in town."

"Right?" Christian grinned. "I had a ride yesterday—cool guy, gave me a pretty damn good tip—and he had me take him to the theater so he could join the open auditions. Told me all about it. I couldn't get it out of my head. I just climbed out of bed today, took a headshot in the bathroom, threw a résumé together, and drove right over."

"Oh." Logan set the knife in the sink. "How'd it go?"

"I dunno. Okay, I guess. I made a fool of myself, for once."

Logan rolled his eyes. "You've done it a hell of a lot more than once. But never on a stage."

Christian pointed the sandwich at him. "You're *supposed* to say that. I suck your balls."

"And you do a pretty good job of that." Logan dropped into the chair across from him. "But you've always done better with your acting. That's a fact."

"Whatever. I haven't been on stage since middle school, and we both know it." Christian wouldn't look at him. He ate chip after chip, his cheeks taking on warm color. It was rare to see him flush. Apparently this audition meant more to him than he was letting on.

It shouldn't have been a surprise, but it was. He hadn't talked about it for years, just like Logan hadn't talked about playwriting. The second Logan's parents made it clear they wouldn't pay for him to go to school to pursue writing, he and Christian both discarded their dreams. Between them, they had solidarity, knowing that if one of them had to give up their future, the other would follow suit.

Logan knew it was a selfish, nasty thought, but the sharp stab in his gut—the resentment that Christian had pursued something without asking Logan what he thought about it—came quick. He swallowed it down and leaned forward, reaching for one of Christian's hands. "So you went to an audition. It probably went well. Don't kid yourself, Christian, you're—"

"I haven't acted since I was thirteen years old. There's people coming into these auditions who do this for their living, I bet. I don't even know why I went. I almost woke you up so you'd tell me it wasn't worth my time."

"But you didn't."

Quiet stretched between them. Christian picked up a chip, then flicked it away and sighed. "But I didn't."

"Because it was something you really wanted to do. And you knew you didn't want me to try and stop you."

Christian met his gaze. "Would you?"

Logan shook his head. "Absolutely not."

As Christian stared him down, Logan took a long moment to ask himself if he meant it. This was something Christian was doing without him. It wasn't the same as soccer—eventually that would end, and they both knew it. Acting was something that had sunk its claws into Christian and refused to let him go.

Logan understood that. He'd burned once, blazing to the skies, drawing unlimited muse from the concept of Christian performing his plays. Everything he wrote had him in mind. He'd been an amateur, and a kid at that, but writing a story Christian couldn't be a part of was never his plan. He'd be there until the end. Logan knew that. He just hadn't understood why.

Passion was a dangerous thing sometimes. By the time Logan and Christian had their first kiss, they hadn't been able to go long without sharing another, and another, until Logan's day wasn't complete without tasting him. They needed each other. And now, Christian remembered he needed acting.

That scared the shit out of Logan.

Christian intertwined their fingers. "I kinda hope they'll give me a callback. They won't—I know they won't—but a dude can dream, right? Like, just imagine it. I'd finally have something worthwhile on my acting résumé."

"I didn't even know you needed that," Logan said softly.

Christian squeezed his hand. "Yeah. Me neither."

What else do you need that I can't give you?

Logan pressed on. "Do you think you're gonna pursue it? Acting, I mean. Are you gonna go out for plays once we're back in school?"

Christian snorted. "FSU doesn't need amateurs trying out for their plays, man. They've got people majoring in acting. I'm not gonna be on stage next to Daiki doing high kicks or something—they don't even hold open auditions."

But you could change your major. The words froze on Logan's tongue. Inviting Christian to take that chance terrified him. Christian's soccer scholarship already paid for school as long as he kept his grades up and his performance on the field pristine. He could change anything he wanted. He didn't have to ask his parents' permission.

Christian was the lucky one. For once, him being poor as shit saved his ass—and Logan envied it.

Logan let out as quiet a sigh as he could. "What about plays at this theater, though? Even if you don't get a callback, the opportunity's there for the future."

Christian shook his head. "Nah." He took his hand back and focused full attention on eating. "Not that easy. I humiliated myself. Went and ran my mouth as if I was begging for them to put me on a reality show. I let myself get carried away through the whole monologue, too—barely even knew they were in the room with me. That's not somebody they're gonna want. They need people who can take direction."

Logan disagreed with that entirely. If he ever did write plays, he likely wouldn't have a hand in the directing or producing process. But if he did, he'd want someone who adored his work to take charge. He'd want to see how they could take his characters and turn them into reality.

Somehow he couldn't give those words life right now.

Instead, he took a deep breath and forced himself to take a bite of his sandwich. He chewed, and Christian didn't break the silence to comment. When he finally swallowed, the words bubbled up. "You're gonna get the callback."

Christian scoffed. "Don't kid yourself—"

"I'm not. I know you. I know what you look like on a stage. You're gonna get it, and the part too, and you'll end up stealing the show without even trying." Logan dug his fingers into the bread and felt it cave. "Whoever's doing the casting, they'd be a fool if they didn't see what was right in front of their noses."

The heat of Christian's gaze on his skin was unmistakable, but he didn't look up at him. Not even when Christian murmured, "Thanks."

They finished eating in silence, both staring at their plates. Christian got up first, and he held out a hand for Logan's empty plate before he carried them both into the kitchen. Only then did Logan watch him.

He was tall—too tall, he imagined some directors would say, but imposing enough to make a statement on the stage. He had a certain knack for his voice carrying across the whole damn soccer field; he'd fill up a theater with his lines without any trouble. His body was toned and beautiful. And his eyes—those incredible eyes—they'd make the whole damn world fall in love with him.

"I'm gonna turn on the TV. Might play a game." Christian came back to the living room. "You in?"

Logan trailed after him, shoving his hands in his pockets. They collapsed on the couch together, and Christian slung an arm around Logan's shoulders.

This is how it ends, isn't it?

A man who shone as brilliantly as Christian had a brighter future than Logan could give him. Just last year, Logan had understood that college would likely be when everything changed. Christian made friends—and, at the time, a girlfriend—and Logan coasted by with nothing at all. He wasn't made to hold Christian down. Logan always had everything handed to him, and Christian actually worked for it.

That made him strong and tenacious and hungry for more.

Christian's life was accelerating. He was taking chances and chasing dreams. He was throwing himself into the great beyond and knowing that even if nothing caught him, he'd be able to get back on his feet.

At any other time, it'd be beautiful to watch. But for Logan, whose dreams and desires all centered around Christian, it was terrifying.

He had no idea what he was going to do if these dreams pulled Christian far, far away. He didn't know how he'd find something to keep him pushing forward.

Shit. I got in too deep.

Christian buried his fingers in Logan's curls, tousling them gently as he watched the screen, and Logan leaned into his touch.

Depending on that callback, they might not have long. But at least he had tonight.

*

Though Christian didn't have to take days off, he knew he'd drive himself up a wall if he didn't. While Logan and Noah were still snoozing at ten o'clock in the morning, Christian had the TV turned down low and his hands around a controller, watching his enemies try to avoid his sword.

It was something to do—anything was better than checking his phone every few minutes to see if he'd missed a call.

The likelihood that he'd get a callback so soon was silly. He'd only auditioned the day before, and they had other people to see before they made their decisions. But he couldn't get the idea out of his head. He carried his phone with him to the bathroom when he had to take a piss, for God's sake. If Logan could see what he was doing, he'd never let him hear the end of it.

Or maybe he would.

Logan was quiet about his acting. Besides the encouragement he'd given him the night before, he hadn't had much to say. He'd stayed up when Christian went to bed, not even coming for a few minutes to lie together as Christian dropped off to sleep. Christian was too much of a baby to ask for cuddles.

He wouldn't be such a coward if Logan hadn't looked so fucking scared during lunch.

Christian saw it, of course. He knew every look that Logan wore. The fear was the last thing he'd expected.

He couldn't figure it out. It wasn't as though Christian could pack up and move to California, like they'd both dreamed of as kids—he had college and a scholarship to adhere to. A transfer wasn't in the cards. The only other thing he could imagine Logan being scared of was if Christian fell in love with one of his cast mates. But what did it matter if he didn't even get a callback? Besides, they hadn't ever once agreed to be monogamous when they began dating.

That was something he hadn't thought about in months. He paused the game and set the controller down, elbows on his knees.

He was happy with Logan. He wasn't interested in a new partner right now, and cheating disgusted him. Both were as far from reality as the likelihood of him and Logan getting married tomorrow. They were still kids. They were figuring shit out, and Christian wasn't looking for a way to complicate things even more.

He couldn't think what else might stress Logan out, and that bothered Christian like hell.

Talk to him.

He pushed the thought away. If it was that easy, they'd never have fought in the past. They were stubborn. Neither of them could open up and speak their mind easily. They needed to stew on their thoughts and put them together, and then, finally, let it all blurt out.

Most of the time, it was in the middle of sex. Something about being that close to Logan dropped Christian's internal walls and made the words pour forth. *I should just go in there and fuck the shit out of him. Maybe we'll both start blabbing.*

Before the thought fully materialized, his phone rang.

Christian dove for it, nearly toppling to the floor, and put it to his ear. "Hello?"

"Ugh, you sound out of breath."

Christian wrinkled his brow. This was what he got for not checking the number before he answered. "Daiki."

"Please tell me I didn't interrupt sex."

"If I said you did, what would you do?"

Daiki laughed. "I'd call Noah and see if we could give you guys a run for your money."

Fucking firecracker. Christian rolled his eyes. "Good to know. What do you want?"

"Ouch. You're my roommate. I can't just call and check on you every once and a while?"

"You've never done it before." Being blunt with Daiki came easily. Every time Christian even looked at the guy, his tongue cut across a whetstone, sharp and ready to draw blood at a moment's notice. He didn't need to be pissed at him—it was just as fun to verbally spar when they were both in a good mood. "Which means you need something."

Daiki sighed. "Possibly. How's Noah? Is he doing okay?"

Of all things. "Yeah, he's fine. You could just call him yourself and find out."

"What, and wake him up? He's still getting his sleep schedule figured out, you monster. Is that what you do? Just go in there and wake up Logan whenever you want for a little fun?"

"I have no idea why we're talking about this." He was definitely not going in there and fucking him after *this.* "Noah sleeps when I'm awake, so I haven't really gotten to talk to him. But I'm sure he's doing all right."

"You should check in on him more. For me." Daiki's voice went quieter. "Or for you. I don't really care which one. But he could use the friendship."

"I'm already his friend."

"Well, you should totally show it more. Go in there, ruffle his hair, tuck him in, give him a good-night kiss—"

"What the fuck are you talking about?" Heat came to his cheeks.

"Or don't, I guess, if you're gonna be a quitter. You're embarrassing, Christian."

Christian's phone beeped against his ear, informing him of an incoming call. "Listen, I've got somebody on the other line, and I'm *real* fucking happy about it, if you're gonna keep being weird."

Daiki laughed. "Fine, fine, I'll just call back later. Not tonight, maybe, but—"

"Bye, Daiki." Christian switched to the other call with a quick sigh of relief. "Hello?"

"Hey, is this Christian?"

Something about the woman's voice sounded familiar. "Yeah."

"Oh, good! This is Amanda!"

Oh. The relief of escaping Daiki vanished, propelling Christian straight into nauseated adrenaline. "Oh, hey." *Sound casual. Don't let your voice crack.*

"How are you doing?"

I'm about to piss my pants. "Uh, doing all right. Pretty good day so far. You?"

"Good!"

How could she sound that brightly vibrant when she held his summer's future in her grasp? The possibility that she might've called him just for idle conversation scared him to death. He didn't think he could make small talk when he was shaking.

She had him covered. "Hey, are you available on Friday between noon and four o'clock?"

"I-I am, yes." *Stammering. Very confident.*

"Could you come by the playhouse for a callback? Anytime in there is fine—we don't have a whole lot of people to see."

The ground dropped from under Christian's feet until he was floating in space. "Yes, yes, ma'am, I'll be there, absolutely no problem."

"Good, I'm looking forward to it!" Amanda's voice wrapped around him, giving him protection—soft pillows hugging his brittle bones for when he inevitably hit the ground. "We'll be having you read against one of the leads already cast, so just bring yourself, and we'll take care of the rest."

"Yes, ma'am, sounds great."

"Awesome. Have a good night, Christian!"

"You too."

And that was that. As if it was that easy. As if Christian could ever come back to the ground.

The unthinkable had happened: he had a callback.

"Shit," he whispered, dropping the phone in his lap and leaning to tent his hands against his lips.

Now what? Where did he go from here? Which way was up? How did his legs work?

What the hell am I gonna wear?

Christian stood up and stumbled to the bedroom. He flooded the room in light, and Logan grunted, rolling over immediately and frowning at him. "Sorry," Christian murmured. He shut the door behind him, plunging the room into near darkness—only the light of the morning shining through the blinds. "Go back to sleep."

"Everything okay?" Logan sat up halfway, his bare torso curving beautifully.

"Yeah, I, uh..." Christian hurried toward the closet. "I-I got a callback."

"Seriously?"

"Yeah."

"I'm not surprised." Logan rubbed his eyes and hung his legs over the edge of the bed. "It's you we're talking about."

Christian still had no idea what that meant. He shot him a look and faltered, taking in the gorgeous lines of him as he stretched. Logan was softer than Christian. He'd never been an athlete, and even his jogging wasn't enough to tone him up. There was enough lovely plushness on his torso to make Christian want to run his fingers up his skin and let his fingers pillow into him.

It was better to focus on that—on anything but how he was going to bomb this callback.

"I dunno what I'm gonna wear." Christian opened the closet door. He could barely see anything, and he swore under his breath. "I've got nothing, man. I'm gonna look like a joke."

"So we'll get you something else." The mattress creaked as Logan stood up.

Christian shook his head. "I need to save my money. We've got rent coming up soon."

"It's fine." Arms wrapped snugly around his waist from behind. "I'll spot you."

"You don't have to—"

"I want to. C'mon, babe, lemme do this for you."

He squeezed his eyes shut and took a deep breath. With every second that they touched, the adrenaline in his body started filtering. It wasn't enough time to calm him down completely, but it was...better. He could see the end of the tunnel now. He could prepare.

What the fuck do you do to prepare for a callback?

"I'm so out of my depth, Logan. I dunno why I thought I could do this."

Logan pressed one kiss, then two against the back of Christian's neck. His body took a sharp internal turn, fixating on the feel of his lover against him, and his voice as well. "Because you can. Because this is the first of many. You're gonna take off. You'll be a star. Find some great friends in the industry who will help you get a leg up. Everybody'll fall in love with you."

Christian snorted. "That sounds like hell. I can barely handle you, sometimes, with how work is."

Logan was quiet. After a few seconds of silence that Christian spent searching through his shirts, Logan simply tugged at his neckline and kissed the shoulder that he bared. "You'll see. Things'll go well." He pulled harder at his shirt. "Let's celebrate."

God, yes. Anything to keep his mind from running wild. But all he could remember was that phone call with Daiki, and the last thing he wanted to do was take advantage of him. "You need to sleep."

"You think I give a fuck about sleeping when you're here?" Logan pressed his hips against Christian's, flush against his ass, and though he wasn't hard yet, it was all Christian could think about feeling. "You think I wanna spend my time dreaming about fucking you instead of doing it?"

Please get me out of my head, Logan.

Christian turned in his arms and dug a hand in his curls, pulling him in for a kiss. As their lips met, he melted against Logan, and for once his lover was the one to hold him up.

They had a system they went through. Christian topped, because it was easier that way. Logan preferred to bottom—he had a hair trigger on his prostate. It worked for them, and Christian didn't question it because he enjoyed being in charge. But now? Taking control? He couldn't fathom it.

Christian sagged into him and broke the kiss, burying his face in Logan's neck. "I-I...Logan, could you..."

Logan's hands rubbed up and down his back. His fingers quested to his hem, then tugged at it. "What do you need, babe?"

The mere thought of begging Logan to top him bled Christian clean of any bravado. "I don't…"

When Logan's palm grazed around to Christian's front, it froze right over his soft cock. "You okay?"

Christian turned his face toward the wall.

"If you don't want this, we don't have to—"

"I want you," Christian blurted out, then followed it with a quiet, "Shit." More than anything, he wanted to harden for Logan and fuck him like he always had, but…

Logan took a few steps backward, and Christian chased him, his heart hammering in his chest. Logan furrowed his brow. The expression he wore was easy for Christian to pick apart: the confusion pairing with his desperate attempt to figure out exactly what Christian needed. Logan finally spoke softly. "Maybe you just need a little encouragement, huh?"

Maybe he did. It was possible that all he needed was for Logan to drag his tongue along his dick a few times and the rest would fall into place. He could get in the mood. He could fuck Logan. He could do anything, if he just swallowed his fear.

Why is this so goddamn hard?

Logan pulled him close by his belt loop and turned him, pushed him down on the bed. As Logan dropped to his knees, he met Christian's eyes. *"I'll do anything for you,"* he might as well have been saying, and the heat in his gaze called to Christian.

Christian just fucking wished he could talk to him.

Chapter Five

Something was wrong. Logan didn't know what, but the way Christian looked at him was unfamiliar. Initially, Logan thought he might be able to fix it with a little sex, but when Christian didn't so much as twitch as he was disrobed, Logan started to doubt himself.

I asked. Logan tugged Christian's jeans down little by little, exposing his slate gray boxer briefs. *He wants this. He wouldn't let me do this if he didn't want it.*

But that wasn't enough for him. He needed Christian to give him *more*.

Logan tossed the pants away, then cupped Christian's calves in each hand. The thought of touching him without getting a little more verbal consent made him sick.

"You say you want this, but you look like...like you're scared." Logan shook his head. "You don't owe me this, babe. I mean it. We can stop right now."

Christian shook his head furiously. "It's not that. I promise."

"But something's wrong."

"I..."

The hesitation only proved him right. Something wasn't working. "Christian, please—"

"I can't fuck you."

Though disappointment stung Logan, he sat back on the floor. "That's fine. I told you we can stop—"

"No, no, that's not..." Christian reached out, and Logan grabbed his hand in midair, squeezing it. "Ugh, it's just...fucking weird that I'm freaking out about it."

Logan's heart skipped a beat. It was worse than what he thought, whatever it was. "Say it. I need you to speak up."

Christian closed his eyes, held his breath for a moment, and let it flow out. "I don't wanna be on top tonight."

That's it? Logan blinked. "Okay. I can ride you—"

"No, I mean, I want you to fuck me."

Logan's eyes widened.

"I want...I want you inside me. I need it. I-I can't, there's so much happening, okay? And I feel like I'm gonna lose it, and I wanna know that you can hold me down—keep me on the ground—"

"Shh, shh." Logan came to his feet and sat on the bed beside him. He pulled Christian into a hug. "I got it, it's okay. You don't have to keep going. I understand."

He really fucking did.

He'd always thought their whole relationship would involve him bottoming. There wasn't anything wrong with it. Hell, one of his favorite things in the world was feeling Christian move inside him—their bodies meeting in the middle with a slap and their skin going slick with sweat. He couldn't dream of asking for more. It had been so hard just to get him to make their relationship official, much less ask him for a twist on how they had sex.

And now Christian wanted Logan to fuck him?

Logan had fantasized about it extensively. He'd had sleepless nights where he jerked off and came in seconds just thinking about being inside Christian.

Christian took a deep and shaky breath. "You don't have to if you don't want to. The same thing goes for you as me. If you don't—"

"What part of me looks like it wouldn't want to be inside you?" Logan asked on a shocked laugh. "Do you think I'm trying to get away from your mouth when you blow me, man? C'mon."

"Okay."

Christian was shaking, trembling in his arms as though he was terrified. Logan cupped his face and sought his eyes. "I'd love to fuck you. Right here, right now, or...or *anywhere*. You just tell me, and I'll do it."

"You're sure?"

Logan's fingers pressed harder into his skin. "I'm damn sure."

Christian gave a curt nod, licking his lips. "Okay. Fuck me."

"Gladly."

Logan pushed him down, finding his mouth immediately. *It would be easy to roll him over and take him.* Logan had enough restless energy licking his veins to drive him to worship Christian all day long, straight through to the night. But as he rolled his hips downward, he felt that Christian *still* wasn't hard.

Logan retreated, tilting his head to the side and coaxing Christian into slow, warm, luxurious kisses that had him shivering with a moan. *I don't have anywhere to be but here with you. Take your time, sweetheart.*

He might not have long to enjoy these experiences. He'd meant what he said. Christian was going to go off and make the whole damn world fall in love with him. Logan wasn't going to look tempting compared to that since he was just some kid with floppy hair. But, until then, he'd treasure this, every single second.

He broke the kiss to push Christian's shirt over his head. Christian arched to try to steal another kiss from Logan—but there were other plans in mind. Logan trailed his lips down Christian's neck, letting them fall as gently as raindrops. When he found Christian's pounding pulse beneath his mouth, he sucked a mark into his skin where no one would see it at the audition the next day.

Christian would know it was there. He'd understand he was marked—that a piece of Logan was with him.

God willing, it'd stay there for days. And, if it didn't, Logan would redo it, as many times as it took for him to be satisfied.

He sucked one of Christian's nipples until it hardened, flicking his tongue over it, feeding on the way his lover arched beneath him with a shivery sigh.

We both need this. He slid his hand down Christian's arm until their fingers met and entwined. *You need to escape. I need to know you're here with me—all of you. I need to know we're damn good together, babe. I need to remember the look on your face for the rest of my goddamn life.*

The warmth of their bodies against each other as he climbed Christian's body made Logan catch his breath. He managed to push their boxers down between kisses without fumbling. It was easy now. They knew the other instinctively, after so many years. Part of him wished they'd started experimenting sooner—that they could've stolen kisses behind the bleachers in high school and held their breath while they made love in their bedrooms so their parents didn't hear.

And then he remembered that their families would never accept this. Not ever.

If they'd been discovered as lovers in high school, they would've been dragged into church and prayed over to exorcise whatever demon was affecting them. They would've been sent to those horrific camps Logan always heard of—the ones that tried to rewrite the truth of a child, traumatizing them to the point they truly believed they were evil. Logan knew his family would never beat him physically, but the words he could imagine them saying were bad enough.

Christian touched his cheek, and Logan jolted back into reality, realizing he was panting and digging up fistfuls of the sheets.

"Hey." Christian turned his head to meet his gaze. "Hey, sweetheart, where are you? What's wrong?"

As Logan drank in the sight of him, he swallowed down the knot in his throat. "I love you. I love you so fucking much. And I don't ever want anybody to take that away from us."

"They won't." The strength in Christian's voice brooked no argument. "I wanna see them try. I'll kick their ass. I'll burn the fucking world down for you. Nothing's ever gonna keep me away."

Logan's eyes burned. As Christian's face blurred, Logan squeezed his lids shut. He didn't fucking cry. This was a moment he might never have again with Christian, and he wasn't going to ruin it with his own shit.

He was going to show him how much those words meant to him, even if he couldn't speak.

Their bodies rocked together as they kissed, a primal rhythm that made them harder and harder. Logan ate up Christian's response to him and held it close to his heart. Christian wanted him, and he couldn't pretend he didn't. Each passing second brought a desperate thrashing inside Logan's chest. He understood the deep desire to possess someone now, because, goddamn, if he didn't get to have Christian right this fucking second, he was going to lose his mind. Logan pulled back, then wrapped his mouth around Christian's cock with a groan.

"Fuck!" Christian dug his fingers into Logan's hair and yanked, singeing his scalp with pleasant pain.

That's it. Show me how much you need me. Logan bobbed his head. Months of discomfort at the taste of precum had finally fallen away. Now, he only focused on the taste of Christian's skin. *Tell me what you want. Tell me what I can give you.*

Christian's body twitched as Logan blew him. His abs leapt and spasmed, matching the accidental jolts in his hips that threatened to gag Logan every time. Logan didn't complain. If his throat ended swollen and raw, then so be it. He'd wear it as a private badge of honor.

Besides, Christian looked fucking gorgeous as he lost himself. With his legs spread so wide that his thick, muscular thighs strained, he was a wanton mess, not bothering to hide his sharp moans.

Noah could absolutely hear them. A familiar jolt came into Logan's belly, making his cock twitch against the bed, and he closed his eyes and leaned into it.

I want you to hear.

He dipped as far down Christian's cock as he could, his throat convulsing before it accepted the intrusion. His breathing cut off, and he trembled as he held firm, swallowing around it again and again.

Logan couldn't take it anymore. If he didn't fuck Christian now, he was going to explode.

Logan pulled off and reached for the end table. "You're still sure?"

"Never been more sure." Christian reached over and snagged a pillow from the head of the bed and shoved it under his hips. "Make me feel it, Logan. I wanna ache for the rest of the month."

With a rough sound, Logan dripped lube all over his fingers and rubbed them together, trying to warm them as quickly as he could. "You act as if I wasn't gonna come inside you, babe."

"Fuck…" Christian pushed down, presenting his hips to Logan, and stared up at him with dilated eyes. "Do it. Fuck the condoms. Throw them all out."

Logan snorted. He touched Christian's thigh and pushed his legs open just a touch more. "You say that now. When you're feeling all sticky and gross…"

"Nah. I mean it. I want it. I want you t—" Christian's words morphed into a sharp exhale as Logan touched his hole. "C'mon, c'mon…"

"I'm in charge here." Logan tilted his head to the side and watched how Christian's muscles reacted—opening wide as though he was trying to suck his fingers in. "Look at you. Look at your greedy asshole. Jesus Christ. How have I never fucked you before? Have you been wanting it this bad this whole damn time?"

"I-I dunno, I..." Christian licked his lips. With his eyes closed, his eyelashes fanned against his cheeks, and the vein in his neck thick and prominent, he looked as if he was barely holding himself together. "I'm not gonna beg you."

"Oh, no?" Logan tried not to fixate on the idea, but the thought of Christian desperately asking for whatever Logan was willing to give him sent a shock of power straight up his spine. It electrified his brain. Suddenly it was all he could imagine. "Not tonight. But this is gonna happen again. I know you."

Christian turned his head away and grabbed hold of the edges of the pillow under his cheek. He tugged at it, arms flexing. "Logan...babe..."

"I know, I know. I've got you."

With patience wearing thin, he pushed his finger inside Christian and watched him melt into the sheets. Logan might have never given anal at all, but he'd fingered himself enough to know the logistics of it. Those weeks where he and Christian weren't lovers—were on break while Christian figured out what he wanted—were tinged with memories of Logan fucking himself with anything he could get his hands on. It had never quite been the same as Christian, just a cheap substitute.

Christian opened for him slowly. His muscles squeezed around Logan's fingers, then relaxed in a concentrated effort. Christian was clearly trying to take him in as quickly as he could—even to the point of pain, if the expression he wore was any sign.

"Don't hurt yourself."

"Fuck you." A smirk spread across Christian's lips. "Fuck *me*."

"Trying to."

Logan shook his head and put his other hand on Christian's firm hip. The strength tied up in this man's body never ceased to amaze him. He was all lean musculature, a body made for chasing a ball down a field and sending it flying past whatever hapless goalie regretted facing Christian Daniels. But parts of him were so much bigger than Logan expected. Those legs could nearly break him in half if they wrapped around Logan's waist just so. The curve of his ass was stunning and inviting enough that he wished he had the patience to eat him out right then and there. And his hands, gripping the pillowcase so hard they shook, only made Logan think of how incredible they felt around his hips.

There was a quiet temptation not to let Christian come. Maybe he could keep him right at the edge, then ride him all afternoon. But he thought about what a spectacle it might be if he could make Christian come on his cock alone, and his mind changed immediately.

Logan pushed a second finger inside him and scissored them apart, watching his lover's reaction. "Stop being better at this than I was my first time."

Christian burst out laughing. "I had Charlotte, man, and you didn't have anybody. As if Kelly Anne was gonna go poking around in your ass."

Not for the first time, the thought of Charlotte infuriated Logan—even more than the mention of his own former girlfriend—and he pushed the memory of both of them away. "Whatever. You're mine now."

"I am. Now make good on it and fuck me."

"You're not ready."

"I know when I'm ready." Christian opened his eyes and pinned Logan with his gaze. "It's gonna hurt, and I want it to, and I want your dick inside me right the fuck now, Logan, so help me God."

The control of the situation mattered far less to him now than being inside Christian. For whatever reason, Christian was so stirred up he wanted to take Logan straight to the hilt. Logan knew how that felt. He understood the desperation of getting Christian inside him just to confirm it was real—that this relationship, whatever it was, was more than just a fantasy.

Is that what you're worrying about? Logan eased his fingers out and wiped them on the bedspread. *Do you think I'm not here with you right now? Do you think I'd rather be anywhere else but here?*

Logan was selfish. He wanted to make sure he took Christian so thoroughly that he couldn't think of anything, not even his callback. But now, pushing past that, was his deep need for Christian to understand that everything was *okay*.

Logan slid his arms under Christian's knees and pushed them high until their hips aligned. "Look at me. Don't look away."

Christian did. He held that eye contact even when his eyelashes fluttered.

"I love you." Logan reached between them to press his cock against Christian's opening. "I always will. You're the most important person in my life."

Christian's eyes widened, and his mouth dropped open.

"No matter what else happens, you're gonna be part of me forever. I mean it." The tears were coming back, and Logan pushed them away with one quick thrust of his hips.

Christian cried out. He threw his head back and let out ragged, uneven hisses.

"Too much?"

"N-no." Christian shook his head.

Logan tried not to think about how *tight* Christian was around him. He reveled in the rich color of his skin, the sweat starting to shine on his chest, and the way his Adam's apple bobbed. "Breathe."

In one rush, all of Christian's air flowed out, and he shook for a second on the bed until he went completely boneless on the sheets. "Move. Fuck me. I need you."

Logan couldn't tell him no. Though he kept his hips slow and careful, he filled Christian inch by inch until his hipbones pressed against the curve of his ass. He shifted Christian's legs over his shoulders, leaned down to press them against his chest, and craned for a kiss.

As Logan tasted him, Christian opened his mouth, inviting him in. Their tongues twisted together as Logan began shallow thrusts, barely sliding out of him before he was aching to be back inside. This was what he needed—what they *both* needed. He grabbed Christian's sharp shoulders and held tight enough to bruise. He never wanted to come up again.

It was difficult and clumsy, fucking him this closely, but neither of them could get far apart. They groaned past each other's lips as they moved together with the bed squeaking beneath them. The headboard softly hit the wall with each thrust, just enough to make noise—just enough to make it all real.

Don't go. Please don't leave me. Logan held Christian's face between both hands. *Please don't find somebody else who deserves you more, not yet, I can't take it.*

A maelstrom built inside his chest, thrashing and coiling and swelling until he thought it might carry them both away. There was no escaping it this time. As the tears came, he met them, letting them drip onto Christian's cheeks even as he gasped out an apology.

In time, Christian's passion for Logan would wane, replaced by whatever he found on the stage. The unspoken rule they'd conceived for giving up their dreams would be broken. Christian would change the world. Logan would suffer in a middle school, impatient with his bored students and watching bootlegs of Christian's performances on Broadway while everyone took a test that they would fail due to his bad temper. He'd witness Christian's acceptance speech for his Tony awards and he'd hear him thank a million lovers and never once breathe Logan's name.

Please, Christian...

He buried his face in Christian's shoulder and let out quiet, weak sobs as he fucked him. He couldn't stop.

And neither, he realized, could Christian.

They'd cried together only twice in their thirteen years of friendship. Once, in bed after a miserable fight that had nearly broken them both. Once, while Christian was still inside Logan, after Logan had seduced him out of fear of being left behind. And now the third time, here, with both of them terrified of something they couldn't even say to the other. Logan kept his thoughts tied down and locked away, and when Christian did nothing but whimper, Logan knew he was doing the same.

Secrets. Even after all this time, they had their secrets. And there was something terrifying about that.

Logan came first, his orgasm taking him by surprise in the middle of his fear, and Christian clung to him, sharp and punched out moans breaking the sounds of their crying as if it had never happened in the first place. Just like that, it was buried away. Gone, whisked away on the wind.

"Let me touch you," Logan whispered thickly.

Christian nodded without a word. He loosened his arms just enough for Logan to pull back and get his hand around Christian's dick.

It was the least he could do. If he couldn't hold out and make Christian come on his cock, then he could make sure he felt *something* by the end of this—more than just their joined tears. With a few tugs, Christian came with nothing more than hitched breaths, not a single moan to speak of.

Logan tried not to take that as a failure.

"Let me go get cleaned u—"

"Fuck that." Christian dragged him down. Logan hit the mattress, and Christian pulled up the sheet, wiping his jizz off on it. "I'll wash the damn sheets later, but you're not leaving me right now."

Thank God. As they wrapped around each other, Logan drew strength from the air around them, trying to rebuild himself before he was questioned. He didn't know what the hell he was going to say when he had to answer to crying for no real apparent reason.

But the questions never came. No words did. Christian held him tight and came down with him, bit by bit.

It wasn't a huge surprise. Christian didn't rock the boat. He used silence as a vicious weapon. But the relief that Logan should've felt was held at bay, left with a quiet disappointment he couldn't identify.

*

Christian straddled a line between relief and despair. On one hand, he was no longer anxious about the callback. On the other hand, something was still definitely wrong. The air in the apartment was thick with something he couldn't identify, leaving him impatient. How could he sit on the couch with Noah and Logan and watch TV as though nothing was different? Like he didn't feel itchy as if he had hives?

The night before, sex with Logan had dissipated the fear of Christian's future, but that was only a fraction of what hung silently between them. The second Christian woke up, the tension grew. Maybe it was only a matter of time before the source of it emerged, but waiting wasn't one of Christian's strengths. If the past was any indication, eventually Logan would bring up whatever was bothering him, they'd fight about it, and then they'd move on.

Christian just hoped Noah wouldn't be around to hear the blowout.

The TV buffered the silence Christian couldn't figure out how to break through, and he was selfishly grateful for the distraction. He was still worn thin, and the others seemed to be as well. The game they'd put on—football, not his favorite—played on, keeping his attention off the inevitable confrontation with Logan. When a phone rang, they all reached for theirs before Christian grunted, "It's me."

It was his mom.

He couldn't remember the last time he'd talked to her. His last contact with his dad had been in middle school, but leaving home gave Christian an excuse to put distance between himself and his mom as well. He hadn't even called her when they moved in—had only sent her a picture of the living room. The bedroom was off limits, and he'd pretended not to see her text asking for a picture of it instead. No way in hell was he explaining why he had a massive bed, and why Logan's shit was on one of the nightstands.

"You okay?" Logan asked.

Christian nodded. "My mom." He let it ring one more time before he huffed and headed for the bedroom, bringing the phone to his ear. "Hello?"

"Hey! About time you answered."

Why do parents always do this? Do they think guilt tripping makes us want *to call them*? He bit his tongue and recentered himself. "I was busy."

"Uh-huh. Are you working right now?"

"No."

"Then you're not too busy to answer your mom's calls."

"Mom," he murmured as he shut the bedroom door behind him. Obviously this was going to be one of *those* chats—the ones that left him wanting to bury himself alive. "I'm talking to you now, aren't I?"

"That's no excuse. It's been months. I almost thought you were dead." She managed to still sound pleasant when she was saying these things, as if she was kidding around. It grated on him. Any other friend, he'd want to punch them in the face for that tone, but because she was his mom she apparently deserved respect just for existing.

He dug his teeth into his bottom lip hard enough to taste blood.

"You there?"

"Yes, ma'am."

"Good. Tell me about your life. I don't know what's going on anymore."

There's a reason for that. He sat on the edge of the bed and stared at the wall, trying to figure out what the hell he could bring up safely. "There's not much going on. Just been busy. Work is work."

"How's Logan?"

His stomach twisted. "He's fine. He and our roommate are still working nights stocking shelves."

His mom clicked her tongue. "That's not safe. He could get a better job than that. He's got a brain."

Another quiet barb pierced his skin. Christian slouched. "He likes his job. Says it gives him the freedom he wants with a pretty good paycheck."

"More than you make?"

"I dunno."

Similar to every other time they spoke, he felt the walls starting to close in around him. Something about his mom and stepdad felt as though they were trying to keep him in a cage. If he ever got too close to picking the lock, they put him right back where he deserved to be.

She sighed. "Well, I can talk some sense into him when I come visit."

Absolutely not. "Mom, seriously, we're both busy as hell. I wouldn't even have time to see you."

"You can't make time for your own mother who birthed you?"

He couldn't think of anything worse.

Times like this, he had no idea what attachment he still had to his family. It was only guilt that made him answer his phone. He couldn't cut himself off from the family, the world said. He was ungrateful. He would be the worst son on the face of the planet if he denied his own mother the information and love and control she desired.

He clenched his jaw. "It's just...there's a lot going on."

"Oh, name one thing," she said, voice full of skepticism.

Do you really think I can't have a life without you? Even if he *wasn't* dating Logan or working his ass off to make ends meet, it wasn't as if all he wanted to do was play video games and never leave his apartment. He had passions. He had dreams. He had desires.

"I'm auditioning for a play," he blurted. There. It was out: the safest thing he could say.

But the silence she gave him didn't bode well for the rest of the conversation. As tempted as he was to hang up and pretend his phone had dropped the call, he gulped. "Mom?"

"When on earth do you have the time to do that?"

"I dunno. I found time. They need actors, and... and I act, so..."

"You haven't acted in years."

"So? I can pick it up again."

"The likelihood they'd give you a role is slim to none. It's a waste of your time. You don't even have any professional experience."

"I got a callback." He couldn't keep the venom out of his voice. Her desperation to shut him down left bugs crawling on his skin, and he needed to cut the conversation as quickly as possible. "I'm going in tomorrow for it. Everything's already arranged."

"A callback isn't a role."

"Doesn't matter. I'm gonna get one." For the first time since his plan to audition had started, Christian believed he was speaking the truth. He *was* getting a role. He was going to go in there and knock them dead, no matter what he had to do. Even if he was only an extra who didn't have a single line, he'd get on that stage just so he could get a picture of himself sent to his mom.

It wasn't as if she'd do anything with it. She'd delete it, not frame it. She'd pretend she never even saw it. But she couldn't wipe it from existence. No matter what, it would be there—on his social media, in his résumé, and deep within his very soul.

"When are you even going to have time to act? I guess you'll be taking off work, won't you?"

Christian rolled his eyes. "My job is flexible. I make my own hours—"

"Oh, so you planned this from the beginning?" Her voice rang out sharply. "You knew you were going to do this when you started the summer? You know you can't keep it up once you go back to college. Your number one priority is your education."

"Mom—"

"Don't interrupt me. I'm not finished speaking."

He dug his fingers into the edge of the mattress. He knew how this game was played. She'd hear what she wanted to hear, and he could never change it.

She took a deep breath. "You're making a mistake. You're not a child anymore, Christian. You're a grown man. And your entire future is at stake. If you put your energy into this...*acting*, you're not going to be able to focus on anything else. I know you. You don't have the mind to balance things."

It didn't matter how much she infuriated him and how desperately he tried not to take her opinions as fact—those words still punched him right in the gut.

She thought he was stupid. Just a fucking idiot. Some guy who couldn't ever make his life shine.

In that moment, he almost believed her.

"We'll see," he mumbled.

"Christian?"

"I said *we'll see*. I'm looking forward to it. I think it'd be good for me."

"Well, you've been wrong before."

I can't keep doing this. "Mom, I've gotta go."

"Seriously?"

"Yeah. I'll call you later."

"No, you won't."

He held his breath for a second so he wouldn't scream. "Bye." Then he hung up.

He considered if it would help to punch a hole in the wall. They could patch it up fine before they moved. Logan could help him paint it, and Noah could supervise.

God, he was a mess if that was what he was thinking about.

He tossed his phone aside, stood up, and went back into the living room. Logan and Noah were already looking at him, going quiet immediately, and he clenched one of his hands into a fist. *You two were talking about me.* It pissed him off.

"Everything okay?" Logan asked gently.

"What do you think?" Christian threw himself on the sofa and leaned into Logan, nuzzling his neck. "What happened in the game while I was gone?"

Noah cleared his throat. "I still have no idea what's going on. Somebody got a touchdown—that's all I know."

"Our team or theirs?"

"We have a team?"

Christian snorted. Though he was still furious, his lips quirked, and the heavy stones tied around his neck seemed to lighten. "I don't know. Maybe we don't."

"Oh." Noah chuckled, a distinct nervousness in his tone. "Uh, well...do, um, do you guys want to finish off the cookies?"

"That's the best idea I've ever heard in my whole damn life," Christian murmured as he made to stand.

"No, no, I'll get them! Don't worry." Noah flew to his feet. As he passed Christian, he hesitated, then touched his shoulder and gave him a warm smile.

Something about the look unsettled Christian. He watched Noah the whole time as he walked to the kitchen. For some reason, it was as if those heavy layers had been pulled back and pinned, as though a light had been turned on him to expose every thought he'd had. As if Noah knew everything, but didn't judge him.

What is that like? He stared at Noah over the kitchen bar. *What's it like to see something in me and not hate it?*

As if he felt the gaze, Noah looked at him and blinked—but then he smiled. His eyes sparkled, turning the full force of a spotlight on Christian.

He's trying to help me, isn't he? Even though he had a thing or two to say about Logan and Noah discussing him when he wasn't there, the way Logan had held him and how Noah was getting food told him they hadn't been rude about it. They'd been concerned. They *cared.*

Noah came back with a plate full of iced cookies and a tall glass of milk. He pressed the drink into Christian's hand and set the plate on the coffee table closest to him.

"Are you guys not having any?" Christian asked.

Noah shrugged. "I guess I will."

"Yeah." Logan grabbed two cookies and passed one to Noah, then popped his in his mouth. But neither of them reached for any more, as if they were leaving all of that therapeutic sugar for Christian instead.

Hell, I don't need to start my training diet for another two months. He ate a cookie and drank the milk just so he could push away the quiet discomfort from being taken care of. Once he felt more stable, he pressed a kiss to Logan's temple in silent gratitude and caught Noah looking at him again. He had the instinct to lean over Logan and kiss Noah's forehead, but he drowned it immediately.

It was because he didn't want to thank them out loud. He didn't want to make a big deal about what he was feeling, or how shitty the night could've been if they weren't there with him. It had absolutely nothing to do with that pleasant blush on Noah's cheeks.

"You think that guy's gonna score?" Logan asked as he set a hand firmly on Christian's knee.

"Hell if I know." Grateful for the subject change, Christian took two cookies in hand and worked on them one at a time.

Tomorrow he'd have his callback. He'd go in there and knock them dead—if not for himself, then to make his mom eat shit. And then he'd come home and cuddle Logan and...and he might even buy Noah something in gratitude. It would be enough.

Chapter Six

It didn't matter that it was past midnight or that their street wasn't well lit or that Christian was asleep and waiting for cuddles. Sometimes Logan needed to run.

Sitting on the couch, he yanked on his running shoes and tied them snugly, his lips drawn in a thin line. The Georgia evening air would keep him warm enough, but not too hot to sweat. He wouldn't go very far anyway—only around the block a few times.

Enough to shake his mind from where it was.

"Hey."

Logan looked toward the hallway and blinked at Noah. "Yeah?"

"You going for a run?" Noah asked, tugging at his tank top.

Logan nodded. "Just for a little while."

"Oh." Noah rubbed the back of his calf with one foot and tilted his head to the side. "Can...can I come too?"

Logan wasn't sure anyone had ever asked to jog with him before—not even Christian, who was the real athlete out of the both of them. He sat a little taller and tried to figure out if he *did* actually want company. But Noah was watching him with something nervous in his gaze and waiting so patiently, and Logan couldn't make himself tell him no. At the very least, he'd have someone to keep pace with. "Sure. That'd be cool."

"Sweet." Noah immediately beamed, his entire body seeming to light up, and hurried to grab his shoes by the door. They weren't the best running shoes, but they'd do the trick.

"You do much running?"

"Not anymore," Noah admitted with a laugh. "I ran cross-country in middle school. They wouldn't let me run with the guys though."

It was so casual, how he put that—a whole world Logan wasn't familiar with. Was it the same as when the nervous white parents wouldn't let their kids play with Logan during kindergarten when his family had first moved to Greenbarrow? He thought there might be shades of gray there where he and Noah could meet in the middle with their experiences, but he didn't want to assume. "I'm sorry to hear that."

Noah shrugged, but he didn't look up from his laces. "It's okay. My dad always told me they wouldn't let me run with the guys because they knew I'd beat them all so bad. I didn't believe him, of course, but he tried."

Logan nodded. He wasn't sure what to say to that. "Have your parents always supported you?"

"Oh, always. They never questioned me. They accepted that I knew who I was better than they ever could. They couldn't exactly read my mind, could they?" He chuckled. "They like Daiki too. They think he'll be good for me—that he'll make me open up a little more or something. I'm glad. They never gave me problems for being queer, but...I think some little part of us is always afraid even if our family *is* supportive."

Logan didn't reply. He looked at the wall as he smoothed his curls back into a ponytail and secured it with the band around his wrist.

"I'm sorry."

"Why?" Logan forced a quiet laugh.

"Your...family. It's just..."

"That obvious, huh?" When he glanced over, Noah was watching him with something soft and vulnerable in his expression.

After a few seconds of quiet, Noah nodded. "Christian made it pretty clear when I offered for you guys to move in over the summer. He didn't have to say everything—it was all over his face. It just...it sucks."

"Yeah." Logan wasn't going to talk about it all night, not when he wanted to clear his mind. He stood and held a hand out for Noah, which he grabbed and used to pull himself up. "Let's see if you still remember how to run, huh?"

As they went outside, Noah chatted, as if he was trying to fill the air. "It'll probably be easier now that I don't have a couple of weights strapped to my chest."

Logan locked the door behind them. He never knew how to navigate these conversations, but if

Noah was talking about it so casually, that had to stand as some form of permission. "When did you have your...your surgery?"

"Top?"

"Yeah—is that okay to ask? You don't have to answer—"

"It's fine." Noah grinned at him as they headed down the path to the sidewalk. "I got it a couple of months after I graduated from high school. My family had the money for it already saved up, and...I guess it was sort of my graduation present."

Logan paused on the sidewalk to give his legs a quick stretch. "Must've been a long summer."

"Try *a long year*. There was a reason I took a gap year before I started at FSU. It seemed to take ages for everything to heal up. I might not have gone outside for a whole month, truth be told." He stood tall once his legs were warmed up and ran a hand through his auburn curls. "It worked out. I got lucky, having that much recovery time and a family to support me financially. And, after I quit running, I never really got active again."

Logan nodded.

"Has Christian always been active? Did he ever try to drag you along?"

Logan chuckled. "Christian tried to drag me kicking and screaming into soccer more times than I can count. Sports just weren't for me. I played in a kiddy league with him to keep him happy, but the day I got to drop out, I was so happy. But no, he's always lived, breathed, and eaten soccer. Worked out for him, I guess. His coach always said he could make pro if he wanted to chase it, but he never did."

"Why not?"

That was the exact thing Logan wanted to get his thoughts *away* from. He started jogging, making sure Noah followed suit, beginning with an easy pace—he'd push himself later to make sure it really burned the bad thoughts away. "Well. He wanted to act. We were gonna go off to California together, and...I don't know. Things changed."

Noah hummed. "This was before you guys knew you wanted to date?"

"Way before." Logan listened closely to Noah, making sure he wasn't too winded to talk, before he continued. "I *think* it was, at least. Part of me wonders if I always kinda knew? I wanted him around all the time. Just sort of figured we'd get married and have two houses next door to each other so our kids could be best friends too."

Noah laughed breathlessly. "That's so cute, oh my God. At least now you guys get to do that in the same house, right?"

Silence.

Some people liked to talk while they jogged, and some were silent. He'd hoped Noah would think he was one of the latter.

Suddenly, Noah stuck his hand out and brushed Logan's arm. Logan looked at him, wondering if Noah needed to slow down or take a break, but as they continued to keep pace with each other, Logan frowned in confusion.

Noah spoke gently. "You only jog when you're upset. Did you know that?"

Logan jerked away on instinct. He lost his footing, legs tangling up, and reached out and caught himself on a lamppost before he could fall. "Fuck," he whispered, stretching out his ankle to make sure it was only aching, not twisted.

"I'm sorry. I shouldn't have said that."

You're goddamn right, you shouldn't have. But Logan bit back the thoughts before they could become a reality. Yes, he knew that he only jogged when he was upset—but no one else seemed to notice. It was always Logan's little secret, something he could do when times were rough without people questioning him. But now, he'd been seen—perhaps too seen.

"That's why you came," Logan murmured. "You thought I was pissed, so you wanted to come with me."

"Hey..."

"Maybe I wanted some privacy, huh?" He turned a scowl on his roommate. "Maybe I wanted to get out here in the dark, where nobody was gonna bother me, and figure some things out."

Noah drew back a few inches and rubbed the back of his neck with a frown. "I asked. You said yes. You could've told me no." He flicked his gaze away. "So, tell me to go back. That's what you want?"

Logan opened his mouth, ready to tell Noah to get the hell away from him, but the words died instantly on his tongue, and he let out a huff. "No. Fuck. I'm just being a prick."

Noah didn't reply, but he didn't have to. The expression on his face said it all.

"I'm sorry. You're right. I only go for a run when I've got something on my mind. But...nobody's ever noticed that before. If they have, they never called me on it. They just let it go."

"Even Christian?"

Logan dug his teeth into his bottom lip and looked away once more. He hated lying. He was shit at it, and Noah had known him long enough to recognize it. "Yeah. Even Christian."

Noah sucked in a breath through his teeth in apparent sympathy, but he didn't say anything.

"In fact, I'm out here because I'm trying to think through some shit with Christian, so you'll forgive me if I'm a little quieter than usual."

"It's okay. We can keep going." Noah picked up speed, jogging away, and Logan joined him shoulder to shoulder. They drifted away from the apartment complex and toward Fulton proper. "Do you want to talk about it? See if you can figure some stuff out that way?"

Surprisingly, Logan found that he did. Not thinking about it wasn't going to happen, and he damn well couldn't fix things if he just kept everything in his head. Noah had technically been in a relationship longer than Logan and Christian anyway. He could offer a fresh perspective. "Tell me something. Does it ever scare the shit out of you, those big dreams Daiki has?"

Noah gave it a few seconds of thought. They'd passed the convenience store around the corner from their apartment before he finally spoke again. "No, not really."

"Even though he could up and leave you anytime? Even though his life might not have enough room for you to be in it someday?"

Noah chuckled. "I mean, we've only been dating for half a year. I'm not going to lie and say I can't see a future with Daiki, but we're not so far along that we're trying to plan out the rest of our lives together."

That was different. Logan and Christian were two peas in a pod. They had inside jokes. Their families knew one another. They'd had the exact same close friends through all their years of schooling. It always seemed inevitable their lives would go the same way.

"Daiki's an ambitious guy," Noah continued. "As soon as we graduate, I know he wants to move to New York City and start pounding the pavement. Maybe I'll go with him. Maybe I won't. But I know it's not going to be easy either way."

Noah sighed. "He's going to need someone to hold his hand when he's failing and to be patient when he's succeeding. Hours are rough during shows, and so are the jobs actors have to work around them to make ends meet. It's going to be hell on earth for him."

He shot Logan a look. "But I might be the guy that sticks with him through it all, you know? I'd be doing both him and me a disservice if I didn't at least consider the idea."

"He'll be meeting people though," Logan pointed out. "He'll have a hundred love scenes he needs to act out. A thousand kisses he'll have to share on stage with some other leading actor. Doesn't that scare the shit out of you, knowing he might find somebody on the side?"

When the silence kept stretching out, Logan glanced at Noah and then blinked when Noah looked away immediately. As they jogged beneath a streetlight, Logan caught the color on Noah's cheeks and made himself pull the pace back a little bit, afraid he might've been exhausting him before they'd even really gotten started.

Noah cleared his throat. "No. That doesn't worry me. On stage is one thing—it's a job, and it doesn't mean anything besides that. Daiki and I are honest with each other. We made a commitment, one hundred percent. Nothing's going to happen without one of us knowing about it."

"You say that now."

Noah pulled ahead, enough to look over his shoulder with a piercing gaze. "And how many times have you cheated on a partner?"

"Excuse me?"

"If it's such an inevitable thing, then how many times have you done it?"

"I haven't," Logan snapped, though he knew he'd dug himself a hole.

"So tell me why Daiki is so different from you—or Christian, for that matter." Noah's voice went softer. "I know what we're really talking about right now. It's okay."

"Do you know what it feels like to think I'm just a stepping stone for the rest of his life?" The words flew from Logan's lips before he'd even fully thought them through. "That I'm just the training wheels? I'm not as special as half the people he's gonna be meeting, Noah, and I know that."

"Where is this even coming from?"

"He auditioned for a play. Without telling me. He's got a callback tomorrow, and I-I *know* him, okay? I know how good he is at what he does. He thinks he isn't worth shit, but I'm telling you, he's gonna go right up in front of those people, and they're gonna fall in love with him, if they already haven't."

Logan's throat went tight, and he made himself swallow around it. "I don't wanna hold him back. I know he deserves it. But, goddammit, I hate just *waiting* for him to move past me."

For a few seconds, there was nothing but the sound of their shoes hitting the sidewalk. Logan's legs itched. He wanted to take off and sprint into the distance where the darkness would swallow him, and he didn't have to deal with this stress anymore. But as hard as it was to let Noah hear all of this shit, it'd be harder still to leave him behind just so Logan could preserve his dignity.

And, he realized now, he didn't want to be alone. Not at all. Noah was the one person he wanted there to see him vulnerable.

"Can I ask you something?" Noah asked.

"Go on."

"Has Christian ever done or said anything to indicate that he's leaving you?"

Logan sighed. "Since we got together officially, you mean?"

"Yeah."

Logan forced himself to think past those silent weeks freshman year, the painful ones where Christian acted as though he never knew him. Those dark days hadn't repeated; that was true enough. "No. No, he hasn't."

"Okay."

"That doesn't mean—"

"I'm not finished." Though Noah never raised his voice, there was a firm strength in his tone, so solid that Logan didn't dream of trying to speak over him again. "I don't think you see the way Christian looks at you, or how he treats you, or the limits he's willing to go to just to make sure you're safe and happy. Did he ever tell you how I offered for you guys to move in with me?"

"He said you needed somebody to help with the rent, and he told you we needed a place to stay."

Noah shook his head with a sound of disbelief. "Not even close. Logan, he took me to get coffee that day—when you guys became *official*—and told me how scared he was of what was ahead of you two. He knew he wanted a relationship with you. He knew he loved you, even if he didn't have the words for it yet. And he knew the second you two went home, the likelihood of you both being able to conceal what you felt was slim to none. Your town would see you. Your parents, your pastor, your former classmates, everybody would see you two together, and they'd say things. And it wouldn't be safe to be there anymore."

Having his greatest nightmares spoken into life and waved in front of him like a flag made acid spread on the back of Logan's tongue.

"He did it for you—to make sure you stayed happy and thriving and...and *alive*. So why would he throw that away just because some new flavor of the week checked him out?"

"It's not that simple. Not for me."

Noah breathed a sigh, but he didn't comment again. They continued their jog, the starry sky stretching out infinitely above them, and Logan took the time to think about how bizarre his relationship with Christian had been all along. What was the likelihood they'd be the only two black mixed kids in their whole damn town? That their personalities would be compatible even for a friendship from the beginning? Added to the strange way they'd hooked up for the first time, the fact that they continued to do well together was incredible.

"Maybe it's because of how we started," Logan finally admitted, the words coming slowly. "Did he ever tell you how we got together?"

Noah blinked. "No, actually. I never thought to ask."

"He probably wouldn't have wanted to tell you anyway. It was a rough start." A car drove past, quieting Logan's words, making it seem safer to say them. "We both had girls. You remember them, right? Charlotte and Kelly Anne?"

Noah made a sound of acknowledgment.

"I know. Kelly Anne didn't exactly stick around for long. I guess I gave her something she couldn't really take. See, we had a date with both those girls once—just a night to hang out in our dorm and watch a movie—but we all started getting handsy with one another, and...well. Things happened."

"Happened?"

"Yes, Noah, we all rolled into the bedroom and had a good old fuck," he snapped. "God, you're gonna make me spell out every goddamn thing. Need me to tell you how long we lasted too?"

Noah chuckled and shook his head. "No, that's okay. Go on."

"The girls asked us to kiss. Charlotte asked Christian first, and he turned her down flat. But Kelly Anne *told* me to do it, and I went right the fuck for it. How could I not? I was so turned on I couldn't see straight, and just... I thought it'd be hot if the girls got turned on by it. That was it. I didn't let myself think he was good-looking. Not until I kissed him. And then I wanted to drop everything and keep doing that for the rest of my life."

He almost forgot that Noah was there, revisiting those old memories one by one, but when he heard him hum in sympathy, Logan came rocketing back to the present before Noah even began to speak.

"So that's how it started?" Noah asked, panting as he kept pace with him.

"Nearly. It was more than that. I wanted to keep messing around. When I asked Kelly Anne if she was cool with it, she kicked me to the curb for being bi—even before I knew I was. Fucking bitch." Logan scoffed. How she'd be getting along for the next three years on a campus as filled with queer couples as squirrels and trees, he had no idea. "Charlotte was different. She was...the term was *ethically nonmonogamous*, Christian ended up telling me. She was used to that shit—people having more than one partner—and she wanted Christian to feel free about experimenting with me, I guess."

When Logan turned his head to see Noah's face, his roommate was staring straight ahead. He was breathing harder than before as well—possibly the jog finally starting to catch up to him.

"Need to slow down, man?"

"No, no, I like it," Noah said quickly. "It's challenging. Keep going."

Logan nodded, furrowing his brow. "Well, it...we were just playing around, you know? Charlotte was his girlfriend. I was just the friend. But it worked for us. I still don't understand why she broke up with him when we were just doing what she wanted, but it happened, and now it's just us. There's nobody else. But I can't help but think eventually somebody's gonna come along and catch Christian's eye. That's what I did when he was with Charlotte."

They came to a street crossing and stopped to wait for the light to change. Noah reached a hand toward Logan, then let it drop between them. "Wish I knew what to say to make you less scared."

"It's all right." Logan shrugged. "Just...it seems pretty inevitable. There's always a cycle. It's gonna keep rolling, and I dunno if I can stop it."

"But would it be so bad? If you had to share him with someone?"

Logan frowned. "Depends on the person. If it's some cast member I've never seen before, then hell yeah, it'd feel weird. I wouldn't know anything about them."

"But if you knew them, it'd be easier?"

Logan rubbed the back of his neck, considering. "I dunno. I really don't. I guess I've never been there. Don't even know why Christian would stay with me, if somebody else was pretty enough to catch his eye."

There was something intense in Noah's gaze—focused, different from how Logan had always seen him. Noah was a gentle kind of guy, one who rolled with the punches rather than throwing fits or making demands, and seeing a rigid concentration in his gaze made Logan zero in on him past the worried thoughts. When Noah spoke, it was so muted Logan could barely hear him.

"He was happy with Charlotte and you at the same time. Right?"

Logan had never thought to ask, but the pleased expression Christian always wore when he was getting ready for a date had spoken multitudes. "I guess."

"He never made you feel as if you had to be her, yeah?"

"How exactly do you know that?"

"Just conjecturing."

"Well, no, I guess he didn't."

"So who's to say Christian couldn't find something worth loving in you and somebody else too? That the feelings can't coexist?"

That was something Logan hadn't let himself consider. It wasn't safe. If he let his thoughts linger on a world where Christian fell in love with someone else, he always pictured himself being out in the cold. "I dunno. I didn't have that experience." He huffed and looked up, realizing the crosswalk light had changed, and they'd nearly missed it. Without another comment, he led the jog once more.

"Not even with Kelly Anne?" Noah asked.

"I didn't love Kelly Anne. I think I barely even liked her." As angry as he still felt with her, he had to admit he hadn't exactly pursued her with the best intentions. "Christian found someone to date at orientation. He was hooking up with her that night. And I was jealous as hell. Kelly Anne gave me a wink and a smile, and I went after her for a distraction. I figured if I had her, I wouldn't keep fearing I'd lose him."

The buildings faded away, leading into a stretch of long, open road, which led, in turn, to a freeway. Not the most ideal jogging area, and Logan knew they'd have to turn back for that very reason, but he found he was enjoying the run with Noah all the same. Having him there was better than being alone with the hills stretching infinitely into the distance, taking his soul with them.

"Do you think it would change"—Noah spoke into the silence—"if you found someone else you liked?"

"I don't think that'll ever happen. Christian's got me by the balls, man. One hand around them, the other on my heart. If anybody could get past that grip, hell, I'd like to see them try—I'd probably marry them right then and there. But it's not gonna go that way. Not unless Christian lets go first."

"Oh." Noah nodded. "Yeah. Makes sense."

"We should probably cross back here."

"Yep." Noah looked both ways with him and took off across the street. "Just remember when somebody like Christian loves you as hard as he does, he's not going to cut ties for no reason. I can see he wants to keep you around. And it could be why he's chasing this dream now, with the audition and the callback."

"What do you mean?"

Noah shot him a smile. "If he didn't feel safe, he wouldn't be going after something that made him feel scared as hell, would he?"

Logan opened his mouth and then shut it. "I didn't think about that."

"Well, obviously." Noah bumped against him with a breathless laugh, but the action made Noah stumble again. "Can we stop for a second? Just need to stretch."

"Sure." Logan stood to the side, reaching toward the sky to lengthen his spine and feel the pleasant burn of it. "Hey, uh...thanks. You gave me something to think about. Doesn't happen very often."

Noah chuckled again. "No problem. Happy to help."

Noah set a foot on the edge of the curb and stretched toward it. Logan glanced over him, checking out his form and making sure he wouldn't strain anything by pushing too far. The edge of Noah's shorts rode up, giving him a peek at plush thighs—ones that looked a bit more supple than the massive weapons Christian wielded—and something stirred in the pit of his stomach.

Heat, warming him enough to make his muscles pliable, spreading just a bit further...

Logan froze, then stared at his feet, his heart pounding. They'd been out too long. Both of them needed to catch a few winks before their shift the next day, and standing here stretching wasn't getting them back any faster. "C'mon, let's keep going. We're not that far from home anyway."

"Good point." Noah stood nice and tall and brightened. "Lead on?"

"Sure enough."

It would keep Noah behind him, out of sight, where Logan wouldn't have to deal with whatever had just happened for a second time.

Chapter Seven

If we're gonna make shit happen, the first step's today, ain't it?

With his thoughts racing, Christian concentrated on taking strong, even steps down the playhouse hallway. He wasn't afraid of getting lost. He had a fine visual memory, and he'd walked these halls every night in his sleep. It was nice to think he'd prepared for this by dreaming of his audition over and over again. He might not know what to expect at a professional callback, but maybe he could roll with the punches.

"You're wasting your time."

His mother's voice rang out in his head, and he remembered the expression she always wore when he told her about his plays as a kid—that pinched, impatient look. No wonder he'd stopped telling her about what he was working on once he was in middle school.

She always seemed to like Logan better. He was smart, she'd said. Studied. Intelligent. He'd go off and make a name for himself. Everyone would remember Logan Brown when he died.

I wish you were here now, Logan.

A door opened in front of him, and Christian looked up at the man coming out of the audition room—a white boy, shorter than Christian—who gave him a grin and a nod as he walked past. That guy was his competition. Cockiness radiated off him, and Christian could believe he'd just wowed everyone inside.

Christian stopped outside the door and took a deep breath. He could give a whole damn team a pep talk before they took the field at the last game of a tournament, but he had no fucking idea what to say to himself.

"Oh, Christian!"

He jerked back a step and blinked, Amanda's face coming into focus before him.

She smiled at him, exposing both teeth and gums in her enthusiasm. "I was just about to step out to go grab some water, but you can come on in. We're ready for you."

"Thank you, ma'am." He forced himself to smile and waited for her to step past him before he entered.

He recognized Sage and Kumar, but five new people sat behind a table in the back of the room used for auditioning, all holding clipboards and talking among themselves as if he hadn't entered. Only one woman about his age sat at the front in a chair facing them.

Great. Even more people to witness my failure.

"Hey." The girl at the front popped her chin at him. "What's your name?"

"Christian."

"I'm Priya." When she grinned, the room lit up around her. "Playing the role of Harleen. It's nice to meet you. Are you excited?"

Christian shot a look to the others in the room. They were still talking rather than acknowledging him. "I dunno yet."

"Nervous?"

That was the last goddamn thing he wanted to admit, but he jerked his head in a quick nod.

"Well, that just means you want it, right? I like that."

The door shut, and Christian turned his head to see Amanda sweeping back into the room, her long skirt flowing as elegantly as a princess's and a tall glass of water in her hand. "Okay! I'm back. Thanks for waiting, Christian."

"No problem, ma'am." He stood taller, hoping he looked braver than he felt. "I didn't mind."

She slid past the row of people to the chair at the center of the table and then sat. "You've met Priya?"

"Yeah." When Christian looked at Priya, she nodded as well.

"She's already been given the role of Harleen, so you'll be reading with her today for her adopted brother, Samyak. Here." Amanda held out a few pages, and Christian quickly crossed to take them from her. "Sit across from her and read this scene."

"I sure will." Christian hesitated when he saw a résumé and headshot lying in the middle of the table—one that matched the man who'd just left. "I didn't know I was supposed to bring those again. I'm—"

"Shh, shh." Amanda whisked him away with one generous wave of her hand. "You're here to act for us, Christian, not apologize, please." The grin she wore softened the words into a tease, putting his mind at ease.

He sat in the chair next to Priya and, on instinct, turned it to face her a little more. She acted in turn, sitting almost knee to knee with him, and smoothed out the papers in her hands.

"You ready?" Priya asked.

Because there was no other option, Christian nodded.

*

"If you do that again, I'm gonna kill you," Logan growled.

Noah laughed, an effervescent sound that was completely unfair given the current state of events. "I guess you'll have to do it," he teased back. "It's the only way you can kill *anything* at this point."

For four long matches, Logan and Noah had gone head-to-head in their favorite shooter. Though it was the first time they'd played since before final exams in May, Logan could see after four losses that his roommate certainly hadn't gotten any worse. "Have you been practicing when I wasn't looking?"

"Maybe. You shouldn't let down your guard, man."

Logan shot him a glare as Noah hit the button for a rematch. "I'm gonna get you this time. Mark my words. I've been learning your strategy. I see all your weak spots now. You're not prepared for what's about to happen to you."

"That's a lot of words to cover your own ass. You could've just put on some pants."

Logan elbowed Noah so hard that he toppled off the couch. The match started, and Logan shot forward. By the time he found where Noah had spawned, Noah had only just managed to get back on the couch, and he wasn't too happy about watching his character get taken down.

"Hey! What the hell!"

"Call it strategy," Logan quipped as he took off for a stockpile of ammo while Noah waited to respawn.

This used to be what they did all the time during freshman year, and even in this new environment, it was like coming home. They treated one another with a solid level of respect, no matter how playful they were feeling at the time. Noah never acted as cocky or sullen a loser as Christian had when they were kids. Instead, he rolled with every punch. He winced at his own defeats but celebrated Logan's just as highly. He turned Logan into a badass, simple as that.

It was amazing. Even when Noah got behind Logan's character and put a knife through him, it was still a million times better than Christian's crowing successes.

In the beginning of their friendship, Logan played these games with Noah for a completely different reason. When they'd first gotten to college, Christian had had his hands full with Charlotte. Any of his free time had been spent with her, not Logan, and it was rankling. Hanging out with Noah was a way to put a middle finger in Christian's face, as if to say, *"Look, I have a new friend! Doesn't that piss you off?"*

As Logan swore under his breath, waiting for yet another respawn, his thoughts strayed. *Am I doing that again? Do I want Christian to walk in from his callback and see us playing? Do I want him to get mad?*

He couldn't answer that question. But he wasn't sure if it was because he didn't know the answer or because he refused to acknowledge it.

On and on the fight went, a vicious back and forth, but even halfway through the match Logan knew he was beat. He stewed on it, clenching his jaw, as Noah took shot after shot, kill after kill. Noah didn't do anything dirty or cheat. He just swept the rug out from under Logan's feet time and time again, as if it was easy.

Maybe it was. But if Noah was bored spending this time with Logan, he never said a word about it. If anything, when Logan shot a glance at him while he waited, nothing but blissful happiness was written across his roommate's face.

Noah *always* looked happy around him.

It was better than how Christian used to look. He always had his head up his own ass—cocky, surefooted, and confident about where he was going. It didn't piss Logan off; to the contrary, he'd always been drawn to that part of Christian and craved it for himself. But it did make it seem as though Christian thought his time was a gift he was generously bestowing on his best friend. It led to a lot of missteps when they were kids, such as Logan asking Christian once a week if he still wanted to be friends with him.

"I'll tell you when I don't wanna be friends with you," Christian had said. *"Promise."*

Logan trusted him. He never asked again. Not even when the fear crept through him that Christian was just there to waste his free time until he could get where he really wanted to be.

Christian didn't even have time to play games with Logan anymore. He was working or sleeping or practicing soccer. And therein was another thought: Logan might be trying to replace those easy days of friendship with Noah instead.

It wasn't the same, being around Noah. They were still getting to know one another, even after almost a year of friendship. Secrets came out day to day that they hadn't shared before. But Logan found himself wondering if Noah could stand in for Christian anyway—and if Christian might be jealous.

"Ha!" Noah took the last kill he needed to end the match, and the screen filled with the statistics of his victory. "Nice try. You got better—"

Logan wrapped an arm around Noah's neck and took him straight to the floor.

This, more than anything, was how Christian and Logan communicated—wrestling. They grappled for everything: where they would eat lunch, whose house they'd sleep over at, and who'd do the homework and let the other copy. Looking back, it made perfect sense. They didn't know how the fuck to figure out what they felt for each other. Girls could sit around and cuddle and do their nails, but a couple of teenage guys didn't have many excuses for touching other dudes in a little homophobic town.

Wrestling was the only way they could have any contact at all. It was playful, but also a sign that they knew the other could take a few playful blows. They didn't grapple with anybody else, and that was done for a distinct reason.

There was a difference though. When Logan took Christian down, he immediately faced a tumultuous fight, one they both had a chance of winning.

The second Noah's back hit the carpet, however, he froze.

Logan moved on instinct to put his hands on Noah's shoulders and pin them down, but even as he waited for the thrashing to start, nothing happened. A second passed—too long for strategizing—and Logan looked straight into Noah's eyes.

His terrified eyes.

Logan pulled back as though he'd been burned and scrambled back an inch or two. "You okay?"

"I-I..." Noah gulped and sat up slowly with beet-red cheeks and a gaze that refused to linger on anything.

"What's wrong?"

Noah shook his head and held up a hand for silence. Logan stayed where he was, and so did Noah, the quiet stretching out until it rippled with tension.

A thousand apologies were on Logan's tongue, and he didn't know why. There were a *lot* of things he didn't understand. Why did Noah look shell-shocked? Why was he breathing oddly? Why was he curved in on himself protectively?

When Logan began to stand, Noah looked at him so quickly that he stopped. Logan gestured toward the couch wordlessly. Noah followed his hand, understanding lighting in his gaze, then got up enough to sit on the couch with plenty of space between them.

Finally, Noah cleared his throat. "I need to talk to you about something. I'm not mad," he clarified quickly. "Or, at least I don't think I am, but...but we need to talk."

Logan nodded, furrowing his brow. "Yeah, man, anything."

"That wasn't okay." Noah dragged his knees to his chest and pinned Logan with his gaze. "What you did. You didn't ask if that was okay. You just did it."

Confusion spread through Logan, clenching his gut. "I, there's, we... I have physical boundaries, and you didn't ask about them, and that... Okay, no, yeah,

I *am* a little mad, actually." Noah dragged a hand through his hair and let out a shaky sigh. "I know I didn't specify what my boundaries were, so maybe some of the blame is on me, too, but you didn't ask—you just assumed I'd be okay with you throwing me down and pinning me."

Logan nodded slowly, trying to show Noah that he was listening. He hoped his sharp pang of fear didn't show on his face.

"So, okay, I'll tell you these boundaries now, and that way you'll know them, and if you forget and do what you just did again, I'll get *really* mad, so..." Noah tented his hands and pressed them against his lips. His breathing finally began to regulate, little by little, until it evened out audibly. "I don't...feel comfortable with full-body contact. I *especially* don't feel comfortable with you just taking it without asking. Do you understand?"

Suddenly, Logan was watching Noah shrink back against the wall at work, with that asshole cornering him and making him look scared shitless, all because Noah wanted to use his own fucking bathroom. Logan sank back against the arm of the couch, boneless with how thoughtless he'd been. "Yeah. Yeah, I understand. I-I'm sorry. I didn't think."

"I know you didn't."

"I didn't mean anything by it, is what I mean," he hurried to say. "Christian and I wrestled all the time, every goddamn time I lost at games with him, a-and it was just...it was instinct. Because you're my friend.

Because I was treating you like I treated my best friend."

"Not your best friend. Your boyfriend. The guy you know everything about already without asking." Noah shook his head. "It's different. *Everybody* is different, and...I really hope you don't do that to someone again without asking first."

That was a humiliating idea, having to sit some guy down and ask if he liked wrestling dudes or something, but Logan wouldn't say that out loud. Not to the guy he'd been willing to kick ass for just to keep him safe. If Logan did a single thing that made Noah feel *unsafe,* then he'd failed. He nodded again. "Yeah. I'll ask. I promise."

"Okay." Noah looked away, his mouth in a thin line.

"Does that..." The ridiculousness of what he was about to ask made him bite his tongue.

"No, go on, say it." Noah crossed his arms.

Shame spread through Logan from head to toe. But Noah was waiting, and Logan couldn't walk away as if he hadn't just started something. "Just, for the record, does that mean I shouldn't, like...hug you or whatever?"

Noah visibly relaxed. "Hugs are fine. They're different. Just make sure I have a chance to pull away or say no."

Logan nodded. That much he could do.

The guilt swarmed him—a horde of bees—and he did his best to push it away even as Noah picked up the controller and ended the game. Logan didn't have anything else to say. There was nothing inside him but humiliation, mortification, and the disappointment that he'd never feel Noah's body against his like-—

Whoa, whoa, back up. Logan stood up abruptly and went to the kitchen before a cold sweat could break over his skin. *No, I don't want that. I don't wanna be up on Noah for any goddamn reason. It doesn't make any sense.*

He grabbed a cup from the cabinet and filled it with soda, wishing they had some beer in the apartment—something he could guzzle down and get out of his system before they had to go to work.

He shot a look over the kitchen bar, staring at Noah where he leaned into the couch again. Noah had one leg drawn to his chest, knee pointing at the ceiling, and sprawled the other on the floor. One thin arm lay over his knee, and the other hand held his phone as he typed something out silently on the keypad. He looked strong. Held together. The vulnerable man of a few seconds ago was gone, replaced by this easy sense of self.

He looked good.

Logan whipped around so his back was to him and chugged down soda until the bubbles burned his throat. Okay. So he was attracted to his goddamn roommate. That was good to know. It meant that all those nights of wondering if Christian was the only man he was attracted to were over. Apparently, he found at least one other guy on the face of the planet appealing, and that meant his whole bisexuality crisis wasn't a fluke after all.

Unfortunately, it also seemed to implicate that Logan was a dirty, rotten cheater, and he needed to go throw himself in the dumpster.

He pulled out a few bags of chips and started filling bowls with them automatically, letting his vision haze over as he combated the thoughts. Sure, he'd thought other girls were hot when he had a girlfriend, but this felt different. Goddammit, he'd thought about *marrying* Christian. He wanted a life with him, and every time he thought about the possibility of not having it, he felt sick. This wasn't just playing around for him, not anymore. He loved the man.

And Noah had Daiki, the man he loved as well. The very man they would all be living with after the summer was over.

I've fucked up. I scared Noah, which might've damaged our friendship. And now I think he's hot. Goddammit. Logan thought about living in the kitchen from then on, buried in the pantry so he wouldn't have to see either Christian or Noah again. But his legs were long and lanky, and they needed room to stretch out. That meant he needed to face the attraction—and bury it quickly before things became awkward.

Easy enough.

Logan juggled the four bowls of chips and the cup of soda all the way into the living room and spread all of it out on the coffee table. Wordlessly, he picked up a sour cream and onion chip and ate it.

Noah snorted. "What's this?"

"Snacks."

"For how many people?"

"Us," Logan muttered.

Though he felt Noah staring at him, he didn't so much as look at him. If he did, he was sure that somehow Noah would be able to read every part of his expression, every thought he wanted to hide.

When Noah chuckled and grabbed a handful of chips for himself, Logan relaxed. "Well. Thanks." Noah slid closer, just enough for their thighs to touch.

It was a blanket of forgiveness and smoldering flames all at once.

*

"Don't ask me again. I've said it enough."

"And what if I need to hear it again?"

"Then that's your goddamn fault. Not mine." Priya swept to her feet and stormed toward the door.

Christian rose and then staggered back into his chair with a wince and a pain he swore he could *feel* in his knee. As he grabbed his leg, he craned forward, hiding his face, and let his ragged breathing speak for itself.

After that, there was nothing but silence.

"Wow."

The first word came from Sage, and Christian took it as a sign that the scene had officially ended. It didn't matter, really. His mind was still buried in Samyak's, the injured pilot. The man who couldn't chase after his sister and beg for her forgiveness because of pride and physical agony alike.

As he stirred back to the present, the first thing Christian realized was that his face was wet. Whether it was sweat or tears, he couldn't say, but he wiped it away quickly and hoped the score of people watching him hadn't seen. It was one thing to get into character during an audition, and another to be buried in it. He mumbled something; he meant it as an apology, but the sound came out clumsy and wordless.

"Thank you, Christian," Amanda said, and he risked a glance up at her. "We'll be making the decision soon, okay?"

That was all he'd get from them. "Thank you, ma'am."

He came to his feet quickly and went to shake her hand. When more hands filled his frame of vision—every single person sitting in the row—he shook all of them, prickling nerves stabbing him. He needed to get out. He needed to breathe in some fresh air and forget what this felt like.

It was as if they were thanking him for what he could give. As if they wanted more. And he couldn't let himself linger on that for long.

As he left, he saw Dottie out of the corner of his eye, but he blew past her. Only when he was out in the baking summer heat, beneath the great blue sky, did he stop at the edge of the sidewalk and take a deep breath. Thick, humid air filled his lungs—heavy enough he could chew it. As much as his body craved air conditioning, the last thing he wanted was to be in his car, trapped by the four doors and heading home. He wasn't ready to explain what he'd experienced, nor was he willing to think about what would happen if he didn't get the role.

Because he wanted it. He admitted that there and then. He craved that role so badly he could feel it in his bones. Each cell in his body was imprinted with a letter, a line, a feeling, an expression, until his blood coursed with it. And if anyone dared to suggest he wouldn't get it, he'd bite their head off.

No, the only person who was allowed to say he couldn't get the role was himself.

He let his feet guide him where they wanted as he replayed the highs and lows of the callback. Priya was an addictive actress to behold. He'd never shared the stage with someone who had a similar passion for acting. They'd all just been kids in middle school, and his counterparts mostly only wanted to go home. But Priya? Intoxicating. He'd fed off her energy and recycled it, using it as his own, building their scene until the force of it scraped the ceiling. Yet, he could tell she had more hiding beneath the surface. She wouldn't give everything she had during rehearsal. She would tuck some away, deep within her heart, to explode out of her during performances.

She'd earned that leading role. And he hadn't even thanked her when he left.

I'll go to a show. I'll bring her some flowers and thank her there. She'll deserve a bouquet on opening night.

But even as he thought it, he knew he wouldn't be there. He couldn't fall so deeply in love with an experience and then go watch other people play it out for him after he'd been dropped.

Another show, then. He knew Priya would rack up roles at Bay Playhouse, impressing audiences and agents until her career took off. He'd always treasure the opportunity to act against her for even just a few minutes in the callback.

He wasn't sure where his feet were taking him until he turned a corner and saw the facade of his old dorm building scraping the clouds. His legs didn't ache, even after a few miles of walking. Soccer had done well by him.

For the first time, Christian didn't feel the itch to return to the field. There were other things he craved—things he could never tell his teammates. God knew they shouldn't find out he had a boyfriend. Fulton was incredibly queer, but his teammates still said shit in the showers. Coach Atkinson was doing what he could to waylay that—outright removing people from the squad for any slurs they spread—but it wasn't enough. Atkinson couldn't cut the entire team if he didn't have bodies to pick up the slack.

I'll handle them finding out when it happens. He picked up the pace, moving into the campus proper.

Stop panicking about that. Just enjoy the view. You've got a few months before you need to be back on the team.

Fulton State was gorgeous. Christian hadn't noticed it as much last year, but after the few weeks they'd spent in the urban side of Fulton, he felt a deeper appreciation for the thick trees, lush flowers, and beautiful pathways. In the center of campus, surrounded by classroom buildings and dorms alike, lay an extensive green area, complete with a fountain and a gazebo where most of the students spent their free time.

Christian climbed the stairs to the gazebo and stopped in the entryway, resting one of his hands reverently on the nearest pillar. If he closed his eyes, he could imagine Charlotte there with him. She'd met him there time and again to walk to dinner or enjoy the fall breeze between classes. It was there that she granted him permission to start messing around with Logan.

No. Not just permission. She'd put the whole damn idea in his head.

Did you know what was gonna happen? He tipped his head back, basking in the shade. *Did you know I was already in love with him? Why didn't you say anything to prepare me? Was it all part of some secret plan you had?*

It was strange, his first experience with polyamory. His girlfriend both introduced him to it and broke his heart when he wasn't letting himself get deep enough with Logan. And she seemed so sanctimonious about it, as if she was doing it for Christian's own good. The whole memory of her breaking up with him still pissed him off.

I'll never be like that. The thought slipped out of his mind just as quickly as it came, before he could register it.

Christian slipped into the gazebo and sat on one of the benches, heaving a sigh. He'd be back here in only a couple of months. Though the four of them, including Daiki, would stay in their apartment rather than return to a dorm, hours of every day would be spent on campus, doing drills with the team or cramming in the library or sitting in classes.

Pursuing accounting.

Nausea swept through him so suddenly he leaned forward and put his elbows on his knees, breathing through it. It didn't make sense for it to come on. He hadn't eaten anything shitty. He hadn't had any alcohol in a week and a half. He drank plenty of water.

The pain came next, right in his gut, and he grabbed his stomach, wrinkling his brow. Little by little it spread, straight up his throat, until...until his vision blurred, and he realized what was happening.

He never let himself experience this kind of disappointment. It had no place in his life and neither did tears. There was nothing to fucking cry about. Everyone had to give up their dreams when they grew up.

But could he come back in a couple of months and return to crunching numbers? Christian couldn't even imagine himself wearing a tie. He was made for sweats and a T-shirt, something he could move around in.

It doesn't matter, though, does it? Life's decided. It's done. A little callback doesn't mean shit. It won't change the world.

He stared at the trees. Wind whistled through them, rustling the bright green leaves and making shadows dance on the ground.

And Christian fought to understand exactly what his double life was going to cost.

Chapter Eight

After a few days of watching Christian mope around the apartment, Logan couldn't take it anymore. He only had one night off that entire week, but he took advantage of it to drag Christian out on the town while Noah had a quiet night in. It gave Noah a chance to watch long distance movies with Daiki, Christian the opportunity to clear his head, and Logan time to pretend he wasn't thinking of their roommate the whole time.

A bowling alley worked as a distraction. Not only did it get their blood pumping from the competition, they were able to split a cheap pizza. They devoured it slice by slice, groaning over the rich cheese stringing from their mouths.

"We need to do this more often," Christian said as he tossed his napkin onto his empty plate.

"What, go out?"

"Yeah. Just you and me." He reached toward Logan. "I don't get to kick your ass often enough anymore, man."

"Hey, hey, greasy hand." Logan pushed it away, but Christian snagged his shirt anyway with a laugh. "Fuck you!"

"Is that any way to talk to your boyfriend?" Christian leaned across the table and pulled Logan into a kiss with one strong fist.

All his annoyance falling away, Logan melted, letting Christian take what he wanted.

It was only when Christian pulled back with a smirk that Logan realized his submission was exactly what he'd planned. "Fuck you," Logan repeated. "C'mon, lemme throw you down our lane. Your big head would get a strike for sure."

"Uh-huh." Christian rolled his eyes, but he was smiling all the same—the first big grin he'd worn in days. As Christian tossed an arm around his shoulders, Logan leaned into him with a satisfied sigh.

They threw their trash away and retook another lane, finding balls that fit perfectly in their hands. Christian took the first frame, bowling a strike—*of course he would*, Logan thought with a good-natured frown. But as Christian stepped back, he pulled his phone out of his pocket and stood stock-still staring at it.

"...I've gotta take this, uh, hold..." Christian took off in a jog with the phone pressed to his ear, as he answered, "Hello?"

Immediately assuming his stricken look meant there was an emergency, Logan quickly checked his phone. But he didn't have a single alert from Noah, Daiki, or his parents. As he put his phone away, he stared down the alley, able to see Christian pacing outside the building through the large glass doors. Christian froze after a few seconds, pressing his fist to his mouth, and Logan knew exactly what the call was.

Logan sat and pulled his hair with a deep sigh. *You knew he'd get that role. It's okay. Just roll with it. You need to be proud of him.* And he was. How could he not be proud of his lover for taking the first step toward the rest of his life? But fear still lurked there, and given how his relationship with Noah had changed in the past few days, he couldn't calm down.

If Logan could feel so drawn to someone else, then what would stop Christian from feeling the same and leaving him?

Logan took his bowling ball in his hands, focusing on the weight of it and rolling it between his palms. He didn't stop until two massive feet in obnoxious blue bowling shoes stepped in front of him. "So?" He looked up at Christian.

Christian sank to his knees, hands on Logan's legs, and whispered, "I got it, babe. They gave me the fucking role. Can you believe that shit?"

Surprisingly, the smile that crossed Logan's lips wasn't forced. As fearful as he was, it took just one look at the man he adored to remember how much Christian needed to be on stage. "I knew you'd get it. Didn't I tell you?"

"Yeah, yeah, you told me so." Christian rested his cheek on Logan's thigh and closed his eyes. A dazzling grin lit the room. "Rehearsals start next week. I'm gonna be busy as fuck."

"You think you'll be able to keep your hours like you have?"

"Oh, absolutely. I'm not gonna drop my job for this; don't worry. It's not exactly a paid gig."

"Not yet." Logan ran his hand over Christian's scalp, his freshly shaved hair just barely tickling his palm. "Soon, though. Guess you and Daiki can move to New York together, huh? Make a name for yourselves."

"Fuck you. Not unless you're going with me."

Logan's heart began to warm. "They don't need more teachers in New York. They need actors."

"What, you think people there just come out of the womb on a kick line? C'mon. Even if they don't need you, *I* do."

The pleasant burning spread, catching the edges of his chest aflame. The longer Logan waited, the less he had to say. He opened his mouth, then snapped it shut again. His hand trembled against Christian's neck.

When Christian peeked up at him through those unfathomable brown eyes—a gaze that made Logan breathless—he knew he was a fucking goner. Christian might want him now, but Logan would *always* want Christian, and even now he couldn't stop feeling as though he'd eventually have to say goodbye. Noah would leave, Christian would leave, and then it would just be Logan, knowing he deserved the abandonment—that he'd played with fire the second he realized he was attracted to Noah.

His full attention should've been on Christian this whole damn time.

"Logan?"

Logan sucked in a sharp breath, set the ball on the rack beside them, and cupped Christian's face. "Look at you. You're gonna take the world by storm. You're gonna make millions of people fall in love with you, and you're gonna forget all about me."

Christian's eyes widened. "What'd you just say?"

"I'm scared. Goddammit, I hate it when I'm scared of you."

"What? Baby, hey." Christian grabbed his shoulders before Logan could stand up and hurry away. "No, wait, what's wrong? What do you mean, scared of me?"

"Of you and everything you're gonna do, just..." Logan dragged him into a hug and buried his face in his neck. "Don't leave. Please don't leave."

"I'm not gonna fucking leave you! What the hell are you talking about?"

"We both gave it up, didn't we? Writing, acting, California, everything we dreamed about. We threw it all away so we could be together, even if it wasn't gonna be as good as we hoped. But now look at you. You're on your way there. You don't need me beside you. Every time I look at you, all I can see is you running off to have all your dreams and leaving me in the dirt."

"Listen. No, you listen to me." He guided Logan to look at him, their foreheads pressed together, both of them shaking with intensity. "I didn't go to that audition because I wanted to leave you. It wasn't me saying you weren't enough for me. Do you fucking hear yourself? You changed my life, asshole. Every second I've spent with you has been a million times better than when we were apart. Do you know you gave me a reason to keep going when my parents split? That you're the whole reason I went to college in the first place? Fuck you if you're trying to say I did this because you weren't good enough. I can want something. I can go after it because you believe in me. I can do it *because* you love me, not in spite of it."

Logan refused to cry in the middle of a goddamn bowling alley, where anyone could see them having a moment right there in a lane—but shit, it was hard to hold back. "Why are you doing it when I can't?" he asked desperately. "I can't write for you. I can't do anything. That's all I ever wanted. To see you performing something I wrote. Didn't you want that too?"

"Of course I do. Yeah, I said *do*, not *did*. Did you hear that?" As Christian pulled back, he took Logan's hands and brought him to his feet. "Fuck bowling. We've gotta talk, and I'm not doing it in front of the whole world."

God, I love you. Christian knew exactly what they both needed, even when Logan was two steps away from falling apart. As Christian guided him through the bowling alley, Logan kept his gaze on the floor and tried to figure out what was going to happen next.

Relying on Christian was too familiar. Without hesitation, he could pick up Logan and whisk him away from whatever trouble he was in. *Have I ever done that for you?* He couldn't remember a single moment.

They burst outside, where the air had cooled with the setting sun. Logan wished he had the chill of winter to breathe in. Maybe some cold air would bring his mind back where it needed to be, rather than mired in fear. Christian let his hand go and turned to face him, and Logan waited for a cue about where they were going, hating his helplessness.

"I know this is hard," Christian finally said, his voice rough. "I didn't know *how* hard, but…I'm here with you now. So you can stop doing that thing where you try to hide it."

"Hide what?"

"This. All of it. Everything that just came out in there. Nobody just decides all of that in the spur of the moment." Christian shook his head. "No, you've been feeling it for a while, haven't you? And you didn't even talk to me about it."

Logan opened his mouth, closed it again, then leaned against the nearby concrete wall. "You had a lot on your plate."

"Fuck that. I'm your boyfriend." Christian crossed his arms.

"That doesn't take it away. You were worried about your audition. Your mom pissed you off. I don't even know how work is going because you won't ever talk about it."

Christian rolled his eyes. "It's work. I don't always have to talk about it."

"But if I don't bring something up, I'm the bad guy?"

"No, Logan," he growled. "Our *relationship* is a little more relevant to both of us than me having a bad night at work." Christian kicked a rock beside them and sent it flying across the parking lot, soaring over a nearby car before it skittered safely along the pavement. "If you'd told me this audition freaked you out, we could've talked about it and figured out why. Hell, maybe I wouldn't have even gone to the callback, if it was that bad."

Something cold pinched him, and Logan shook his head. "I didn't wanna make it all about me."

"What do you think we're doing right now?"

He was right. Logan hadn't even thought about that. Christian had taken the first step toward the future—angling for opportunities that would shape the rest of his life—and Logan was putting all the attention on himself, being a little pissant. But he couldn't stop. And if Christian wanted to hear the worst of it, then he would.

Logan put his feet firmly on the ground, looked Christian right in the eyes, and forced himself to speak. "It's as if you don't need me."

Christian's eyes widened. He took a step back.

"You need soccer. You need acting. But you don't need me. And that scares the shit out of me,

Christian, I-I don't know what I'm gonna do when you realize you don't want me around anymore. Your life is so fucking full already, and mine is so small, and...I just keep thinking that soon you're gonna be gone, and that's it. The second I do one wrong thing, it'll be done. Finished."

The sound of the cars driving by on the distant road filled the air. The longer it took for Christian to respond, the more fear rose up in Logan, strangling him. This was why he'd never said anything. He knew the second he gave the words life, Christian would know that everything he said was true, and he'd make this prophecy a reality.

Finally, Christian spoke. "Why do I have to *need* you for our relationship to be good?"

The words stunned Logan. "What?"

"Do you need me?"

He didn't think that was a question that needed to be asked. "Yeah."

"No you don't." Christian shook his head. The dark slashes of his eyebrows came down with dangerous intensity. "You don't fucking need me, man. What the hell are you on about? If something happened to me, your life wouldn't stop. The whole world wouldn't quit spinning if I walked over there and got hit by a car."

The mere mental image made Logan's heart skip a beat. "Don't say that," he murmured.

"Apparently I need to! If you're sitting right here and saying the only thing giving your life meaning is me, we've gotta talk about that shit!"

Christian took two massive steps forward and grabbed Logan's hands, squeezing them painfully. "You're Logan fucking Brown. You've got the best smile I've ever seen. You kick ass at video games. You're the only person I know who can make a room of strangers feel calm the second you walk in. You can memorize poems better than I can learn a monologue—hell, you *wrote* the first monologue that ever gave me real joy when I learned it, and you..."

As Christian trailed off, realization filled his gaze, and Logan shook in the face of it.

Don't see me, he wanted to say. *Look away, don't read me, don't know my secrets.* But it was too late.

"Did you do that? You had to choose between making your life big in California, or making it small here with me, and you chose—"

"I couldn't let you go," Logan gritted out through his tight throat, swollen with the tears he refused to let fall. "You have more power and life in your pinkie than the whole city of Los Angeles. I would've given everything up for that. I *did*."

"No, no, no, I never asked you to do that." Christian's hands flew to Logan's face and held it still. The warmth of his touch singed Logan's soul. "I didn't tell you to give up everything for me."

"I didn't want you to ask me to. I did it all on my own." Before the words even fully left Logan's mouth, something tense and furious crossed Christian's expression. Logan dug his fingers into his wrists, holding him there so he couldn't get away. "Christian, please."

"I'm not mad at you, I promise. I'm pissed at the whole fucking world for making you sure you had to choose." Christian leaned against the wall and touched his temple to Logan's. "You had opportunities. Your family has money. They would've sent you anywhere—hell, they probably would've been happy to get you away from me. The last thing they wanted was you in some dingy state school."

"It's not dingy."

"It is to them. They never even came with you to tour it. Just sent you with me." Christian laced their hands, and Logan clung to that connection. "Why didn't you tell me? Didn't you trust me?"

Logan turned his head away. It was getting harder and harder to keep his cheeks dry; his eyes were too full. "I trust you more than anybody else alive. I don't trust myself. You were always the hotshot; you know that? All through school. People knew your name because of what you did—but they knew mine because I was attached to you. From the first day we moved into our dorm, I was just waiting for you to replace me."

Christian snorted. "Stop. Nobody likes me more than you. My mom wishes you were her son instead of me."

"Fuck your mom," Logan muttered with no small level of disgust. "If she doesn't know what she's got with you, then fuck her."

"You don't know what *you've* got in yourself either."

Logan didn't reply.

"I'm not looking for a reason to get rid of you, man. Waking up next to you is sometimes the best part of my day. It's the whole reason I keep doing this awful job that makes me wanna throw a brick through my windshield. And I've missed the shit out of you since you started your new gig too, trust me."

Christian clenched his hand, as though he was putting the period on a promise. "But you can't make your world all about me. You're better than that. You should have more than just some asshole who sucks your dick every week."

Logan slid closer, pressing their sides flush together. "I like it when you suck my dick."

"Who doesn't?" But even the little attempt at humor didn't lighten Christian's tone. "Will it make you feel better if I promise that if you piss me off, we'll talk about it instead of me jumping ship?"

"You sure?"

"Why wouldn't I?" After a moment, he made a thoughtful sound. "You're not still thinking about when I ran off, are you?"

How am I supposed to forget it? Back then, the weeks of silence had only confirmed Logan's fears. It wasn't an easy thing to move past. If it happened once, it could happen again.

"I was an asshole then. I fucked up. I didn't treat you the way you deserved—but I learned from it. And I'll do whatever I can to show you I'm not going anywhere." Christian paused. "But Logan...it can't just be me. Your life's gotta be bigger than that. You'll go bonkers if it isn't."

The mere idea was terrifying. There was a reason Logan hadn't tried to connect with anyone in his college classes. Noah and Daiki had been exceptions. He lived with them, which made it impossible to keep a distance so he could focus on maintaining Christian's friendship. Anyone else? He never hung out with them. He finished group projects as quickly as he could. He did his homework in their room, preferably in Christian's bed. It was a habit that had morphed into a desperate need.

He couldn't just drop all of that.

Logan came back to the moment. "Are you trying to put distance between us?"

"No. Yeah. I don't fucking know." Christian heaved a sigh. "I don't wanna have to do that. I want you to figure it out on your own. This isn't an ultimatum or whatever. It's me being freaked out about what'll happen if we have to be apart. What if you got an internship offer for the summer that took you out of state? You couldn't turn that down just because I wouldn't be able to go with you."

The panic bubbling up in Logan's chest took the air from his lungs. Logan leaned forward and put his head in his hands.

"Logan."

"I'm okay, I'm okay," he mumbled because he had to. Because if he showed this weakness, he'd be giving Christian more reasons to hurt him in order to help him. "You're right. You're fucking right. I can't keep doing this. I-I don't even know who I am if you're not there. It scares the shit out of me. If you were gone, I feel as though I'd just vanish into dust."

"You wouldn't. I promise. You've got life in you, too, y'know. You've got inspiration and power and passion and love, and... I know I sound sappy as shit right now, and I'm sorry about that, but you're more than what you think you are. Just gotta take steps to find it."

"How?"

"Hell if I know. But we'll figure it out."

"I wanna believe that," Logan forced himself to admit. "But it's just so goddamn hard. How do I know you won't leave if I fuck up?"

Christian threw his arm around Logan's shoulder and pulled him close. "Easy. Tell me something you've been holding back because you're afraid it'd piss me off, and I'll show you I'm not going. We'll talk about it."

That's not true. But even as Logan thought the words, he blurted, "I think I'm into Noah."

"...You're what?"

There. It was out. He hadn't intended to say it, but there was no taking it back. Logan pushed the heels of his palms against his eyes and released a shaky sound. "No, there's no thinking; I *know* I'm into Noah."

Though Christian took time to respond, he didn't pull away. "Like...like *into* into?"

"Yeah."

"Like, wanna tap that, into?"

"Yeah! What else do you want me to say?" Logan's voice cracked in frustration. "I didn't plan it. It just happened. One day I looked up and thought he was hot, and that's that."

Christian's hand found the back of Logan's neck and squeezed. Tension immediately flooded out of his body, and Logan sagged against him.

"Okay, listen," Christian said, the gentle lull of his voice bringing a fuzzy blanket of cobwebs over Logan's brain. "I get looking at somebody and wanting to fuck them, but that doesn't mean you *like* like them, right?"

Logan turned his head away. "You think I don't know how it feels? I spent my whole damn life looking at you and experiencing this. It isn't the same as it feels with girls, but I know it now, and it's real, and...and I'm sorry."

Christian sighed. "The fuck are you sorry for?"

That was the last thing he'd expected to hear him say. Logan frowned. "Because I'm dating you. Because you're the guy I'm in love with."

"Okay?" Christian flashed him a little smile. "So you're in love with me, *and* you think some other guy's pretty cool."

This wasn't supposed to happen. They were supposed to have a blowout fight. They should be screaming their lungs out. "Why aren't you freaked out about this?"

"Why should I be? Logan, we already *did* this. Did you forget Charlotte?"

"How am I supposed to forget the girl who broke your heart because you did exactly what she said you should do, which was to start dating me?"

Christian narrowed his eyes in thought and tipped his head to the side. "Okay, I see your point."

"Oh, *now* you do?"

"Shut up." Christian ruffled his hair. "Listen to me. You're not gonna lose me just because you're interested in somebody else—not as long as you're still interested in me too. We'll figure it out."

Logan wanted to walk away and have some space to think, but it felt so nice to be next to Christian that he couldn't bring himself to pull away. That hand around the back of his neck, the smell of Christian's T-shirt, and the confidence in his words were all a balm on the anxiety tripping through Logan. "I don't understand. I really don't. I was scared shitless of you finding out. I never thought you'd be this cool about it. It doesn't really matter, but it's...it's nice to know, I guess."

"Why doesn't it matter?"

"Did you forget the part where Noah has a boyfriend?"

"I mean, you've got one too," Christian pointed out. "Daiki could be polyamorous—we don't know."

Logan shot him a look. "Is this just part of your plan to get me to have a bigger life? Trying to get me in bed with another guy?"

The stunned expression that crossed Christian's face was admittedly cute. "Shit, why didn't I think of that? This is why you're the smart guy, babe, and not me." He kissed Logan's temple. "I don't know what's going on in my life right now. I don't know where it's going. But I'm gonna be pissed off if you're not there with me just because you decided to shoot yourself in the foot by breaking up with me. So stop. Let's just...figure it out, okay? Make our lives bigger, then tell each other about it. I'll act. You'll do something. Write, I hope."

"I don't have time to do that."

"You can. You will. I'll kick your ass if you don't."

Logan barked a surprised laugh. "Very inspiring, thank you."

"You still wanna play tonight?"

After considering the state of his mind—fragile, shaken, and so exhausted he doubted he'd get enough sleep before his shift tomorrow—Logan shook his head.

"All right. C'mon, let's go change our shoes and head out." Christian grabbed his hand and led him back into the bowling alley.

The environment inside was flashy and loud, but when Logan pulled in closer, Christian didn't laugh at him or push him away. He seemed to puff up protectively, bigger than a bird with sheltering wings.

With each step they took together, Logan focused on trying to find his footing in the world again. He was still lost. Nothing had gone how he thought it would, and the fact that Christian was challenging him to grow beyond their relationship was horrifying. Logan would never ask him to do the same.

But that could be the problem. Look at everything you put on hold for Christian. You didn't even ask if that was what he wanted. What if you had gone off and done something big? He would've been so proud of you.

The matter of Noah continued to rankle Logan. Christian wasn't angry about it, but he hadn't exactly given Logan explicit permission to figure out how much he wanted Noah either. "Can I ask you something?"

"Yeah, what's up?"

"Noah. You're okay if I keep liking him?"

Christian squeezed his hand again. "Yeah."

"What if he was interested in me, and I dated him?"

"I'd say *hell* yeah." Christian grinned at him. "Why?"

"Just wondering. I don't know. I don't think I'll do anything about it."

"Well, you don't have to. But it'd sure be less awkward when he hears us fucking if y'all were too."

"Fuck you!" The entire idea of sleeping with Noah was dizzying and confusing, especially after that line he'd drawn in the sand about full-body contact. "Are you saying you wouldn't be jealous if you heard us having sex?"

Christian snorted as he sat and removed his bowling shoes. "I dunno. Doubt it. It'd be you having sex. That's pretty damn hot for me to think about. If you were cool with it, I'd probably be jerking off the whole time I'd hear y'all through the wall."

Logan shot his gaze to Christian. "Would you be thinking about Noah too?"

Christian's hands slowed. He leaned forward in contemplation, pursing his lips and shoelaces going ignored. "I dunno," he said again. "Never really thought about it."

I don't exactly see how you could keep *from thinking about it.* Noah was cute. Handsome, even. He had a nice mouth, and once Logan noticed it, he hadn't been able to stop thinking about those lips around his cock. Christian didn't have any hair for him to grab hold of, but the curls on top of Noah's head looked inviting—messier than his own and shorter, but perfect for his fingers to slide through.

No, he looked damn good—enough that Logan didn't realize he was staring into space until Christian waved a hand in front of his eyes. Logan slapped it away just to hear his boyfriend laugh and then stood up with his bowling shoes in hand.

As they walked to the counter to return them, Logan bumped against Christian's side companionably. "Hey...thanks. Seriously."

"No problem, babe. That's what I'm here for."

Christian slid his hand into Logan's back pocket. The sense of ownership in it made Logan's cheeks flush. It was exactly what he needed.

Chapter Nine

It didn't take a genius to know that Noah was sick. When Christian woke up, he'd heard Noah going up and down the hallway, to the bathroom and back to bed. Logan might've been able to sleep through it, but Christian hadn't been so lucky.

Damn disgusting, that was what it was. Throwing up that much? Awful to hear—but worse on the body.

Somewhere around noon, sympathy started to trickle in, and hours later, as Logan sat on the couch next to Christian, bleary eyed, Noah had yet to show his face.

"What's up?"

"He's sick," Christian murmured as he put his arm around Logan. A whole week might've passed since their conversation at the bowling alley, but he wasn't finished with making sure Logan knew he was loved and wanted. "Noah's been up and down all day. Was anything wrong with him at work last night?"

Logan sat up, craning his neck to look past Christian with wide eyes as if trying to see Noah through the wall. "I dunno. He wasn't eating much. He said the lunch he brought smelled a little funny, but...shit, you don't think he has food poisoning, do you?"

"Well, he's sure not dancing in the streets," Christian drawled. "Just chill. If it's food poisoning, it's not gonna be contagious."

"Yeah, but he could probably use some help."

If Logan was showing interest in doing something that *didn't* involve Christian, even if it was just checking on the other guy he wanted to suck off, then Christian sure as hell wasn't going to be the one to stop him. "Okay, go on."

Logan flew to his feet and hurried down the hall. He knocked gently on Noah's bedroom door before disappearing behind it. Christian kept his eyes on the TV.

It wasn't that Christian hadn't wanted to see if Noah needed anything. But goddamn, Christian hated it when people saw him at less than his best. Whether he was sick, tired, injured, or stressed, he wanted to keep it all under wraps. Even Logan rarely saw it. Call it force of habit, but it kept Christian from offering a hand to people who were struggling. Pair it with how people stared at him too much—too tall and frowny for his own good—and it was better if he left well enough alone.

But Noah could be different. Christian rolled his eyes as he considered that he shouldn't have let his own pride keep him from checking on him all day.

Logan sighed as he came back down the hall. "He's staying home from work tonight. Already called out."

"I figured," Christian murmured. "Can't be filling the shelves if he's turning the aisles into a slip and slide."

"That's *disgusting*."

"Writer Boy, you'd think you'd be happy with my metaphors."

Logan put a hand on Christian's head and pushed. "I don't like gross shit," he reminded him. As Logan perched on the edge of the couch arm, his mind was clearly elsewhere. "...I don't wanna just leave him here while I go work. Maybe I should call out too."

"Dude." Christian didn't bother trying to hide his annoyance. "You've got a job to do. We've got bills to pay. Noah's a whole year older than us. He can probably handle himself."

"Yeah, yeah, I know, I just..." Logan fiddled with a string hanging from his shirt hemline, foot tapping on the ground. "...I don't want it to get worse without either of us knowing."

You've got more than just a crush, don't you? Christian studied his profile. The evidence was written all over his face. Whatever Logan felt for Noah, he might've been able to hide it for a while. But now, every time Christian so much as glanced his way, he could see it. "I was gonna take the night off anyway. I'll stick around and keep an eye on him."

Logan stared at him. "You'd do that?"

"If you're gonna be a big fucking baby, then, yeah, I'll do it. If I don't, you're gonna be sweating about it all night, breaking shit, not hitting your quotas—"

"God, you're an asshole." Logan's tone was affectionate, and he grabbed Christian by the jaw and pulled him into a quick kiss. "You don't need to do a lot. It'd probably embarrass him. Just see if he needs anything or if he should have something to drink…"

"You're gonna be pathetic when we have kids," Christian drawled. The words had the exact effect he wanted, stunning Logan into silence, and Christian pushed him off the edge of the couch with a smirk. "You've gotta go get ready for work, don't you? Shower, scarf something down, and all that."

"Fuck, you're right." Logan fled the room again, and Christian shook his head and turned his attention back to the TV show.

Kids. He'd never talked about kids before. Hadn't breathed a word about marriage either. Why should he? He didn't need to do that. He might've spent a good eighteen years just messing around with girls for fun and attention, but Logan was different. They'd been tied at the hip for most of their lives. At this point, Logan should know exactly what he meant to Christian.

Guys who know their place in a relationship don't have a meltdown outside a bowling alley because they're afraid they're gonna get left, y'know.

Christian sank into the couch so far it almost swallowed him. All right, so maybe there was more he needed to do to prove it to Logan, but...how was he going to juggle that now? He'd seen codependent people make life a living hell for their partners. He'd watched people tear one another apart in high school for the dumbest shit. One girl came to mind who'd go through her boyfriend's phone every day just to make sure he wasn't flirting with someone else. And what about the guy who'd get a new girlfriend, then tell her she couldn't hang out with another guy ever again? Over and over, Christian saw the effects ripple until all parties involved were convinced it was how relationships worked.

It scared the shit out of Christian that he'd let Logan get so far into isolating himself.

Logan never went out unless Christian was there. He didn't go to parties by himself or hang out with people from classes. He was just...in their dorm, first, and then in their apartment, always watching for Christian, always eager to be as close to him as possible.

And that had to change. They had a hell of a lot of college to go. With this first role under his belt, Christian was already dreaming about where it could take him. He could go overseas, maybe, if he was able to save up the money, and study acting elsewhere for the summer. He could get an internship at a theater in a completely different state. The sky was the limit. But Logan couldn't go there with him. No, Logan had to trust him while he was away and have his own life to pay attention to.

Noah could be good for that. He could give Logan someone else to focus on. They might have new adventures of their own.

Or he might just replace one bad habit with another one.

It was a damn shame, really, that it wasn't Daiki that Logan had his heart pounding over. Daiki didn't take any shit. He'd grab Logan by the scruff of his neck and throw him into the world and demand he take notes on something new so he could tell Daiki all about it. Noah was kind. He was a sweet guy, but he had a massive heart, like Logan's, and he'd probably baby the shit out of him.

Christian shifted in the cushions. *That* was something to think about—Noah and Logan tangled up in the sheets, cuddled close, whispering sweet nothings to each other, taking away the pain of the day. It was a cute image. Christian was the man who always wanted to grit his teeth and push through a fight like a bulldozer. But that was too harsh for Logan sometimes.

Logan and Noah would be a fine fit. Noah would instinctively know exactly what Logan needed to hear when he was hurting. It'd be better than Christian ham-fisting his way through everything.

Something gentle and content was spreading through Christian's chest. The second he became aware of it, he pushed it away in confusion.

Logan came whipping down the hall, still pulling a shirt over his head. The sounds of the fridge opening and Tupperware being shoved around turned him into a tornado tearing through everything.

"Just take the leftover ravioli, dude," Christian called.

"Noah might want it!" Logan shouted back.

Christian rolled his eyes. "He'll puke his brains out all over again if he sees that. Take the goddamn ravioli."

"Fine." Logan appeared in the living room again with a plastic bag, shoving a can of soda inside it. "Let me know how he's doing?"

Christian got to his feet, snagged Logan as he hurried toward the door, and pulled him in for a deep kiss. The freshness of Logan's toothpaste, the spiciness of his soap, the way Logan sagged against him with a moan—all threatened to overwhelm Christian. What Christian wouldn't give to carry him back to bed right now and get all those little worries off his mind.

"I'll take care of him," Christian murmured the second he broke the kiss. "You're pathetic when you've got heart eyes."

"You're one to talk." Logan pinched him, then darted out of his reach with an incorrigible smile. "Love you, babe."

"Love you too." Christian waved him off and locked the door behind him once he'd left.

I can't believe I'm taking care of your future boyfriend tonight as if he's a fucking child.

Christian had already decided it was only inevitable that Daiki and Noah would both be receptive to the idea of opening their relationship. Charlotte was out there infecting the college campus with ethical nonmonogamy one step at a time. The last time he'd seen her, she had two girlfriends, all three of them together in a triad. Obviously, she was dosing the water with something.

Why else would Christian be so okay with the idea?

He'd never been a possessive asshole. His girlfriends in high school, they could talk to whoever the hell they wanted. When they'd tried to make him jealous by flirting with somebody else, he'd been unaffected, and if they went so far as to cheat on him, he broke it off then and there. It hurt like hell, but he never took it as a reason to tighten down the hatches the next time he found a partner. He didn't fucking own anybody, and they didn't own him.

Times like this, when he was feeling contemplative, he wondered if there was a genetic reason for that.

There was a difference between him wanting to mark someone up so everybody knew they were taken, and insisting that they only ever spend time with him. The first was exciting—kinky, even. It was all part of making Logan flustered if anyone teased him about his hickeys. The second was disgusting and unnecessary. Every time he'd discovered he was one of the few people in his high school who didn't dictate his girlfriend's behavior, he'd been horrified. Now he couldn't help but think he might be wired differently from them entirely.

He hoped not. He hoped the world just had fucked-up ideas; those at least could be changed one day. But if he was one of the few different ones, then he didn't know if the tide would ever shift.

A door clicked open in the hallway, and Christian looked over his shoulder and caught sight of Noah making his way slowly toward the living area. When Noah saw him, he froze, supporting himself with one hand on the wall. He was pale and looked miserable.

"You look awful."

Noah scoffed, but the edges of his lips curved upward. "I should be mad at you for saying that—but you're right. I look like an unseasoned bowl of oatmeal."

Christian burst out laughing. They didn't joke around with each other, and hearing him say something so ridiculous took him by surprise. "You're not wrong. Go on; go lie down again. Tell me what you need. I'll bring it."

"It's okay. You're not my mom." Step by shaky step, Noah emerged into the lamplight. "I've been in there for, like, a year or something. I don't want to stay in bed any longer. Have pity."

"Even if I have to look at your ugly ass out here with me?"

Noah rolled his eyes. The grin widened. "Yes."

"All right, fine." Christian stood up. "Have a seat, man. But I'm still getting you shit."

"I don't need you to trouble yourself—"

"Did I say it was trouble?" Christian tossed over his shoulder as he went into the kitchen. "If you're not gonna tell me what you need, you're just gonna sit down and be surprised by what I give you."

The couch creaking as Noah sat was his only response. Christian went through the cabinets. There had to be something for a sick guy in there. With each moment that he came up empty, Christian was forced to confront the fact that they didn't have any of their moms doing the shopping for them anymore—that there were things they hadn't bought in advance of certain situations. "C'mon, c'mon," Christian murmured, a senseless chant, until he let out a satisfied sound when he found a can of chicken noodle soup.

It would do for now.

Christian dumped it and some water in a pot and set it to warm on the stove. He then went for a glass of ginger ale—something tall so Noah would be nursing it for a damn long time. He brought it out and gave Noah a stern frown until he finally took it.

"You'll drink all of that."

Noah blinked. "Seriously?"

"That's a threat, Noah Kramer."

As rough as he looked, Noah clearly didn't have another ounce of fight in him. He sagged into the couch and sipped the ginger ale, eyes on the TV.

Seeing that he'd left the soccer match on—one of many sports Noah professed not to understand—

Christian rolled his eyes and reached to hit the power button on one of the controllers. Their game system powered on, and he tossed the controller onto the cushion next to Noah. "Put something interesting on. A movie."

"Anything in particular that you command me to watch?" Noah drawled.

Christian responded by throwing an afghan on him he'd gotten out of the nearby closet.

As far as Christian knew, babysitting a pot of chicken noodle soup wasn't exactly necessary, but he did it anyway, watching it with a frown as he stirred. Otherwise, he'd be hovering over Noah. Noah never let any damage show in his armor. Christian had never once seen him give in to fear—not even the day he came out as trans to Christian with his chin in the air and his eyes full of challenge.

He was a sweet kid, sure, but he was strong too. For the first time, Christian found himself wondering if Noah was *too* strong. If the softness he gave others was something he never gave himself.

Noah was fighting the help Christian wanted to give him. He deflected and teased rather than outright telling him to stop, but even that felt too familiar. Christian was trying to defuse the situation without getting into a fight, and Noah seemed to recognize how stubborn Christian was as well, and how he wasn't willing to step back even an inch.

How much do you hide from us?

Christian poured the steaming soup into a bowl, grabbed a thick sleeve of crackers and a spoon, and headed for the living room. He put the bowl right in Noah's lap, on top of his thighs, and watched him shift and grab hold of it, startled.

Christian leaned down and waited until Noah was looking at him. "Eat it."

The last thing Christian expected was for Noah's cheeks to flush. His pupils wide, Noah flicked his gaze from Christian's face to the bowl and back again, then nodded as he took the spoon from his hand. "Okay. Thanks."

"No problem."

Christian sat and watched him while he ate, the movie going unnoticed in the background. Noah worked his way through the soup gradually—each spoonful taken slowly, as if it caused him pain. The way he sat didn't look entirely comfortable either, as though he was trying to prove how much better he was feeling.

"You act as if nobody's ever made you soup before," Christian drawled.

Noah shot him a look. "No one's ever put it in my hands and told me to swallow."

Christian opened his mouth, then snapped it shut, pressing two fingers to his lips to keep his comments inside. There was a time and place for that shit, and making fun of the guy talking about *swallowing* when he was only a few hours out of a puking hellhole didn't seem right.

Noah simply looked back at the screen and slurped the noodles out of his soup, but the color in his cheeks never faded.

Do you have a fever or what? Before he wasted his time weighing the possibilities, Christian pulled his phone out of his pocket and shot Daiki a text.

"I'm sitting here taking care of your man, and you haven't even called to see how he's doing. I know you're not that busy this late at night."

He tapped his phone restlessly on his knee as he glanced at Noah again.

He hadn't shaved that day. His facial hair always came in patchy, as far as Christian could see, but maybe it would change over time. Noah's body was still adjusting, he figured, trying to decide how to react to the amount of testosterone in his system in just the past couple of years. But Noah was doing better about the shaving now—better than last year. He'd finally thrown out his cheap plastic razor and gotten himself something a little more high quality: the nice shaving brush, soap, oils, and a gorgeous razor that would last him a lifetime. It made his skin look so much better, the razor burn and bumps gone.

Normally, Noah looked as smooth as a baby, but the red dusting his chin and cheeks didn't look too bad either. Christian could almost imagine the scratchiness against his own hands.

For one lingering moment, his awareness jacked up in intensity, like a floodlight spilled into the room onto the line of Noah's jaw, the rich pink of his lips, the freckles dusting his cheeks—

Christian's phone vibrated. He was ejected from his distraction and stared at it instead with a deep breath.

"Taking care of him? What's wrong with him?"

Daiki had texted back. Even before Christian could open up a reply, his phone rang with Daiki's name attached.

Christian considered mentioning it to Noah but took the call to the bedroom instead. He answered as soon as he had the door shut. "Hello?"

"What's wrong with Noah?"

"Nice way to greet a guy."

"Yeah, nice way to tell somebody his boyfriend's needing to be taken care of. It's nothing bad, is it?"

Christian rolled his eyes and collapsed backward on the bed. "He's fine. He's got a tummy ache. Food poisoning, maybe. Been up puking all night. What, he didn't tell you?"

Daiki scoffed. "Of course he didn't tell me. Why would Noah tell me something as little as him being sick all night?" There was a bite of sarcasm and something disappointed in his voice. "Is he still throwing up, or is he doing better now?"

"He's eating. I made him soup and got him some ginger ale."

"Well, thank God for that." Daiki sighed. "Thanks."

"No problem."

Christian could hear sounds in the background of the call—someone shouting, then a piano striking up a lively song that was followed by a thick chorus of voices. "Are you in rehearsal right now?"

"Yeah. I've got a break. I'm not in this number."

"What time is it?"

"Late as fuck. It happens." The noise quieted, and then there was nothing but Daiki's voice. "Just keep an eye on Noah, okay? I'm worried now."

"You don't need to be. It's really not that bad. Don't be so nervous. God."

"Fuck you."

Christian smiled despite himself, but something about Daiki's response to the whole situation still itched at him. "So he really didn't tell you? Why not?"

"Because he's Noah." A breeze buffeted against the phone, overwhelming Daiki's voice. For a moment, Christian closed his eyes and vividly saw the image of Daiki beneath the stars, his sleek hair blowing around his thin face, a taxi driving by. Without hesitation, Christian pictured himself sitting outside a theater in between rehearsals with Daiki.

Shit, I didn't even tell him about the audition.

Daiki continued, bringing Christian back to reality. "We've lived with him the exact same amount of time, Christian, come on. Don't act as if you don't know how he likes to hide things."

"Hide things?"

"Yeah. He doesn't want to give people trouble. He'd rather pretend he feels nothing at all than actually ask for something."

Suddenly, all Christian could think about was the day he'd offered to buy Noah that damn razor, and how he'd melted into wet eyes and clear gratitude.

Noah had never let those tears fall. He never spoke about that moment again. He did his best to hide whatever it was he'd been feeling, and Christian let him because he knew the humiliation of exposing his heart to someone he barely knew.

The same Noah who snarked at him over the food. The very man who wouldn't even look at him as he ate.

"Does it piss him off when people help?" Christian asked almost on a whisper, furrowing his brow.

Daiki was quiet for a moment. "I don't know. Sometimes. But I think...maybe he likes it too. He's in charge of everything else. If somebody gives him the chance to relax and let someone else have the reins, it takes the load off his shoulders."

Familiarity resonated in Christian's chest. The way it felt when Logan pressed him into the sheets and kissed the tension right out of his body. How humiliated Christian had initially felt to give up the power so fully in that exchange. How brilliantly red Noah's cheeks were, without a single ounce of anger in his gaze.

An apology. Only an apology in his eyes.

"I've got to go. Rehearsal's wrapping up. Tell Noah I'll call him later."

Christian nodded. "Yeah, man, totally."

"And, uh...thanks for taking care of him." Daiki cleared his throat. "Between you and me, a few hickeys tends to calm him right down, so if you wanna—"

"Daiki."

"Just kidding!" His voice surged into something bright and peppy. "Bye, Christian!"

Christian held the phone over him and stared at the screen after Daiki hung up, trying to process if he'd really heard what he thought he had. Those kinds of jokes came too quickly for him to react—especially when they had some basis in the real world.

He made a mental note to quip back next time to see if Logan had hickey permission too. He could imagine worse things than Logan pressing a firm hand to Noah's thigh to steady himself, his face buried in his neck, Noah's expression twisted into painful ecstasy and his eyes opening to stare straight into Christian's—

He shook it off and tossed the phone onto the pillow behind him. That was enough of those thought experiments. The sooner he got them out of his head, the better. He was a busy guy now. He didn't have time to fantasize about threesomes.

Besides, Noah didn't exactly look *scared* of him anymore, but there wasn't anything inviting in his hazel gaze either. He had his own shit to deal with too. Daiki was already a handful.

No, it had to be Logan and Noah, and that was it.

Logan, you're gonna feel so smug when I admit that Noah's hot, aren't you?

Christian rolled out of bed and made his way back to the living room. He sat on the sofa and glanced toward Noah, pleased to see he'd eaten most of the soup. "Daiki says he'll call you later."

Noah jumped. "That was him on the phone?"

"Yeah. I told him you felt like shit."

Noah put the bowl on the coffee table with a resounding, irritated thud. "Don't do that again, please. I'd rather tell him how I'm feeling, not have somebody keeping tabs on me and sharing things I didn't want him to know."

Christian looked him full in the eye. He knew very well the stubbornness staring back at him. "Are you gonna sit there and tell me you don't trust your own boyfriend knowing when you're sick?"

"He's busy," Noah shot back. "I don't want to distract him while he's working."

"It's food poisoning, Noah. You're not telling him you're in the goddamn hospital. And I'm pretty sure he can handle juggling some sympathy for you with his quickstep or tango or whatever the fuck he's learning."

"Still. It's my privacy."

"Yeah, and one day you're gonna have to fucking ask yourself why you think you know what's better for Daiki than Daiki does."

In the tense silence, they stared at each other, neither willing to give in first, and Christian saw himself reflected in Noah's face. He saw the fear he'd felt as a kid when he let himself cry in front of Logan. He saw the bricks he'd built up for years to keep himself safe from the world.

How long until you fall apart?

"I won't do it again," Christian said softly. "I didn't know it was such a big thing for you. I'm sorry."

Noah frowned and looked away. Wordlessly, he picked up the bowl of soup and finished it off. Once it was empty, he cleared his throat. "I'll tell him next time. Promise."

As the movie played on, Christian relaxed back into the couch. One last look told him Noah's afghan had fallen, and he reached for it, offering it to him. Noah took it and wrapped up in it as tight as a cocoon. When one of the edges fell to expose his shoulder, Christian covered it up for him again.

Sometime between putting the blanket back in place and relaxing back into the couch, Christian realized Noah had slid closer. Their legs and shoulders touched. After a long moment of deliberation, Christian put his arm on the back of the couch. Not around Noah—not quite—but close enough. And the way his heart pounded when Noah didn't pull away told him right then and there he was in more trouble than he thought.

Chapter Ten

Though perhaps it should've been obvious, Logan hadn't anticipated how lonely working by himself would be. Even before he realized he had a crush, Noah's constant companionship at work had gotten him through the tedium. The job didn't require a lot of brainpower, just the repetition of pulling a pallet, unloading it, and filling the shelves. Without having any diversion, it was enough to drive a man mad.

And he'd been a fool and forgotten his earbuds at home. *Idiot.*

Still, on he worked. He felt the eyes of his fellow employees and his managers on him. Something told Logan those in charge were expecting higher productivity out of him tonight, since he didn't have a distraction, but somehow he found himself moving slower. With each product that he put on the shelf, he lost a second to missing Noah beside him.

God, I'm fucked, aren't I?

He wasn't comfortable with wanting Noah yet. Nerves rose inside him, bubbling like champagne, and he swallowed them down as best as he could. It didn't make sense that Christian would let him pursue a crush. They were boyfriends. They were in love. They had a future together, if things kept going well. Why would Christian want to introduce a complication?

It's not that serious, man, c'mon. Christian didn't mince words. He didn't hold onto something that was already dead. Once Charlotte was gone, he hadn't exactly wasted time pining for her. He'd accepted the change of the seasons, and if he was sick of Logan, he would've let him go.

Logan couldn't let himself think of the contrary.

"Break time, Logan."

He spun around and locked eyes with his manager, Peter. He even chanced a look at his phone, furrowing his brow. "Damn. Didn't realize it was that time."

"Don't sound so excited," Peter drawled as he continued down the aisles to catch any other stragglers.

Normally, Logan and Noah didn't have to be looked for. They kept an eye on the clock, and as soon as their break began, they embraced it.

My mind's not where it should be. Logan made his way toward the bathrooms with a heavy sigh. His hand squeezed tighter around his phone.

Two in the morning. Noah was probably up, but Logan didn't want to risk texting him if he might be sleeping the sickness off. Christian would've been passed out by now, for sure; it was shocking that he was awake at all when Logan had been getting ready to go to work. He wasn't going to wake Christian up either, not when Logan needed to prove to him that he had plenty of control over his own life. That he wasn't weak or codependent.

Am *I codependent?*

He'd never asked himself that question before. Had he missed some warning signs along the way? If he had, he didn't know how to fix it. The thought of pulling away from Christian choked him, and forcing himself to put his phone in his pocket instead of texting him seemed impossible. His arm was as heavy and thick as molasses. It couldn't move much slower.

But he did it. And when the anxiety bathed his throat in acid, he pushed it down one more time and focused on the goal ahead.

Working here was physical labor. It would wear him out and keep his thoughts from stirring too far in the wrong direction. He'd rather feel the burn of his muscles than the terror of losing the one person who mattered to him in life—or the fear of disappointing a second important person.

As Logan caught sight of the bathrooms, he also spotted a man standing in his path—massively muscular, blond, and watching him with a smirk. It was the very asshole who'd given Noah problems, the one whose name he still didn't know.

Apparently he was bored without Noah to mess with. Logan didn't even have time to take a steeling breath and drop his eyes before Blondie stepped in his path.

"Where's your *boyfriend*?" Blondie piped up.

"Fuck off," Logan muttered under his breath.

Hands landed on Logan's shoulders, and then were gone, replaced with the sharp pain in his back as he hit the wall. He flashed his gaze upward as Blondie hovered over him, seeming to almost scrape the ceiling. "What did you just say to me?"

Logan's mouth went dry. There were only a few ways this could go, and every single one led to Logan not keeping his job. All he needed was to throw one punch before he got labeled as a pissed-off black guy and booked for assault. Just one wrong move, and sirens would come pounding up the road, bringing with them guns and dogs and a special on the evening news all about him.

"Where's your respect?" Blondie spat. "You know how you and your little boyfriend walk around here with your noses up in the air? Think y'all are better than us?"

Logan curled his hands into fists. He couldn't breathe. He'd never dealt with this shit alone. Christian had always been there, and he could intimidate people with just one look. Not Logan. He hadn't realized exactly how powerless he was until right here, right now, when he couldn't move an inch.

"How about this? You apologize."

No. Even with the nausea in his gut, Logan refused to look this asshole in the eye and mumble out some pissy little apology. The punch would be better. Hell, even a concussion would be worth it. He lifted his head, gritted his teeth, and said it again, nice and clear this time. "Fuck. Off."

The second the fist came up, something else came through the air, light and bird-like. "Oh, don't you dare!"

Blondie staggered backward, whipping his head around. Logan looked with him, searching for the source of the voice, but he couldn't see around the corner. All he knew was that Blondie was going to hurry off and talk his way out of whatever shit he'd started—

"What's going on here?" Another voice, but familiar. Peter came into view, frowning, looking between him and Blondie.

Blondie scoffed. "Nothing. Just playing around here with Logan." He slapped Logan on the shoulder, and Logan smacked his hand away with a glare. "Break's over, right? Time to get back to work."

Before Blondie could take two steps, a girl stepped up beside Peter. She was familiar—the girl who often kept to herself with a book in the break room. She wore a scowl that looked far too expansive for such a tiny face. "No, *no*, that's not what he was doing, Peter. He was about to punch Logan."

"No shit." Peter's voice was tired. Logan could practically read the exhaustion in every part of his body—the realization that his night had just become filled with a hell of a lot more paperwork. "That true, Logan?"

Snitching didn't go well for guys in high school, and Logan had no idea what the protocol was now that he had a job in the adult world. Still shell-shocked from the entire altercation, he simply crossed his arms and stared at the floor.

"Oh, c'mon, he started messing around with me first!" Blondie snapped. "She didn't even show up until the very end. It was all just fun!"

"That's not true!" The girl waggled her finger at Peter. "Don't listen to him! I was right there, next to the frozen foods, and I saw the whole thing!"

Blondie took a step toward her, and Peter held up a hand as he spoke. "Okay, you know what? How about you and me go to the office and take a few notes about this, and then I can check out the cameras."

When silence from all parties greeted him, Peter cleared his throat. "Logan, I'm going to need to talk to you later too."

I didn't wanna get mixed up in shit. I just wanted to do my job and go home and cuddle my boyfriend. He nodded. Didn't seem as though there was any other way around it. As Peter and Blondie walked away, their footsteps heavy on the tile, Logan slowly released his fists and saw the nail marks left behind on his palms. *Fuck.*

"Hey."

The girl was still there, though, apparently. He shot her a look.

"You okay?"

Logan opened his mouth, closed it again, and settled for one last nod. He was turning into nothing but a bobblehead, and it pissed him off.

"Okay."

He didn't want to be stationary anymore. He pushed away from the wall.

"Is, um, is Noah okay?" she asked.

Logan froze.

"He's not here today. It's the first day he hasn't been here. I was worried maybe...maybe something happened to him."

Logan had no idea anyone had even noticed the two of them enough to learn their names. Did she already know him? Or was she just fixated on Noah for some reason? She might have a crush on him. He glanced over. She was cute, pixie cut and all, but he didn't want to break her heart and tell her that not only was Noah taken but also gay.

When she met his stare with the same stoic intensity he realized he was giving her, Logan remembered he hadn't said a word. "No, he's okay. He's sick. I can let him know you asked about him. What's your name?"

"Oh, he won't know who I am," she said with a laugh. "You two kind of keep to yourselves, don't you?" Her black eyes sparkled as brightly as Daiki's did when he laughed, the same narrow shape.

He needed some air, and badly. He wasn't allowed to leave the fucking building until his shift was over, but goddamn, did he wish he could go out front and catch a whiff of the honeysuckle to cleanse his palate. Anything to replace the stench of the fight.

It was still quiet, and she wasn't filling the silence. He cleared his throat and forced himself to speak. "Yeah, but I can tell him anyway. He might like that."

Her smile was a bit crooked. "Fine. Chelsea. You're sure he's just sick? He's coming back?"

Why do you care? Logan wanted to ask, but he kept it at bay. "Yeah. Promise. Just a stomach thing."

"Okay." Chelsea let out a heavy sigh. "I...I thought Joe drove him off."

"Joe?"

"The guy who was picking a fight with you. He's picked them with Noah, too, hasn't he?" Her expression went serious. "He talks about Noah in the back sometimes."

Logan's blood began boiling all over again. "I take it he didn't say very nice things."

Her lips thinned as she shook her head.

"Figures." Logan took a deep breath and let it out slowly, all too aware that venting against the asshole might put a target on his back, if Chelsea was as free with information with the rest of their coworkers as him. "Well. Noah's too tough to quit over something like that. Don't worry about him. He'll be back with me soon."

"Then I'll tell him I'm glad he's back the next time I see him," she said simply. "I'm glad to see you still here too. I know it's not easy working here sometimes."

She spoke with a sort of confidence Logan found himself envying. She hadn't even flinched when she called out Blondie. She looked as if she'd been ready to jump into the fray, even though Blondie had a good few inches on her, and she looked more thick than strong. And now, here she was, speaking plainly to Logan without any embarrassment at how he might take the words.

He didn't know how to reply to that kind of frankness. He'd just met her. He couldn't exactly start teasing her right off the bat. So Logan shrugged. "It's a job. They're never easy."

"I think they can be sometimes, if you love what you're doing."

I'm never gonna know how that feels. He simply gave her a small, tight smile.

"Do you want to have lunch later?" Chelsea tilted her head to the side.

Logan blinked. "Me and you?"

"Yeah." She gave him that crooked grin again. "You won't have Noah to sit with. And you shouldn't sit alone. It'll make Joe think he won something over you."

She had a point. He couldn't let that asshole think he'd won anything, if he even still had a job at the end of the day. *He will.* The thought flew through Logan's mind instantly. *I bet he fucking will. It'd be just my luck.*

But it was hard to feel that sort of negativity when Chelsea was standing right there, beaming, waiting so patiently for his answer to her invitation. So he nodded. "Yeah, okay. Sure."

"Cool. I'll come find you, then." She started taking a few steps backward. "We need to get back to work. I'm in canned goods right now."

"I'm in, uh, shampoo and shit."

Chelsea chuckled. "At least you'll have good smells around you while you're working. Bye, Logan."

"Bye."

It took him a few seconds to remember to head back to his section. Somehow, he realized, he'd just made a friend.

Weird.

*

Just take a melatonin or something, dude. It wasn't the first time sleep had evaded Christian, but it was annoying him a lot more than usual. For some reason, his body was restless, all stirred up and keen on Logan getting home, as if it wasn't going to be able to to rest until he saw him.

Normally he wouldn't care, but six in the morning was still a long time away. He checked his phone. *Four. Shit.* He dropped it again and stared at the ceiling.

Part of it, he knew, was because he was eager for something. Affection, maybe. Sex, definitely. Intimacy, more than anything. He didn't know how only sitting with Noah could upend him so easily. They'd made their way through a whole movie with Christian's arm over the back of the sofa and Noah sitting close enough to him that their legs touched, and their eyes never straying toward the other. Christian couldn't say a damn thing about what had happened on the screen.

He could say a hell of a lot about the smell of Noah's shampoo.

Some part of him needed to see Logan to confirm they were still *each other's.* Even though possessiveness didn't fill Christian's veins, the strong physical response he'd had the moment he and Noah shared the couch had almost overwhelmed him. He wanted to remember he could feel that for Logan with one look. That they could keep having it for the rest of their lives.

Because they would, of course. No matter what happened—no matter how many crushes either of them had, or if they acted on them or not—they'd spend all their days together. Christian knew it clearly. Something told him Logan did too.

But nights like this, when his future felt so tangled, he wanted just one quiet reassurance. He wanted to find it in Logan's body, with their hands lacing against the sheets and their hearts pounding, something as familiar to him as breathing. Especially when the rest of his life was so topsy-turvy.

Lusting for his roommate wasn't anything out of the ordinary. Logan wouldn't be the only one to own Christian's desire—other guys would as well. But the idea that Logan might not be disturbed by the idea was new.

As far as other novel things, the play Christian would be acting in was exceptional. The thought of spending the rest of the summer learning lines blew his mind. He didn't deserve it.

Maybe it was because of how different it was here in Fulton. In Greenbarrow, his life was paved out for him. He hadn't even made his own breakfast. He hadn't needed to think. All he'd had to do was keep his eyes forward and his feet moving, and he knew he'd get where he needed to be eventually.

For a long time, he'd considered it normal, having things placed in a simple line for him. That was how it was for everyone there. Eventually, children would take over the family businesses. Farms would stay in the same lineage. One day, everyone would be buried in the same, overcrowded cemetery—Christian could pick out the Daniels plot behind the church with his eyes closed.

Logan's family, really, were the odd ones out of the bunch. They owned the pharmacy and the funeral parlor, but never expected Logan to take up the mantle once they were gone. On the contrary, they demanded that he forge his own path.

But not too individual a path. Christian would never forgive the Browns for that. They had an incredibly talented, driven son, one who could've taken the playwriting world by storm with only a little bit of training, yet they'd forced him into a far smaller hole. Logan wasn't going to be stuck in the same rigid path as every other family in town, but goddammit, they still chose everything for him. Logan's life was on their terms.

And Christian's life on his mother's.

During the first few nights of staying in their dorm, Christian hadn't been able to stop dreaming of Greenbarrow. There was the quiet strip of Main Street, with three stoplights and no chain stores. He remembered the excitement when the next town over, a good thirty minutes away, got a Walmart Supercenter. Whole families would make a day of going to fill up their trucks with things they couldn't get in town. He dreamed of climbing trees with Logan with tiny hands and pushing himself to get one branch above him so Logan would still think he was cool. He recalled the outcropping of greenery near the church, where all the kids would play when the service was over, pushing through the shrubs and low-hanging vines as though they were exploring a jungle. It was all as familiar as the back of his own hand.

Right now, even with his eyes closed, he couldn't envision a damn thing from home.

People would say things about him and Logan when they went back. The townspeople had always thought Logan was a little big for his own britches, with his books and how much louder he talked about his dreams than Christian did, but the fact remained they'd both done the impossible. They'd left. It didn't matter that they were still in Georgia and going to a state school rather than a fancy private one. They'd crossed the borders into a small blue county, surrounded by red, and picked a liberal college. They were uppity now. They had their noses in the air. And nothing they could do would change that perception.

Can I ever go back?

The question took him by surprise. His breathing caught and his eyes flew open. He stared at the ceiling until they ached from drying out.

That he couldn't immediately say *yes* was terrifying.

For a little town surrounded by nothing but long stretches of fields and no buildings over three stories, Greenbarrow was painfully restrictive. No one could step out of line. Everyone remembered every single scandal that had ever rocked the village, from its founding onward. A sinner was brought to the pulpit and prayed over by the whole congregation. From age six to sixteen, there were nights Christian thought about grabbing Logan by the hand and running for the horizon. He could never go through with it only because he imagined that no matter how far they ran, they'd never get out of sight. Greenbarrow was a vacuum. It sucked people back in before they even got a few miles away.

He and Logan had gotten out, but they would be expected to return all the same. They'd gotten around going home for Thanksgiving, Christmas, and the summer, but that would never happen again. Guilt trips were one thing, but threats would soon follow. Logan had everything to lose the second his parents decided he shouldn't be at college, if it was keeping him away from what was most important to them: family. They paid for his tuition. He'd gotten as many scholarships as he could, but nothing need-based, not when they had so much money. They'd suck him in. They'd trap him. Chain him down. Never let him leave.

And Christian? His mom had power too. She...

...No, she doesn't have a goddamn thing over me. Does she?

He sat straight up in bed and grabbed his chest, where his heart burned from how quickly it was racing. Air was hard to find—breathing shallow. A fistful of sheets. Cold sweat.

He'd never thought about it. Not once had he considered the position he'd put himself in the second he came to this school.

He was an adult now. Nineteen years old. He'd won his full scholarship to FSU through his own merit—by the talent of his feet and legs. No loans, no credit cards, no debt beholden to his parents. His own bank account. His own driver's license. His social security card and his birth certificate tucked in a folder in his room, just in case he'd needed them at school.

All they had was a room full of old childhood memories and the power of words. And he could throw all of those in the trash.

Christian's gaze darted around the room. He and Logan had bought everything there with their own fucking money. He had the funds to pay for books for his next semester. Everything else was covered. Even his goddamn accounting major.

That godforsaken, stressful, frustrating, useless major.

It brought him no joy. It was safe. Numbers were simple to understand, and calculators were easy to use. Formulas, he could write down and have reference to. And he was never going to own a business, so he didn't have to worry about entrepreneurial struggles. But, to him, it was soulless. He was sure there were thousands of people who enjoyed their work as accountants, and the promised money was enough to appeal to just as many others. But Christian despised the idea.

He knew how to live for tomorrow. He knew it, because he experienced it every damn day that he woke up with his script on the nightstand. And the thought of going without that cut him to the quick.

"I think..." His mouth was dry. He swallowed hard. The thought was foolish, but more than anything, he needed to verbalize it. He needed to *hear* it in the air, as though he was casting a spell— as if it might actually be possible. "...I'm gonna change my major."

A chill raced through him from head to toe. His lungs were empty.

Christian Daniels was in charge of his own life. Nothing could stop him from doing what he wanted, as long as he put in the time and the passion. He could focus on whatever he fucking wanted to. He could live a worthwhile life.

All he had to do was take a leap.

The sound of a door flying open and hitting a wall made Christian jolt. Next he knew, he was no longer alone in the tower of strength he was building up. He was in an apartment with his roommate, whose normally light footsteps now thundered down the hall and into the bathroom.

Shit, dude. Apparently he wasn't out of the woods yet after all.

"Does it piss him off, when people help?"

"Sometimes. But I think...maybe he likes it too."

Without another thought, Christian came to his feet. There was only one way to find out.

When he opened his bedroom door, the sound of retching was impossible to miss. Yellow light bled into the dark hallway through the crack in the bathroom door. Christian let himself in, pushing it wide open.

"Don't." Noah lifted a hand behind him, the other white-knuckling around the edge of the toilet. "It's gross." His skin had always been pale, but his bare back looked pallid beneath the fluorescent light bulbs.

Tempting as it would've been to shrug and let Noah keep his pride, Christian made himself stay put. "You look like hell. Are you really gonna tell me you don't need anything?"

Noah hung his head. "Right, because what guy wants somebody to see him like this?" His voice was raw.

"I'm not gonna tell anybody you puked your guts out," Christian drawled as he went to the closet beside the sink. "God. Just because your momma's not here to rub your back doesn't mean you've gotta do this alone." He took a washcloth from one of the shelves and ran it under cold water until it was dripping. "I told Logan I'd keep an eye on you, and I intend to."

When Christian knelt beside him, Noah turned his head away. His fingers trembled. "Why does he even care?" he mumbled.

"Does he need a reason?"

Noah didn't reply. Christian pressed the cold cloth to the back of his neck, and Noah sucked in a sharp breath in response, eyes squeezing shut.

"We both care." Christian said the words too softly—too intimately—and before he could let Noah process them, he quickly followed up. "Get used to it."

Noah leaned into Christian's hand with a heavy sigh. As he sat back, he wrapped his arms around his middle, just beneath the twin scars under his pectorals, as if giving himself a hug. "I need you to do something for me, Christian."

"Mm?" He watched Noah closely. His earlier moment of triumph—reclaiming his life, making his own decisions, and steering his ship straight where he wanted it to go—had left him floating in an odd fugue state. He could do anything he wanted here. If Noah needed him to fly, he'd damn well try.

Noah met his gaze, bloodshot eyes looking half drained. He needed strength, and Christian had it in spades to give. In this moment, Christian realized, he would give Noah anything he asked—anything at all. He hung on his breath, watching as Noah opened his mouth.

"Never. Ever. Let me eat that big-ass burger again."

Taken aback, Christian burst out laughing. He squeezed the back of Noah's neck and sent cool droplets streaming down his freckled back. "You know what? I'll do that. I'll slap it right out of your hand next time."

"You're a gem," Noah mumbled, but his quirking lips did Christian a world of good. Noah leaned into him, putting his head on his shoulder and going halfway limp. "Thanks for not calling me disgusting or something."

For some reason, those words felt as though they carried something more than just the fact that there was vomit in the toilet. Christian didn't quite understand it, but he replied anyway, voice as light as a cloud, "Ain't nothing disgusting about you, Noah."

Noah sighed. His eyes closed. Christian made the decision then and there not to move an inch until he was asked, even if they both had to damn well sleep there. If Christian Daniels could do one thing, he wasn't going to let this guy down, no matter how tough he wanted to seem.

He could get back to his own soul-searching later.

Chapter Eleven

The quiet crinkling of the plastic unfolding beside Logan drew his eye. As he worked on his sandwich, he watched Chelsea meticulously open each part of her lunch, separated not just by the walls in her lunch box but by disposable layers as well.

When she caught his look, she smiled. "Some food doesn't taste good when it's all tossed in the same place together."

Logan blinked. "It's all going the same place. It'll just end up in a sludge anyway."

"But I don't have to force myself to endure a sludge," she pointed out with a directness that was quickly becoming familiar. "Peanut butter and pickles might be nice apart, but they wouldn't make a good flavor in my mouth together."

She has a point. "Still can't imagine taking the time to do that every single day."

Chelsea chuckled as she placed the individual raw vegetables back into her box. "It's easier when you have someone you care about helping you."

What a domestic idea that was. Without hesitation, he imagined himself and Christian elbow-to-elbow in the kitchen, making dinner together, sharing kisses over the food as they worked. He'd been prepared to make fun of it, but with each passing second he warmed. "I guess I can see the appeal. Boyfriend?"

She shook her head. "No."

Though he waited for more, she didn't give it, and Logan wasn't in the mood for prying. The past hour had been stressful enough. He popped the top of his soda and took a slurp, then set it back on the floor beside him.

They sat before one of the broad glass windows of the store, the ones that created a wall facing the parking lot. The only cars there belonged to those currently working—no one else had the sense to poke around the parking lot at four in the morning. Though the others had retreated to the company-sanctioned break room, it was too suffocating for Logan. Everyone knew, it seemed, about the earlier confrontation. Everyone gossiped and whispered and stared at him. And Blondie wasn't there. It had taken a good twenty minutes of gentle grilling from Peter in the office before Logan was allowed to leave, and that had been difficult enough. All he could do was tell the facts and affirm that, yes, it *was* him in the security camera footage, and intentionally avoid answering direct questions about how Blondie was harassing Noah.

It wasn't Logan's story to tell. If Peter wanted to ask Noah about it when he got back, then he could.

"What about you?" Chelsea asked, breaking him from his thoughts. "Girlfriend? Boyfriend? Datemate?"

Unfamiliar though he was with the last term, he simply furrowed his brow and stared at his sandwich. "Boyfriend."

"Oh, cool! But not Noah?"

"Not Noah."

"Cool, cool." She took a sharp, loud bite of a carrot stick, straight through the middle. "Do you want to tell me about him?"

The real question was did Logan ever *not* want to talk about Christian. He was Logan's favorite and most-studied subject. Up until recently, that had been a point of pride. Now, he questioned whether or not he should know as much about him as he did.

"He's my best friend. Name's Christian. We've been together for…for a few months, I guess." As if he didn't know the exact hour they'd become official boyfriends, much less the date. "He means everything to me. I'm starting to think that might not be what's best."

Chelsea kicked her feet out, her black nonslip shoes and vibrant green-and-yellow shoelaces at odds with the white-speckled linoleum tiles beneath them. "That sounds like a story waiting to happen."

Maybe it would be better not to rely on a total stranger to listen to Logan's concerns, but who else was he going to discuss them with? Noah? Noah wasn't a safe sounding board anymore—not now that Logan had admitted to himself that he *liked* him. And Logan had been so careful to focus one hundred percent on his classes and Christian, and no one else. So that left…a stranger.

Logan sighed. "I'm codependent on him." He shot Chelsea a look from the corner of his eye.

"Oh yeah?"

"That's what we've both decided." Logan fiddled with the tab on his can of soda. "I didn't plan it, but...here we are."

Chelsea made a thoughtful sound. She crunched on celery, the resounding *crack* loud in the room. "So how do you feel about it?"

"What are you, a therapist?"

She laughed. "Just super empathetic. It helps."

A moment passed, and Logan glanced her way, but she continued staring out of the window.

She finally said, "I know some things about being codependent. I thought maybe I could be of some assistance."

Logan shook his head. "You don't even know me."

"I know. And you don't have to tell me anything you don't want me to hear. But...if you need someone to listen, I'm happy to. And if you need advice, I like giving that as well."

It had been too long since Logan had anyone other than Christian to listen to him without expecting something in return. It might be a low moment to lean on her when he didn't even know her, but...

I need to do this. I promised Christian I'd try to make my life bigger, one step at a time.

"I guess I sort of lost track of what made our relationship healthy. I let it spiral into something bigger." Logan rubbed the back of his neck. "We've been close since we were young. He was the center of my world before I even knew what that meant. My family was always so busy they barely even had time for me, and the other kids weren't all that interested in being friends. So by the time I figured out I actually wanted to be with him? Romantically? He was pretty much *everything else* in my life too."

Chelsea hummed. Just a hum, like she didn't have anything she wanted to say but needed him to know he was being heard.

"So here's the thing. I know we're still teenagers. We're only nineteen. There's a hell of a lot that's gonna change ahead of us. But..." Logan winced. "I had this thought our whole lives would line up together. We'd share as many college classes as we could. We'd get married someday, if we had somewhere safe to do it. Kids, the white picket fence, the whole thing." He hesitated.

Chelsea smiled, finally peeking his way. "And what did Christian have to say about that?"

Logan lifted his brows, reluctant to say. He finally settled on a huff. "Okay, yeah, so planning out our whole futures without asking him what he wanted to do was...shitty."

There. He'd said it. It made his chest hurt like hell, but he'd accepted how presumptuous it had been. "I get it. I know I don't *wanna* be this way. I don't wanna make him think that if he doesn't do what I want, I'll leave. But I get so damn scared sometimes. He wants to go off and be a big actor on the stage, and I dunno if there's room for me there in his life. I'm just some kid from Georgia. I've got an accent. I'm nothing compared to him."

"Hold on. Does he say that to you?"

"No!" Logan blurted. "No, never. H-he makes me feel like I hung the fucking *moon*, but I...I keep thinking maybe he's got it wrong."

Chelsea kicked her foot out again, bumping their shoes together. "Why don't you let him decide that, huh?"

He could practically see Christian grinding his teeth, shaking his head, grunting out that he'd make his *own* decisions—not Logan. That he knew Logan was supposed to be the damn brains, but Christian's head wasn't completely hollow or anything.

Logan settled for a slow nod, even if he wasn't sure he believed it yet.

"So." Chelsea's voice stayed quiet and direct. "You know you're codependent on your boyfriend. Is he okay with you being that way, or does he want...something else?"

"He wants me to change," Logan admitted. "He's not being an asshole about it—I swear to God, Chelsea, I don't deserve him, he's being too good about all my bull—but he *does* want me to try and...I dunno, make my life *bigger* than just him. Other friends, going out by myself sometimes, doing things he doesn't have to hold my hand through."

"I think that sounds smart," Chelsea remarked.

Smart or not, it was all Logan had. "I wanna try. For him."

"Not for you?"

Logan paused, frowning. He hadn't asked himself if any of this was for himself yet. "I dunno."

"Don't you think it'd be good for *you* too, if you have all these experiences? Things you could have just for yourself instead of being based on your boyfriend?"

That sounded so simple. Almost *silly*. Logan's entire life was based around having things to tell Christian at the end of the day, to impress him so he'd see Logan as a worthy friend and stick around.

The silence stretched as Logan parsed through the idea, never quite finding the end of it, until he realized it was getting awkward and scratched at his cheek. "I-I, uh..."

Chelsea bumped their shoes together again. It seemed as companionable as a little punch on the arm from a friend. "I've got a suggestion."

She went for her pocket, rooting around, and pulled out a wallet that she began to sort through. "You don't have to say yes or no, you can *think* about it, but this place has been really good for me, so maybe it could help you too?"

All sorts of scary ideas came to mind. *A church? A cult?*

But what came out of her wallet was a business card, and the moment Logan had it in his hand he blinked in confusion. "Sweet Grounds?"

"It's a coffee shop." Chelsea paused. "A *queer* coffee shop. One of the only ones I've ever been to specifically for LGBTQ people." She smiled and shrugged. "The owner's a really sweet woman. All her staff are super great. And they have events there, like poetry nights and speed dating and ways to get involved with an older mentor, and... I don't know, Logan, it just sounds like it might be a good place for you to meet some new friends."

Logan looked up from the colorful card. "You're queer too?"

"I am! I'm aromantic. Means I don't experience romantic attraction at all. I spend a lot of time at Sweet Grounds—it's really awesome to have a queer space that isn't centered around dating or meeting people, like bars or clubs often seem to be, do you know what I mean?"

Logan was still trying to wrap his head around the concept of being *aromantic.* He cared deeply for Christian and felt equal warmth and fondness for Noah, so he couldn't conceive of never experiencing that attraction for either of them.

I don't have to understand it. Just respect what she's got going on.

He was rubbing the card between his fingers, struggling with a response, when Chelsea looked down at her phone.

"Shit. Break's over, dude, we've gotta get back to work."

"Fuck, I barely ate anything."

Chelsea laughed. "I made you talk too much. That's my fault." She stood up and held out a hand. "Need a lift?"

With anyone else, Logan might've said no. But something about Chelsea was just as warm as the colors of the card in his hand, as the safety that surrounded Christian. Logan let her pull him to his feet. "It's weird. Even without eating, I...I think I feel a little better," he confessed.

Chelsea sighed, but a soft and pleased one that matched the sparkle in her eyes. "Good! Good, I'm so glad to hear it."

She patted him on the arm before gathering up her trash, then made her way toward the trash can. "Listen, just think about it, okay? Sweet Grounds! I'm there all the time!"

"Yeah," Logan called back. He stared at the card for another moment, then pulled out his wallet to put it inside.

Might not be a bad idea after all.

*

By the grace of God alone, Christian didn't have to carry Noah to bed. It had taken time, both of them sitting silently on the floor, Christian's arm around Noah to keep him stabilized, but eventually Noah got to his feet without a word and flushed the toilet. With a quick swish of water in his mouth that he then spat in the sink, Noah seemed right as rain once again. He'd stopped at the bathroom door only to murmur a word of thanks, and then he was gone.

Christian was used to silence. He didn't need everything to be talked about. But the realization that his attraction was steadily growing—and that it had nothing to do with pure platonic gratitude—was something he didn't know how to sit with. He needed to talk it over with Logan. The two of them could find some common ground in that rising heat and figure out exactly what they wanted to do about it.

They'd get there eventually. There was so much else to discuss first. Things had changed for the better. For once, Christian had a course set before him that he *liked*, and all he needed was Logan's approval before he'd know it was the absolute right thing to do.

By the time he heard the front door open, Christian still hadn't slept a wink. It was foolish, since he had rehearsals and a job to think about, but he was too far gone. The sun had risen a half hour before, finally transforming the quiet gray of the skies into a vibrant orange.

Seeing Logan would be far more beautiful.

As Logan snuck into the bedroom with a sleepy gaze, his eyes lit up as soon as they landed on Christian. "Hey. Is Noah doing okay?"

"He's fine. All tucked into bed." He'd keep his promise and not go talking about how Noah had blown chunks. He'd let him have his self-respect, if nothing else. "Didn't even need to put a baby monitor on him."

Logan snorted, but paused at the foot of the bed. "Why the hell are you up so early, if nothing's wrong with him?"

"Up *early*?" Christian laughed and shook his head. "Babe, I haven't slept at all."

"Why not?" Logan stopped fiddling with his belt, concern written all over his face. "What's wrong? What's happened?"

"Nothing, nothing, just..."

Christian didn't even know where to begin. There was a fog in his mind from sleepiness, and only the certainty that he was doing the right thing cut a spotlight through it. He'd had hours to meditate on his decision, but putting words to it wasn't as simple as he thought it would be. *Wish I could just pull you in my head with me.*

"...I've been thinking a lot. Made up my mind about some stuff. Fuck, I don't know why it took me so long to figure it all out, but it's here now, Logan, and it makes sense; I know it does."

Logan sat on the edge of the bed. "Well, c'mon, tell me about it." He reached a hand across the sheets.

It was impossible to think of it all in a line, but as Christian interlaced their fingers, he tried. Seeing Logan there in all his glory—that gorgeous dark skin, the keen gaze, and the way he looked good enough to eat—made his mind fixate instantly. "First things first, I wanna fuck your brains out."

Logan laughed. He squeezed Christian's hand and shook his head, giving him a faux serious frown that never quite reached the sparkle in his eyes. "Talk first, sex later."

Christian couldn't find it in himself to be frustrated. "Fine. I'm never going back home."

Logan's eyes widened. "What?"

"Never. I hate it there. I don't wanna go back. And you know what? My mom can't even make me. No one can. What are they going to do, arrest a full-grown adult for making a place for himself in his own college town? Fuck that. I never have to go back on that turf."

"But..." Logan shook his head. "Your friends, your family—"

"If they give a shit about me, they can come see me here, huh?" Christian sprang up from the bed and paced toward the closet. "I mean, c'mon, man, how many times have you *actually* heard from somebody from home? You think they weren't dying to get rid of us all along? Bet they'll be thrilled in their pants, scrubbing the whole damn town white again—"

"If your family comes here," Logan interrupted firmly, "they'll see this bedroom. One bed. What are they gonna say about that?"

Christian stopped on a dime. He knew the reality of that—and he also knew why it hadn't occurred to him to worry about her seeing it in person. "Logan. Babe. My mom's not gonna come see me. You know she's not."

When Logan stayed silent, Christian looked at him. He was staring at his joined hands, head turned downward, gaze hidden.

Suddenly Christian's concerns were less important. "What's wrong?"

Logan opened his mouth, then closed it, looking away. "Nah, I wanna hear what you've got to say first."

"Babe—"

"I'll talk when you're done." Logan met his gaze. The visible pain in his eyes took Christian's thoughts off course, and he fought to find his way back.

"Anyway, that's...I don't even care if she comes." Christian waved it off, trying to get rid of the pang in the base of his stomach so he could move on to the next, more important subjects. "I'm changing my major too. Accounting is a piece of shit. Always knew it wasn't for me. Just because all the other damn jocks are doing that or, what, sports medicine? That doesn't mean I've gotta do it too. So I'm switching to theater the second I can. Dunno why I didn't do it in the first place."

Logan's brows lifted in clear surprise. "Seriously?"

That shock made Christian's heart thud a little faster. He licked his dry lips and went on. "Nobody can stop me. My scholarship's gonna be fine as long as I don't fuck up my knee or something. That means it's all paid for. I've just gotta juggle my time to make sure I can handle performances and games and practice, and, hell, you can help me with that, right? You're damn good at it, Logan."

Logan nodded silently. He stopped tracking Christian, staring into space. The way he turned his head made the dawn spill over his expression, illuminating it little by little.

"And after school, you and me, we can just go off wherever we want, and we'll make it work, okay? Even if we don't have a lot of money or whatever, we're gonna fucking do great." Christian came quickly back toward the bed, because with each inch of Logan's expression coming into the light, all he could see was his fear. "And..."

There was more. There was Noah. There was the stunning awareness of how similar he and Christian could be, and how he felt drawn to that—to a kindred spirit rather than someone who could complement him. But even as he prepared to say it, Logan fixed him with such a shaky stare that he hesitated.

"What's wrong?" he asked softly, reaching to trail the back of his fingers down Logan's cheek.

Logan shook his head. He didn't lean into Christian's touch.

"Logan."

Nothing came.

Impatience bubbled up inside Christian. "I need you to talk to me. Something's wrong. I can see it all over your face."

"It's not important." Logan locked his eyes on Christian's with a frown. "It's more of the same."

"What?"

"Me being scared or nervous or fucking clingy as shit. You've got these big dreams and ideas, and I..." He shook his head again, and Christian dropped his hand from his cheek. "Shit, I'm afraid to talk about it. I-I'm trying to be better than I was—you know, about being *codependent*. If I talk about it, maybe...maybe I haven't grown at all."

"Are you being real right now?" Christian asked, voice tight. "That's not true at all—" He cut off when he saw Logan look away and drag his legs to his chest. "Hey, hey." A moment ago, Logan had been fearful but open, and now he was closed off. Christian dug through his mind, trying to find the answer to what he'd done wrong.

Their whole friendship, they could brush off their worries, their fears, and move on from them instead of discussing anything too deeply. *Right*? Couldn't they still do that now?

We're not just friends anymore. The memory of sitting across from Logan in the restaurant weeks earlier, holding hands and promising to do better about treating him like a *boyfriend*, came to mind.

Christian knelt in front of him. Even with their height difference, he found himself looking up at Logan. He rested his hands on Logan's thighs. "Babe. I love you. Okay? If you're upset about something, I-I wanna *hear* about it."

Logan made fists—but after a long moment, he nodded. "Yeah. Not exactly *communicating* with you if I keep it all inside, right?"

"Exactly."

It took a bit more time. Seconds turned into a minute. As uncomfortable as it made Christian to wait, he forced himself through it. Logan was worth it.

When Logan quietly spoke, his voice was brittle. "You've got huge ideas about what you wanna do. It's fucking *incredible*. But maybe I won't be able to keep up. Like, think about it. Your college is paid for by your scholarship. I'm not that lucky. If I tried to change my major, my mom could tell me she's not gonna pay for my school anymore. I'd have to drop out until I could raise enough money to come back. Do you know how scary that is?"

Logan lifted his head and revealed brown eyes that were filled to the brim with despair. "I don't wanna teach, man. It's not my bag—you and me both know that. Wh-What if I see you chasing your dream and I get fucking jealous as hell that you get to do it instead of me, and I burn our whole damn relationship to the ground?"

You wouldn't do that, Christian wanted to say. Logan loved him. Logan supported every bit of Christian, from his good parts to his bad. But Logan wasn't perfect, just like Christian wasn't. They both had a mean streak through them, one that had manifested multiple times in their friendship. They were growing up now, and they were figuring out how to have a healthy, long-term relationship, but it didn't mean they wouldn't trip up.

Christian cupped Logan's hand in one of his own and brought it to his lips. He left a kiss right on Logan's knuckles, watching him so closely that he saw the moment Logan looked away with a smile he was trying to hide. "You do that? We'll talk about it. If I make you feel shitty? We'll talk about it. If we fuck up, *we'll talk about it*. Just like we're doing now. You understand?"

Logan hesitated—but he nodded.

"You want me to stop this whole theater thing, sweetheart?"

"No." Logan said it so quickly he couldn't have possibly given himself time to think through it. "I meant what I said before. I wanna see you kick ass. If I've gotta live the boring life, then...then you deserve to shine."

Christian's chest ached. "But I wanna see you happy."

"I'm happy when I'm with you." Logan's words lifted trepidation inside Christian, but before he could voice it, Logan went on. "And I'm gonna *learn* how to be happy with everybody else too. No matter how hard I've gotta work to get there."

"You'd better," Christian blurted without thinking.

Logan rolled his eyes and shook his head. "I'm working on it. I made a friend today and everything."

"Yeah?"

"Her name's Chelsea. She works with me and Noah. She...taught me a lot, actually. We had lunch today. She invited me to hang out with her sometime." Logan chewed on his bottom lip. "I think I'm gonna do it."

I think you should. Christian held the thought back before it reached his mouth. Instead he kissed Logan's hand again—hopefully silent approval wouldn't feel like he was manipulating Logan into doing exactly what Christian wanted rather than letting him make his own decision.

Logan took a deep breath. "Can I tell you something?"

"Yeah, man."

"I wanna thank you. For listening. For hanging in there with me and not cutting me off the second we realized I might've fucked some stuff up."

Christian huffed. "I love you. So. Much. Gotta believe me when I say that. We've both fucked up." He cupped Logan's cheek. "And we're both gonna do it again. But as long as we keep *trying*, then we'll fix it too."

Logan nodded, his eyes falling shut. He was so damn beautiful, but looked so exhausted too. Even in the moment, Noah's tired face came to mind. Was it the right time to mention him? Christian had no idea. But keeping his mouth shut about his other realizations that night seemed foolish now.

"I realized something tonight when I was taking care of your boy," Christian drawled, his lips quirking when he watched Logan roll his eyes. "Hell, maybe it's a bad time to bring it up. But I wanted you to know that I...*get* it now. What you see in him. 'Cuz I might see it too."

Logan jerked, his gaze flying to Christian's. "What?"

"Yeah. Dunno if it's just me seeing what you see, but I'm definitely *feeling* something for him now. Even if it's small." Christian kept his hand on Logan's jaw, studying his expression intently. "How's...how's that make you feel?"

Logan opened his mouth and closed it again, letting out a sharp breath through his nose. "I-I...scared? Nervous you're gonna leave me for him?"

"Nah, nah, listen to me." Christian held Logan's face in both hands and put their foreheads together. "When you felt something for Noah, you knew it wasn't you wanting to leave me. Just something *different*. Remember?"

Logan nodded feverishly, as if he was trying to convince himself.

"This is the same damn thing. Just like when I was interested in both you and Charlotte." He grinned unwillingly, trying to soften the tension in the air. "The difference is neither of us is gonna break up with the other person to make them face what they're feeling. We're gonna figure it out and help each other. Yeah?"

Logan stayed quiet.

"Is that okay?" The last thing Christian wanted to do was trap Logan.

Logan inhaled deeply. "Can I, uh, get back to you about what I'm feeling? Not mad. Promise I'm not mad. I-I wanna work through this first. Okay?"

That wasn't completely promising. Was it Logan closing up and hiding his thoughts again? Would Christian do damage to their relationship if he pushed? He made himself hold back. If Logan was doing better, then Christian had to give him a chance to show it. "Will you talk to me if you need help?"

Logan nodded once more. "Yeah, babe. I mean it."

"Okay. Thanks." Christian leaned in, brushed a tender kiss across Logan's mouth, and pulled him close. "I love you."

"Love you too."

The two of them fell back into the pillows and cuddled up. All of Christian's earlier plans of seduction had left him. Now it was just the two of them finding safety in each other, silently reaffirming everything they loved about being so near they practically shared one body.

Words could come later, after sleep. Right now, this was all they needed.

Chapter Twelve

Logan hesitated outside Noah's open door for a few moments before he knocked. "Hey."

Noah whirled around in his desk chair, grinning. "Hey!" He picked his phone up off his desk and checked it. "Geez, you scared me. Thought maybe I might've lost track of time and we were late to work or something."

"Nah, don't worry about it." Logan leaned against the doorframe and tried to push down the fluttering in his gut. It wasn't easy, accepting that Noah made him nervous in a different, yet familiar way now. Just looking him full in the eye could send Logan's heart racing. "What're you up to?"

"Nothing, really. Catching up with some old friends." He thumbed toward the screen where, even now, a chat client was flying with updated messages. "What about you?"

Logan fought back his frown. Christian was already at work, which seemed like an ideal time for him to go check out this coffee shop Chelsea had pointed him toward. Inviting Noah only made it more appealing—making new friends with someone he cared about by his side—but the last thing he wanted to do was interrupt him. "Uh. Not much." He cleared his throat. "Never mind."

As Logan turned to leave, Noah's laugh stopped him in his tracks. "Come on. Is that it? Just going to pretend you don't have anything else to say?"

"Ah..." Logan crossed his arms and looked over his shoulder. "I mean, you're *busy*."

"Not too busy for *you*." Noah minimized the chat window and stood up. His bright eyes were eager, and his smile unmistakably directed toward Logan with the full force of the sun. "What's with you? What happened to the guy who used to drag me off to play video games even if I was doing homework?"

That was different. It was during the school year when Christian was running around with Charlotte, and Logan was still trying to make him jealous. Now he could recognize that—and he knew what a shithead he'd been at the time. Shithead Logan was the same guy who wanted Christian to give up his dreams so he could spend every second by Logan's side, the two of them suffering through drudgery together for the rest of their lives. And he was trying not to be that asshole anymore. "Just trying to do better, dude."

"Well, I'm all ears. What is it? Play a shooter? Go for another jog?"

Logan's cheeks warmed at the mere thought of their last jog, how obviously Logan had been checking Noah out. "I actually got an invite to a little coffee shop. Sweet Grounds. You heard of it?"

Noah's eyes lit up. "I *have*, actually. Haven't been there yet though. Who asked you?"

"Chelsea? We work with her—"

"Yeah, yeah, I remember her!" Noah nodded. "She's a sweetie."

Logan shrugged, trying to seem nonchalant. "It sounded like it might be your jam. So if I'm already going...do you wanna tag along?"

Noah's lips curved in a small, mischievous smirk. "You just need my car, don't you?"

It'd be an easy out to say that was all he wanted. But Logan scoffed. "No, I actually *like* hanging out with you." He crossed his arms. "If you don't wanna go, you don't have to, but—"

"No, no, I want to go, are you kidding?" Noah looked around, then moved quickly around the room, gathering wallet and keys as he went. "I just...you know, I figured you'd go with Christian or whatever."

Fed up with himself, Logan looked Noah straight in the eye, stopping his roommate in his tracks. "I wanna go with *you*."

For a long moment, Noah stared at him, his bushy auburn brows lifted in surprise. And then unmistakable pleasure bled into his expression. Noah had always been an easy guy to read. Logan just wasn't used to that ease making himself flustered.

"Well, what are we waiting for, then?" Noah grinned, linked elbows with Logan, and began pulling him along.

The drive wasn't long, spent mainly with Noah singing along with the radio in a voice he seemed to still be figuring out the highs and lows of, and Logan staring out the window pretending he wasn't enjoying the sound of it anyway. It was a simple pleasure, being near Noah, not needing to fill the air with conversation.

Logan had spent long weeks trying to stand on his own two feet without Christian's help, and months before that unwittingly clinging to him like a child. It was embarrassing to remember, and exhausting to figure out how to stop.

By the time Noah pulled up to the coffee shop, Logan was half asleep, lulled by the steady sway of the car and the company of the second man he was fond of. The marquee was colorful—cute, even—with a rainbow of small coffee beans tucked under the pastel sign. *Sweet Grounds*. It was so at odds from the gay bars Logan had driven by but been too afraid to go inside, so much *softer* than them, that he wasn't even sure how to parse it.

"You ready?" Noah asked, as if he could sense Logan's trepidation.

Logan took a deep breath, nodded, and got out of the car.

The wide glass windows gave him a peek into the cozy surroundings before they entered, but the opening of the door bathed him in the familiar, comforting aroma of freshly brewed coffee. While he was used to tiny coffee shops with only a few hard seats and tables, maybe a couple of comfy chairs that people often fought to get to first, the atmosphere in Sweet Grounds was completely different.

There was comfort everywhere. Thick, plush chairs were scattered around with couches. Even the tables had an elegant curve to them rather than a sharp contemporary flair. A corkboard covered the entire wall from Logan's waist to the ceiling on his side, stacked with notices. Protests, educational seminars, political gatherings, and invitations to local concerts and poetry readings overlapped. But what drew Logan's eye were the lists to volunteer for events all over town—working at a local homeless shelter, cleaning up the litter by the roads, and delivering food to local homebound people.

Line after line notated names and contact info. As though people here really wanted to help.

There was more. His eyes wandered to the bookshelves lining the back of the vast room, and even from a distance, he could see some of the sections listed: LGBTQ+ History, LGBTQ+ Romance, Cookbooks, How To.

Something about this building suddenly resonated as so unmistakably *right* that Logan's heart finally slowed from its anxious thundering. It was the quiet, the warmth, the *magic* that surrounded him.

How do places like this even exist?

"Hey there."

The voice from behind the counter made Logan jump, but Noah spoke brightly beside him. "Hey, how are you?"

"Good." A woman wiped the counter down, flashing them a crooked smile. She was beautiful, the orange of her dress stunning against the mahogany of her skin, and the wrinkles at the edges of her eyes whispering that this wasn't the only grin she'd flashed recently. "Can I help you find anything?"

Noah immediately looked at Logan, prompting him silently, but he didn't have any words. As safe as the building itself felt, the twisting in his gut wasn't as easily driven away. *What was I hoping for? See Chelsea right off the bat, then move onto hanging out with her? What happened to the guy who could charm anybody he saw?*

He knew the answer to that. He'd always had Christian at his side in those days, someone to attempt to impress with his jokes and the girls he could pull. He didn't have the same familiarity with Noah, nor the ability to distract himself with flirting, and besides, the woman seemed far older than him anyway, enough to be intimidating about hitting on.

Noah touched Logan's back and rubbed it with a smile, then looked back at the woman, unaware that he'd lit Logan's spine with flashy sparks with just one graze. "It's, uh, it's our first time here. We had a friend tell us about it. Wanted to pop in and see what sort of stuff you've got going on."

"Well, I'm glad you stopped by, sweetie." She beamed. "I'm Adele. I own the place. Always happy to see some new faces here."

"Oh, you *own* the whole thing?" Noah asked, his jaw dropping. He moved in a little closer, already carrying on the conversation even while Logan stayed stock-still like a statue.

"I sure do. As far as I could see, a town like Fulton had a big old void in it—most places do, in my opinion." Adele moved to the glass case of confections and reached in through the door in the back to adjust their placement. "It's one thing to have gay bars, gay clubs, places like that to meet queer people. But most of them are swept up in this desire of meeting a partner, or having some drinks, things like that." She stood tall and brushed her hands on her apron. "But there's queer minors out there, or people who don't like the bar atmosphere, or who aren't really looking to hook up with somebody. And they need a safe place to meet up with others just like them. So..." Adele gestured around, beaming. "Here we are."

"That's really incredible!" Noah piped up, his voice tinged with awe. "I've read so many articles and things about needing spaces like that, but I've never actually gotten to *see* one."

Adele lifted one shoulder in a shrug. "It's not always the easiest place to run. We don't have the full support of some mega corporation, like other coffee shops, and that means I can't always afford exactly what I need—but I think it's worth fighting for."

As Noah and Adele continued speaking, Logan rubbed his arms, chasing a chill away. Fuck, he hated this, the piercing envy in his gut. It was too familiar. He'd faced it for years at parties, in classes, when he watched Christian be worshipped by everyone he passed while Logan fought for recognition. Even here, he was in someone else's shadow.

Who was he trying to fool? How the hell was he ever going to stand up and actually be a person worth noticing? For the rest of his life, he'd struggle to draw attention to himself. Christian would be in the spotlight. Someone like Noah would instantly win a smile just from how excited he was to be there. And Logan would flounder in the shadows.

"Logan?"

Logan blinked and looked up. For a few seconds, he stared in confusion at Noah's gesturing hand.

Christian would've teased him for being away on some other island in his own head. He would've forced Logan to laugh it off, to say something clever so he didn't look like an idiot in front of a perfect stranger. But Noah simply quirked his lips in that familiar way and gave another little wave forward. "I'm telling Adele about some of the books we read last year."

Logan's brows lifted. "Oh, uh, yeah?"

"Yeah. Remember the discussion we had about *The Picture of Dorian Gray?*"

Adele spoke up. "Can't go wrong with a little Oscar Wilde gaying up the room," she teased with a chuckle. "I've even got some of him on the back shelves." She tilted her head to the side. "Noah says your roommate acts."

Roommate. It took Logan a moment of offense to realize Noah was being kind—not outing him immediately to a perfect stranger, even in the middle of a queer coffee shop.

"My boyfriend, actually," Logan said with a sense of pride. He stepped forward to the counter. "He's damn good at it."

Adele's eyes wrinkled again with her grin. "Has he corrupted you into reading plays too? Into thinking about the queer subtext of *The Importance of Being Earnest*?"

Logan spoke without thinking. "Does it really count as subtext when the author is fucking *Oscar Wilde*?"

Adele threw her head back and laughed again, a brilliant cackle that lit the air like stars. "All right, you've got me there." She waved her hand vaguely toward some of her machines spread neatly over the counter. "Boys, I was just about to make myself a coffee. Y'all want anything while I'm at it? On the house."

She locked eyes with Logan when she said it. Brought him into focus. And, warmed by her regard and Noah's arm pressed companionably against his while they stood side by side, Logan flashed her a grin in return. "Yeah, I mean, if you're offering, I'd love it, ma'am."

*

After a week and a half of rehearsals, Christian sank into the ebb and flow of his work. It helped that Logan was making an effort to get out of the apartment more. Christian had more time to study his lines and dive into his character.

His character, Samyak, doted on and was very protective of his sister Harleen. He'd missed her dearly when he went to war. A courageous man, he hated everything he'd been forced to fight for, yet his desertion from the army would damage his family.

Christian sat to the side of the theater, waiting for a scene that he wasn't involved in to finish blocking. Hunched over his script, he tried to breathe in the essence of Samyak and commit him to muscle memory. It was far easier said than done.

He hated worrying about Logan like this. Selfish as it sounded, he didn't have a ton of experience with it. Logan had always been well put together, the sensible one to Christian's passion. Logan worried about *Christian*, not the other way around.

Now Christian was stuck wondering if that had been a ruse all along—if perhaps Logan had struggled far more than he ever let Christian see. Or if it was *Christian's* fault. That he'd been too concentrated on himself to notice his best friend's pain.

We're better than we've been in the past. That was Christian's one solace. Even while he worried about Logan's desperate expressions, the fear he carried in his gaze, and his automatic hesitance to share how he felt with Christian, there was still the fact that during the school year they'd handled things far worse than this.

Logan wasn't running from him. Christian wasn't pushing Logan to break so they could both explode together. They were handling it like adults. Like lovers.

Fuck, he hoped he was right.

"That's an interesting face."

Christian jerked his gaze up and frowned at Priya as she sat beside him. "What?"

"You look as if you're about to sob your eyes out." Priya smiled as she slouched in the chair, her long legs stretching forward. She was about as tall as Logan, only a few inches shy of Christian's immensity, and he still wasn't used to having someone else around who he didn't *quite* tower over. She cocked her head to the side, studying him. "Are you getting into character, or should I go beat up whoever made you look like that?"

Christian huffed a sharp laugh and shook his head. "It's fine. Just...life shit."

"Ooh, life shit, my favorite." She set her script aside. "If you've got some drama to unload, by all means, hit me with it. Can't be any worse than what I hear at my job every day."

"What do you do?"

Priya rolled her eyes. "I work retail right now. Maybe not the most glamorous job right out of college, but I need to pay the bills somehow until I can do this acting thing full time, right?"

His chest burned in the wake of a kindred spirit. "I hear you. I spend all day giving rides to strangers and itching to get back here. Not fun."

After a few seconds of silence, Christian looked back at Priya, and her brown eyes hadn't moved from watching his face. She hadn't lost her smile, even when she spoke.

"Are you trying to change the subject? Should I go along with it and stop talking about you being sad?"

Getting into his own business with a stranger wasn't ideal, but...Priya wasn't exactly a stranger now either. On stage, she was his younger sister. They fought like hell when she was his nurse, after he was shot in combat, but she got him out of the army anyway, even at her own risk. They hadn't blocked their scene at the end, when they reunited years later on the farm she shared with her girlfriend, but he sensed that Sage's direction was going to make tears fall.

Even though he and Priya had no personal history, he couldn't ignore the connection they already had through their scenes. And he *had* always wanted a sibling.

He didn't have a chance in hell of holding back.

"I'm just worried about my boyfriend," Christian mumbled, glancing around the room. Theater, he'd come to realize during these rehearsals, was decidedly queerer than he'd been aware of before, but old habits of checking for homophobic assholes died hard. "No big deal."

"Mm-hmm."

He shot her a look. "What?"

"Is that really all it is? You can't even tell your own sister?"

"Are you always gonna be this nosy?"

She chuckled. "Maybe."

She turned her attention toward the stage. Sage had paused the action again to make an additional suggestion for blocking, and when Christian followed Priya's gaze, he knew for a fact they wouldn't be done any time soon.

"Listen," Priya murmured, "you don't *have* to tell me anything. But I'm happy to listen and offer some advice, and you might feel better after you do."

Will I? His whole life, Christian played his cards close to his chest. He didn't let someone else see his hand. He didn't go looking for advice, if only because he wanted to make his *own* decisions instead of letting someone else influence him. But every time he recalled Logan's anxious face as they both realized how codependent their relationship had become, he wondered if he'd done the right thing by sticking around.

"Things ain't as cut and dry as they're supposed to be." Christian crossed his arms, his script crumpling slightly. "I don't know which of us fucked up first. Like, do I say all of this is my fault, or do I blame him? Or does it even matter?"

"Context might help."

"Long story," he countered. He only wanted to tell it once, not be interrupted and have to start again halfway through. But the more he thought about holding it in, the more words flooded his mouth, desperate to flow. He sighed. "There's just a lot going on. My boyfriend needs me more than I thought he did. He's not *clingy*, really, but there's something a little codependent in him, I think? He needs me to weigh in on a lot of decisions he makes. He needs my approval about everything. And he wants all my time. When he found out I was doing this play, he got so pissy about it, and he all but asked me to give it up—"

"Leave him."

Christian whipped his head around. "What?"

Priya was already watching him evenly, her lips in a thin line. "Leave. Him. That's what I tell all my girlfriends. If somebody is going to step all over your dreams, they're not someone you want to take through life with you."

The mere idea was so repulsive that Christian shook his head immediately. "No. No way. I'm not even done telling you what's going on; you can't just jump in and tell me to leave my fucking boyfriend."

"Do I really need to hear the rest? Listen to yourself. If you told him he couldn't do something he loved, wouldn't you hate yourself for it? That's a shitty thing to do, Christian. If we're going to go our whole lives searching for our one and only, we need someone who's going to have our back, not who'll push us down."

One and only? That's a whole other thing. Thoughts of Noah flooded his mind. Remembering Noah tucked under his arm and leaning into him in his most vulnerable moment left his heart racing. When he thought about Noah's warm expression as he offered Christian and Logan a safe place to stay over the summer, Christian melted.

Priya's voice broke through Christian's silence again. "All right. Fine. If there's more to the story, spill. I'll try to keep my judgy ass quiet," she drawled.

Christian shut his eyes, pressure on his chest. "I think I might've driven him into it."

"Why?"

Even now, he could see Logan's shattered expression from fights they'd had in the past. If only he could wipe the slate clean. "When we first got together, I kinda ghosted on him for a few weeks. I got scared. We'd been friends our whole lives, but seeing him as a boyfriend? That was spooky. I knew it was gonna change everything, and I wanted a sign to tell me it was worth risking. But I made him wait while I looked."

He opened his eyes and slapped the script on his chair arm, frustrated. "If he's all codependent on me now, then it's my damn fault for making him think I might just up and run at any moment."

"It's not your fault. He chooses how he's going to respond to whatever he feels."

"But I choose too. Right?" Christian closed his eyes. This time, he pushed past his regret, his memories of Logan's fear. He forced himself to pierce through the darkness. "Like, everybody makes it sound so easy. If somebody's codependent, you gotta cut them off right then. They'll drain you dry. They're not gonna learn if they can keep having you nearby. And I dunno if that's true."

Priya was quiet. "What do you mean?"

"I'm his *best friend*. If anybody wants to see him get better, it's me."

"It's not just you though. What about his family?"

Christian made a face. That was a nonstarter. He shook his head and huffed, slouching further in his chair as he looked away.

"Got it. Understand it better than you know." Her chair creaked as she twisted to catch the corner of his eye. "What I mean is, it's not all on you to carry and fix him. The guy asked you to give up something important to you. You don't think that's a big warning sign?"

Christian couldn't deny the concern. But he wasn't satisfied. The more he spoke, the more solid he became in his decision. "Listen, it's not that I wanna be the big man who fixes the guy I love or anything. That's not what this is about."

"Then what *is* it about?"

"It's..."

Christian imagined Logan again. The determination in his gaze, right behind the fear of his expression. The earnestness of his tone, though the words were clumsily said.

"...it's because he's *trying*. He really is. Who decided that people can't change? Can't heal? Can't do better unless they've been shoved down and shattered?" He scoffed. "Fuck, Priya, we're *nineteen years old*. We've played the field a lot, but we've never been all that serious with a lot of people before. And we've *never* been with a guy before. We're figuring shit out as we go—and that means it's gonna be scary, and we're gonna fuck up a lot, right?"

The silence stretched between them, buffeted by the lush voices on the stage wrapping around them like a blanket.

Finally Priya touched his arm. "I might think chances are overrated in a relationship, but you look as though you're about to cry if you let him get too far out of your sight. Are you sure he's not the only clingy one?"

Christian snorted. Her touch was grounding, bringing his focus back to the movement on stage and the building he already loved so deeply. "I guess I'll find out."

After a moment of quiet, he spoke more quietly. "I think he's my soul mate, Priya. We belong to each other. That's kind of fucked up, and we probably need to talk to each other to get our relationship to a healthier place, but...I can't just cut things off when I might be the reason he acted out in the first place."

She patted his forearm. "If you're sure."

A glance told him that she didn't look very convinced, and it surprised him when she didn't jump on him and try to change his mind. He'd been used to having debates with his mom and stepdad for years. Nobody back home trusted his ability to make decisions for himself, not when they still saw him as a kid. And, though he knew Priya was only a few years older than him, her regard settled him in the decision even further.

Maybe other people could easily let someone they'd loved their whole lives go without giving them a chance to grow first. But not him.

"Christian, Priya?" Sage turned around on stage, scanning the rows. "You're up!"

Christian let out a deep breath to cleanse his thoughts. There'd be time to work on his relationship later. *For now...* He looked at Priya and grinned. "You ready to yell at me, sis?"

"Oh, I've been waiting for it all day," she gushed as she stood and dragged him to his feet behind her.

Chapter Thirteen

For days, *weeks*, waking up hadn't been Logan's favorite thing to do. There was the twinge of panic if Christian wasn't beside him, as if maybe he'd changed his mind in the middle of the night and decided to leave Logan after all. There was the worry he wouldn't have the strength to push past anxiety at work and talk to yet another new coworker who might become a friend. And, ultimately, there was the fear he'd never be happy in his future—that he'd have to watch Christian soar while Logan dropped like a stone behind him.

For some reason, waking up today was not the worst thing.

Maybe it had to do with yesterday, when he and Noah and Chelsea had hung out at Sweet Grounds for a full two hours before it closed, before they had to even *think* about getting ready for work. It turned out Chelsea shared a love for retro games with both Noah and Logan, and she'd pulled Logan so deeply into the conversation he'd started carrying it before he could remember to be nervous about it.

It was good. For only a few hours, he'd been his old self, the guy who could make an entire class laugh with a group presentation that made their grumpy teacher smile.

Fuck, Logan hadn't realized how much he missed being him.

Work had been long. Strenuous. And this morning, as usual, Christian wasn't in bed with him. But Logan's mind touched on logic—*probably at work*—and flitted away equally as quickly.

No fear today. Not yet, at least. Another step forward.

He left the bedroom and padded silently down the hallway. It was nice, he had to admit, being in a quiet apartment. With two busy parents constantly on call in their tiny town—one the sole pharmacist, the other the only funeral director—Logan had gotten used to his sleep or study time or hang outs being interrupted by a pounding on the door or an anxious doorbell or the telltale sign of his parents' cell phones jingling with a new emergency call. Even in their dorm, Daiki was always rehearsing a song, or the trumpeter on the other side of Logan's bedroom wall had something to practice.

No, yeah, this was nice. Better than he thought it could be, to be alone, to exist without living on someone else's schedule.

Logan had a quiet morning ahead of him. He was off work tonight, and so was Noah. No doubt Noah would sleep in, letting Logan build up his strength to see his handsome face once more, and Christian would drive people all over town until he had rehearsal. Maybe Logan could chill out for once. Read, even. It had been so long since he'd read something for *fun*.

Making a plan for the day was typically easy, but seeing Christian sprawled on the couch with a stack of papers threw his mind into disarray.

Exhaling shakily, Logan froze in the doorway, fingers tangling in his shirt. His first instinct was to turn around before he could bother him, but Christian glanced up, and there was no escaping the sweet smile that crossed his lips.

It was so good to see Christian. Better than Logan had anticipated. They'd been missing each other more and more often recently—but of course they had. They worked opposite hours, Christian had his play to focus on, and Logan was doing everything in his power to be *better* than he ever had before.

Though this was his first morning without fear, he couldn't deny the way his body keened to wrap around Christian and fall asleep all over again, tucked against his beating heart.

Logan had been good recently, and he made the conscious decision to answer Christian's smile with one of his own. "Can I read for you?"

Christian blinked. "What?"

Logan's voice was ragged from sleep. He cleared his throat. "Your script. Can I read lines for you?" Logan rubbed the back of his neck. "You...you need to work on memorization, right?"

"Yeah." Christian's tone burst with a surprised sort of pleasure, something that only made Logan ache for him more. Christian shifted, making room on the couch. "Yeah, c'mere, you can help me with this scene."

Logan crossed the room and sank into the cushion. When Christian offered him the script, he paused before he took it from him, staring at the lovely grace of his hands.

He'd spent weeks trying *not* to look at Christian. He'd forgotten how damn handsome he was.

"Where do you want me to start?" Logan risked a glance and found Christian still staring at him. "Like, are you having trouble in any specific place, or...?"

Christian's gaze danced all over Logan's face. A thrill sparked in Logan's gut with each place his eyes rested—his cheek, his lips, his jawline. It had been too long since he was *seen*, truly and deeply. Night stockers didn't have much reason to interact with one another, and they only saw what was on the surface. Chelsea was a new friend, someone Logan still held at arm's length. Noah, especially, couldn't be allowed to go much deeper, not when there were dangerous feelings he might catch hold of. But Christian could see everything. He always had.

Christian took a deep breath. "Middle of the page was where I left off. The place where Harleen starts with *You're full of shit.*"

Logan forced himself to look at the paper. The section Christian described appeared to be a tirade specifically directed at Samyak. He wasn't sure why he needed him to start there. "You're Samyak, right?"

"Yep."

"So you want me to read her last line to go into yours?"

"Nah, do the whole thing."

Is he trying to make fun of me? There was a reason Logan hadn't been an actor, and it had everything to do with how stiff he was when reading a passage aloud. Something told him he hadn't improved since middle school. "Uh...okay, let's...yeah."

As Logan began to read, he was all too aware of how stilted his phrasing was in comparison to Christian's performances in the past. His cheeks burned. He sounded as if he was a goddamn fool, but another peek told him Christian hadn't looked away. Dueling pleasure and embarrassment twined inside him until he couldn't tell which would win out: the joy of being observed by the man he loved most of all or the shame of being so terrible a reader.

"...so don't tell me my choices didn't mean a damn thing when I'm the only nurse here who can still stand you." Logan relaxed as the last words spilled off his tongue, and he waited for Christian's line in response. Nothing came. Just a deep silence accompanied by Christian's searching eyes. "Do you need your line?"

Christian shook his head but didn't respond verbally. He drew his eyebrows together, his lovely lips pursed in thought, and though Logan was sure he was too eagerly obsessed with those small details, he couldn't stop. The magnet of Christian's gaze sucked him in. When Christian spoke, his tone was ragged.

"I missed hearing your voice."

Logan's heart began to pound fast enough to leave him lightheaded. "What?"

"I love your voice. You know that?" Christian wrapped his arms around his long legs and hugged them to his chest. "Used to feel guilty about how you got it in the first place. You didn't always have that accent, remember? You sounded so normal when you first moved to Greenbarrow. Midwestern, I guess, that's probably what they call it. But the first day we were in class together, you were in the desk on my left, and you laughed and said you liked my accent, and I never forgot it. You never second-guessed what you said back then—but I guess just about every six-year-old's like that, aren't they?"

Logan had no idea how to reply. He was too fixated on the memory, thinking about how rare it had been to see Christian smile as a child, and how every time he had, Logan stored them away to think about later. That first week in class, Christian hadn't laughed a single time. But once, Logan tripped over his own feet while they were walking to lunch, and Christian's loud cackle had made the skinned knee worth it. *Why did it take me so long to realize I was in love with you the whole goddamn time?*

"We were about eight when your twang really kicked in, weren't we? Did you spend two whole years studying mine?" Christian grinned, flashing his bright teeth. "I had no idea why you wanted to sound like me, and I kind of figured I must've taken a part of you away. But then the more I thought about it, I felt damn proud that I left a lasting effect on you. It sounded better on you than anybody else, anyway. Even me."

Logan shook his head. "No, no way, are you kidding me? Your voice is amazing—so much better than mine. Do you know how many times I called you on the phone when we were kids only so I could hear you talk? Even if I didn't have a damn thing to talk about? It pisses me off to think that some big vocal coach is gonna take that away from you one day all so you can be *famous*. Why do you think I always went to every single performance of your plays?"

Christian's eyes widened. "You did?"

With his cheeks still warm, Logan nodded. It seemed to be a silly secret to keep. If Logan was doing his best to not only strengthen their relationship but be a better man in general, then Christian deserved to know exactly how long Logan had been worshiping him from afar.

"All of them?"

"I never missed a night. Sometimes I didn't get my homework done, and I didn't care."

Christian's mouth dropped open. "Why didn't you tell me?"

"What, and make you think I was weird?" Logan looked away. "Nah, I couldn't take that risk. Had to make sure you didn't...didn't *know*." The list of things he hadn't wanted Christian to know was as long as the ocean—how he tried to dress like him, how he would ask himself what Christian would do when he was anxious, how he talked more about Christian than any of his girlfriends. Though Logan had believed he was straight all along, he'd still known there was something peculiar about his fervent infatuation.

If he hadn't hidden it so well, they wouldn't be in this situation. Logan wouldn't be clingy, and Christian wouldn't have to wait so patiently for him to be better. The thought brought words to his lips. "I think I might actually be doing better. Is that weird? I'm making friends at work. I haven't been blowing up your phone. I've been running more."

Christian grabbed his hand. "You have. You really have, baby."

Was it wrong to be so pleased at just a few little words? At a moment of recognition? Logan had been fighting hard. He'd been kicking his ass to build healthier boundaries.

For once, it looked like he'd done something right.

Christian pulled Logan in, and Logan rested his cheek on his shoulder. Christian kissed his forehead. "How're things with Noah?"

Logan blinked. "Things?"

"You know. Are they going anywhere?"

Logan was so taken aback that he laughed. "Sorry, uh, why are you asking? Did you think I was making moves on him?"

Christian shrugged. "I mean, wouldn't be surprised or opposed, you know?"

Logan's eyebrows lifted. "Jesus, babe, you know I'm trying to work on not being codependent, right? Not replacing you with somebody else?"

Christian jolted back an inch, jostling Logan into lifting his head. "Nah, for the record, *replacing* me never came to mind. You sound touchy, dude, what's going on?"

"I-I just...I didn't expect you to bring it up."

"Well, somebody had to," Christian pointed out. "Remember when I told you I started feeling something for him too? Remember what you said?"

Let me get back to you about what I'm feeling. Logan nodded slowly.

"And did you ever get back to me?"

"Hey." Logan held up a hand. "I was going through a lot. Remember? So were you. Your first performance is in, what, a couple of weeks, and you're not even off your script yet?"

"Shut up." Christian rolled his eyes, but fondly. Being on time had never worked for him. "Just trying to figure out if we were...waiting on something. If we weren't gonna talk about it. Like, if we were just gonna pretend neither of us felt anything for him or whatever."

The more Logan thought about it—Christian making a move on Noah or vice versa—the more he realized he didn't hate it. He might've been hiding from the idea while he figured his own shit out, but now it was just an interesting thought experiment. "Did you consider it?" Logan blinked up at him.

Christian took a few seconds to respond. "Consider what?"

"Going and asking him if he wanted to fuck when we were still figuring out what was going on with us. Like a rebound or whatever."

Christian scoffed, frowning in confusion. "What? No, I didn't *consider* it. Rebound—listen to you. What part of you thinks I'd be looking for a rebound anyway? It's not like we'd broken up or anything. I wasn't interested in going after him when you were still pissed at me. That's a fucking ridiculous idea."

"Is it?" Logan hesitated. "You're serious? You didn't wanna go after him just because it'd be easier?"

"Where the fuck are you getting this from?" Christian's voice lifted in what was clearly both surprise and confusion, but not as angry as Logan might've expected him to be. "It's *ridiculous* because I'd never cheat on you. If you or I ever fucked around with somebody, it'd be because *all of us* agreed to it in advance. Why would I ever wanna cheat on you? I've never done that before to anybody, and I'm not about to start now with somebody I'm fucking in *love* with."

The passion in Christian's voice left Logan's heart pounding. They'd never remotely discussed something similar to this. He'd been too damn afraid to ask. But given that their entire relationship had started around group sex and ethical nonmonogamy initially, it seemed to be something he would need to bring up. But he hadn't expected Christian to be so vocal about his decision to be committed to him.

What a weird relationship they had. They'd never agreed to only be with each other, and Logan was *surprised* to hear that Christian had made the decision to be monogamous? Logan knew some friends who'd want to take him to therapy just for assuming that eventually Christian's eye would wander—that Logan wouldn't be able to stop it.

Yet here they were. Both of them looking, but hands joined between them, not willing to take a step toward someone else if it jeopardized what they already held so near and dear.

The force of Christian's love washed over Logan so completely for the very first time. He was adored, not an experiment. He was something *real* for Christian, not a plaything.

Christian turned on the couch to face him. "You really thought I'd do that to you?"

"I didn't know what to think, man. That's the whole reason I didn't wanna start feeling something for Noah in the first place. I was scared of you thinking I needed something with him and not you. And for days, all I could think about was your acting career taking off, and you falling in love with somebody you did a play with, somebody so much better than me. Why would you stay with me if that happened? It doesn't make any sense."

"Because you're you. Because nobody's a better Logan Brown than you are." The intensity in Christian's voice turned Logan's focus back to him. "I've spent thirteen damn years wanting you by my side, and that's never gonna change. If I'm into Noah, it's because there's something special about him, not that there's something you're missing. You should understand that by now. What you feel for Noah, is it anything like what you feel for me?"

Logan didn't even have to think about his reply. "Not a bit."

"Tell me how it's different."

Little by little, words floated to the surface, ones he barely was aware of conceiving before they were slipping out. "It's...comfortable with him. As if I could spend a few hours just sitting with him on the couch and not doing anything, and I'd be happy. He understands how hard writing is, and he kicks my ass in video games, and both of those light me up. There's something so sweet about how he is, too—as if he wants to take care of me the way I take care of him. With you, it's...God, it's fucking red-hot. The two of us smoldering. I can't keep my hands off you, and when you're not there, it about kills me. You're inside me all the time, and I don't know how to make it stop."

"Then you get me. You understand exactly how I'm feeling." Christian's hand covered his thigh, connecting them. "There's not a single thing missing in you, babe. I love you because you're *you*. And, no matter what, that's not gonna change just 'cuz somebody else walked into my life."

Logan believed that immediately. Christian didn't lie to him—he was shit at *any* lying, much less to somebody who knew him backwards and forwards. The weight of the truth left him shivering in the middle of a Georgia summer, buried in a hoodie, though the sun had just come out from behind the clouds within him.

"I need you to know something," Logan said quickly. It had become the most vital thing in the universe. "I said it before and I'll say it again. You're made for the stage. I want you up there. I wanna see you succeed. I'll read lines with you every day and night until you're ready. I'll come to each performance, and this time you'll know it. I'm never getting in the way of your dreams again."

"Hey, hey, hey." Christian pulled Logan into his arms and rested a hand on the back of his head, keeping him safe and secure. "I trust you. I forgive you for freaking out. It's okay."

Forgiveness. Logan wasn't sure if he deserved it for so selfishly concentrating on his own fears, but he couldn't turn it down right now. He clung to Christian and buried his face in his neck. "Thank you."

"Do you forgive me too?"

Logan's mind raced, trying to remember what Christian might've done wrong. "For what?"

"For not talking to you about this sooner. For not asking if there was anything you were scared of. I didn't check in with you often enough, and that's on me."

Lifted higher by Christian's words, Logan nuzzled his skin. "I forgive you too. Jesus, this feels good, actually *talking* about this shit."

"Not running from it, you mean?" Christian teased. "Not leaving and crying real pathetically outside while your boyfriend sulks in bed upstairs and forces you to face your fear of heights to finally fix it?"

Logan laughed. "Better than me kicking your ass."

"I don't know. Pretty damn effective. Listen, just shove me to the ground the next time you think I'm not listening."

Logan couldn't help but laugh. "I'm starting to think you get horny as hell when I beat your ass."

Christian prodded Logan in his ticklish side, making him yelp, but held him close so he couldn't pull away. "You can't prove shit."

Neither of them seemed in a hurry to leave the couch. After remembering for so long what it was like to live without Christian being in his life every damn moment of every damn day, Logan soaked up his physical affection like a plant in a sunbeam. He basked in his arms, breathing deeply.

It was only when he opened his eyes that he saw Noah watching them from the hallway with a small smile.

Logan jolted away from Christian, panic immediately racing through him. *What the hell did he hear?* They'd talked so frankly about their attraction to Noah, and Logan hadn't even once considered that the subject of their interest might be in the apartment.

"Hey, it's okay, don't get up on my account." Noah beamed, making his way toward the kitchen. "You guys are really super cute together. Seriously. Don't feel as if you can't cuddle just because I'm here; it's your apartment too."

A glance at Christian's profile showed he was watching Noah with the same feverish intensity that Logan had often been privy to in the beginning of their relationship—as though he wanted to eat him up. Neither of them spoke, but as Noah rooted around in the fridge, Logan grabbed Christian's hand and dragged him to the bedroom, heart pounding.

*

The second the bedroom door shut behind them, Logan was already speaking. "We can't keep acting like nothing is going on." He followed Christian to the bed, and both of them flopped on the mattress. "It's killing me, man. Every goddamn time I'm alone in a room with Noah, I swear I turn into a blushing baby."

Christian poked his leg with his toes, loving the shyness in his boyfriend. "He probably thinks it's cute. Like me."

Logan shot him a look.

"Okay, fine." Christian pulled Logan closer and threw an arm around his shoulders. "You wanna make a game plan about whatever the hell it is we're doing? Is that it?"

"It'd be a fucking start, wouldn't it?" Though Logan put his head on Christian's chest, his leg kept wiggling against the mattress, shaking the bed enough to make a man seasick. "It's not as if he can't tell something's there. He's not an idiot."

Christian grunted. He'd seen it too, the way that Noah watched them both. He didn't think there was an invitation in Noah's gaze. It'd be easier if there were. Logan was a worrier, no doubt always panicking about what would go wrong if his interest became clear. Christian got off easier, he guessed—he was willing to wait and see what happened, not a lick of fear inside him.

Logan, though, acted as if at any moment he might crawl in Noah's lap and stick his tongue down his throat—as if he couldn't hold himself back for much longer. It put pretty pictures in Christian's head, fantasies about how pliant Logan would be for a guy like Noah. He'd roll over for him and whine. Maybe he'd even beg.

"Do you have any ideas?" Logan piped up. "What're you thinking about?"

"Noah fucking you," Christian said.

Logan slapped a hand over Christian's mouth. "Shh! He's in the goddamn kitchen! Do you want him to hear?!"

Christian licked Logan's palm, then laughed when his boyfriend rolled off the bed with a sound of disgust. "It'd make it easier. I can't stand watching you run around like a chicken with your head cut off. If Noah knows anything's up, it's because you don't have a subtle bone in your body." Christian rolled on his stomach and watched Logan pace. "What happened to that high school charmer? The one that had all the nerdy girls buying him lunch and shit?"

"That was different." Logan glared at him. "They were just girls. Noah makes me nervous."

There was a hell of a lot to unpack in that statement, but Christian let it go for the time being. "Okay, fine. So let's talk shop. We should just tell him we want him."

Logan stopped on a dime. An expression of horror crossed his face. "You're kidding."

"No." Christian wrinkled his brow. "It's quick and easy, and there's no miscommunication. I think it's the best way we could go."

"Did you forget the fucking boyfriend he's got?" Logan's voice cracked. He seemed as though he wanted to punch a hole in the wall with exasperation. "I know Daiki's a twig, but that guy can high kick like nobody else's business. He'll hit us square in the jaw."

"Or he could be completely cool with it. Everybody at FSU is different. None of us are pretending to be our parents anymore. If you and me have been in a little polyamorous thing already, who's to say they wouldn't be up for that too?" Christian spread his arms wide.

"So that's your plan. Assume everybody on campus is exactly like us." Logan went to the window and stared outside, arms crossed.

Christian watched him helplessly. Logan could talk all he wanted about Christian being the talented brilliant actor, but at the moment Logan was far more of a drama king.

Christian checked the time on his phone and swore under his breath. He needed to leave for rehearsal soon. "Then they can say no. It's not a big deal, babe. But things are gonna get awkward as hell if we keep dragging it out."

"You don't think it'd be awkward *after* they said no?"

"Nah. We're guys, right? We can all move on."

Logan rolled his eyes. "You're such a... Okay, listen to me. Did you ever think about how Daiki will be moving in with us once summer's over? Four guys in a tiny-ass apartment, trying to deal with the stress of college and jobs and shit. Now think about what happens if we tell Noah we've got a thing for him, and he turns us down. It's gonna make the walls close in on us. They might not know how to talk to us after it's over. Friendship? Gone. Apartment? Bye-bye. And then it's you and me trying to figure out how we're gonna afford a place of our own."

The words spread something cold through Christian's stomach.

"Suddenly, all the freedom you figured out you have disappears. Unless we got lucky and found a dorm that late in the game, we'd have to look into going back home, wouldn't we?" Logan's voice had quieted as he went on, until it was a whisper.

Christian could tell Logan felt that very real fear as strongly as he did. Going home wasn't an option anymore. The mere idea of not being able to touch Logan in public made him sick. He could burn the bridges between himself and his family if he had a safety net to catch him, but if he had to risk for even one second that it would be gone...

Christian leaned forward and rubbed his face with a sigh. "We can't pretend it's not there, though, what we're feeling. We can't choke it dead."

"Maybe we haven't tried hard enough."

"No, I know us. You love like there's no tomorrow. And the second I want something, I can't get it out of my head until I know it's not an option. Believe it or not, the guy watches us, and he doesn't look...scared."

Logan huffed as though he didn't believe him, but he glanced in his direction from the corner of his eye. "Right. What's he look like, then?"

"Like...I don't know. As if he's *thinking*." Christian wrinkled his nose. "I can't count him out yet. We want him, and it's not going anywhere."

"Doesn't change anything."

"Maybe not, but, hell, it's early in the summer, right? It's not even July yet." Funny how he'd dragged his feet for thirteen whole years to figure out what he felt for Logan, but decided he wanted to jump into something with Noah only a month after they'd moved into this apartment together. Things were allowed to be different here. Logan was an exploration—a change in how he perceived the whole world. Now that Christian had gone through that, he could do exactly what he'd done with girls his whole life and dive right in.

"What does the month have to do with anything?" Logan asked.

"It means we've got time to find another place, if we need to." Christian stared at Logan. He didn't want to miss a single expression, not when they were talking about their future. "Things're gonna get weird if we don't talk about them. We need to trust he can handle it. We sit him down, we tell him we both have a thing for him, and we ask if we need to start looking for a new place or whatever."

Logan frowned. "We can't afford all our living expenses with just our two paychecks."

"We can if...if I get a second job."

"No." Logan cut a hand through the air. "Don't. I know what you're gonna say, and I don't wanna hear it."

"I can still drop out of the play. It's not a big—"

"It's a huge fucking deal, shut up," Logan snapped. "I told you not to say it. You're not giving up the fucking play for anything. You'd be miserable."

Christian shook his head. "Not if I'm with you."

"Don't go that route either. You're almost done with rehearsals, and I can see what good it's done you." Logan sat on the edge of the bed with him, grabbing his hand. "*I'd* take on a second job before I let you do that. Okay?"

Something about the words flooded Christian with a deep, passionate regard. "What happened to the guy who wanted me to give up everything I wanted for him?"

Logan looked down at their hands, his thumb moving restlessly over the back of Christian's. "He's trying. He knows what's important right now. And, yeah, maybe he's scared as shit, but...hell, it's *worth* it to try, right? Especially if the only other option is saying goodbye to the guy he loves."

Christian couldn't stop himself. He leaned in and kissed Logan, burying his fingers in his thick curls with a rough moan. "I love you so fucking much," he whispered against his soft lips. "Don't you ever doubt it."

Logan's smile was pained. "Even if me eying some dude up means we end up homeless at the end of this?"

"I'll take care of you. Don't worry."

"And I'm gonna take care of you too."

Being the strong one came easiest to Christian. He'd rather make all of the decisions the whole way.

But knowing that Logan was in his court sure as hell helped. He nodded and gave him another quick kiss. "We tell him. We make it easy. We don't tell him how much we wanna suck him off," he said with a quiet chuckle, just so he could hear Logan laugh too. "And we do it soon, so that if we need to start looking for a backup plan, we can."

When Christian's phone began to jingle, Logan sighed. "Rehearsal?"

"Yeah. I gotta run. Fuck."

"It's okay." Logan stood up and pulled Christian to his feet too. "Kick ass."

"I will." He hesitated. "You and Noah off work today?"

"Yep."

"We should do it when I get back, then."

"Fuck," Logan whispered, his eyes shutting. "Fuck, fuck, *fuck*."

"Quick and easy. Painless."

"Nothing we do is ever painless," Logan drawled. He kissed Christian's cheek. "But...fine. We can try."

Never had Christian wanted to shirk his responsibilities more. As much as he adored this production, all he wanted was to stay in and hold Logan until he stopped looking so terrified. But he knew Logan could handle it. He was taking small steps, gradually getting away from needing to lean on Christian every second of every day. Christian needed to trust Logan to keep going.

It didn't make it any less difficult when he looked over his shoulder just before he left and saw Logan standing in the middle of the room with his arms wrapped around himself like a child.

Chapter Fourteen

Though he didn't *want* it, Logan felt the need for solitude while he waited for Christian's rehearsal to finish. If he'd known a month ago he would develop a crush on Noah, he might have avoided making their schedules exactly the same. Now he had to live with the fact that they were at work *and* home together, always. Due to their exhausting job, Noah rarely went out unless he was with Logan, and it meant he was sitting right in the living room where Logan couldn't avoid him unless he isolated himself.

So he did. For hours, he camped out in the bedroom, unable to do anything but scroll through random articles and wikis on his phone. He didn't know how long Christian's rehearsal would be, but it gave him plenty of time to think about how awkward the conversation with Noah would be. There was no avoiding it. Thinking of more elegant ways to approach the subject came up flat.

It was going to be a crapshoot. *Why is there never an instruction manual for anything in my goddamn life?*

Eventually, his stomach began growling, as if his lot in life wasn't *already* bad enough. He considered going without food as some kind of punishment, but he was a weak man who couldn't resist his stomach.

Logan crept out of the bedroom to forage, doing his best not to look at Noah on the couch. It didn't work very well.

"Yo!" Noah waved at him with a grin—because clearly God didn't exist, and if He did, He wanted Logan to make a complete fool of himself before the night was out. "You've got to get over here and play with me. It's been too long."

Noah was playing their favorite shooter, the one he always dominated Logan in. At the moment, he appeared to be kicking massive amounts of CPU ass. No doubt he was bored to tears. Any other night, Logan would've grabbed a controller and given him slightly more of a challenge. But everything was changing tonight.

"Nah, I'm just grabbing some food. Thanks." Logan went in the kitchen and took a deep breath. If he got himself all stirred up before he got something to eat, he wouldn't be able to stomach it.

When the couch creaked, he steeled himself and looked at the door, seeing Noah come into the frame. He had absolutely no idea how Noah could look so damn good when he was dressed so simply. A tank top, sweat pants, and a beanie? Lazy—and he still looked hot as fuck.

"You want some company while you eat?" Noah asked, smiling.

Logan shook his head. "I'm gonna take it in the bedroom."

"Oh." Noah blinked, his smile faltering. "Everything okay?"

"Sure." Logan opened the fridge just so he had something to do, but nothing inside looked appetizing.

"You just, uh…" Noah leaned against the counter. "You always eat out here. You said you hate eating in bed. It gets crumbs everywhere."

Did I say that? He looked at Noah, brow furrowed. "Yeah?"

"Yeah. A few days after we moved in. Christian was taking some pizza to bed—"

"Fuck. No, yeah, I hate it." Logan closed the fridge and went to the pantry, heart pounding in his chest.

Christian was right. Noah *had* been watching. What the hell did that mean? How did he remember some throwaway comment from over a month before when it wasn't relevant to him at all? Was that just what friends did? Perhaps Logan had been doing it wrong all these years. The only person he remembered those banal details about was Christian, and there was a reason for that—one that came into light as he'd noticed his changing sexuality.

But that didn't make sense in this context. None of it did.

Why were friendships with guys so fucking hard to understand?

When Noah's bare feet slapped on the kitchen tile, Logan looked at him sharply. Noah slowed, then leaned to open the fridge. "Grabbing a soda."

Right. He hadn't been approaching Logan for anything specific. Of course. "Sure."

"Want one?"

"Yeah. Thanks."

"No problem." Noah held the can out, and Logan took it. "Do you wanna talk about something?"

Logan was terrified that it was written all over his face. "Why?" he asked a little too quickly.

"You're just acting a little weird. Last time you did, you were freaking out about...some decision you couldn't talk to me about."

Logan's anxiety began to run wild. Noah wasn't looking at him with interest. Obviously Noah was confused. He didn't understand a goddamn thing Logan was doing, and it was written all over his face.

Join the fucking club. Logan grabbed a random bag of chips and headed toward the living room. *I don't know what the hell I'm doing either.* "It's fine. You busy tonight?"

"Uh, no, just...playing video games. Wild social life when Daiki's not in town."

Though Noah chuckled, Logan couldn't bear to do the same. A spike of sharp jealousy punctured his gut. Besides the one party Logan and Daiki had gone to together early in their freshman year of college, they hadn't hung out much. Logan had put all his attention on Noah. Now he realized he knew very little about his roommate's boyfriend: he did musical theater, he was of Japanese descent, and he drove Christian up a wall with the shit he said. That was it.

Daiki, however, was probably perfect for Noah in every way. That was why they were together in the first place. It was ridiculous that Logan had been considering talking to Noah about this stupid little crush.

I have to call this off. I have to text Christian right now. Logan dropped the bag of chips on the couch and made a beeline for the bedroom.

He made it three steps down the hallway before the front door swung open.

"What's up?" Christian asked with an unfamiliar brightness in his tone. "Everybody having a good night?"

As Logan whipped around and sliced his hand across his own neck, trying to get him to shut up, Noah popped out of the kitchen. "Hey, you're back early."

"Yep! They're done with me for the day." Christian shot Logan a confused look. He tossed an arm around Noah's neck and pulled him into a headlock, rubbing a hand through his short curls.

"Hey! Jerk!" Noah laughed as he slapped Christian in the stomach, giving him a vicious enough jab that he was released. "What's wrong with you?"

"What, a fellow can't be in a good mood? C'mon."

Logan was going to burst out of his skin. Why did he have such a dense boyfriend? "Christian," he said sharply. "Can we talk for a sec?"

Both Christian and Noah stared at him, the latter frozen with his drink halfway to his mouth.

"Please?" Logan tried again.

"Sure..." Christian dragged the word out. As he left the room, he shot Noah a look over his shoulder. "Hey, don't go too far, all right? I've gotta talk to you about something too."

Noah held up his can in silent agreement just before Logan shut the bedroom door.

"We can't do it," Logan blurted out. "It's stupid, Christian, there's no fucking reason he'd be even remotely interested in us."

Christian scoffed out a surprised laugh. "Speak for yourself. Have you seen me recently?" He pulled up the hem of his T-shirt and rubbed his abs, his smirk going coy.

"Don't—" Logan pulled the shirt back down and held it there, leaning in an inch away from Christian's nose. "Can you keep your dick in your pants for five seconds while we talk about this?"

"If there was something to talk about, we would. I think we covered all the bases earlier, didn't we?"

Logan rolled his eyes. He rested his forehead on Christian's shoulder and sighed. "Some. We covered *some* bases. We didn't exactly hit on the topic that Daiki might be perfect for Noah. If he is—if Daiki is everything Noah needs—then we might as well not bother mentioning the whole crush thing."

"Are you saying I'm not perfect for you?" Christian asked, insulted.

Logan looked up at him. "You'll only play two matches of a game with me before you get pissed that

I'm beating you and storm off, and I still don't know what the fuck an offside call is in soccer. We're perfect together, but you and me both know there's some gaps that other people might be able to fill."

Still, Logan drew comfort from the closeness of his lover, and he hugged him. He just needed a little longer with him before they did something stupid that might change the course of their whole life in college. "Could be that Noah and Daiki have all the bases covered, y'know?"

Christian's strong arms wrapped around his waist and squeezed comfortingly. "Hey, listen, we're not having this talk because we're expecting a wedding ring or something. We're doing it because we like the guy, and we don't wanna make him or his boyfriend uncomfortable when they start noticing. We're giving ourselves as much time as we need to get out of here, just in case. Remember?"

Even Christian knew they didn't have a chance, then. How deeply Logan regretted giving Noah a second look. What he wouldn't give to take back how he'd awakened to his new sexuality, if it meant he was going to start losing friendships by being himself.

But then he wouldn't have Christian in his arms, and that was impossible to fathom.

"Let's just go do it, okay?" Christian smoothed Logan's hair down and kissed the top of his head. "Lemme do all the talking, if you want—"

Logan barked out a laugh. "Not a chance. You're good with a script in your hand, but I'm not trusting you with my thoughts."

"Fine. Asshole."

"I love you."

"Love you too." Christian nudged him back far enough to open the door behind him. "Let's do this, babe. Go team." He gave Logan a swat on the ass.

The second the door was fully open, the video game sounds in the living room paused. They came around the corner, and Logan took a deep breath before he let himself look at Noah.

Noah sat on the couch, already staring at them both, his bushy red eyebrows lifted, and the controller resting in his lap.

Logan wished he could throw himself on the couch and rest his cheek on Noah's thigh and tell him he didn't have to look so damn worried about whatever was coming. It would be over quickly, and they'd get out of his hair. But instead, Logan froze. When his feet stayed rooted to the carpet, Christian tried to tug him further into the room, then gave up and shook his head.

This was why Logan needed Christian in his life. Logan could charm and laugh with the best of them when there were no stakes in the game, but when something really mattered? He needed a bull. He needed Christian to put his head down and charge into the china shop because, otherwise, they'd never make it through the door.

"Can we talk for a few minutes, man?" Christian asked quietly.

Noah let out a deep sigh. "Yeah. Go for it."

"Cool." Christian grabbed Logan's hand and gave him one more tug, and this time, his legs loosened. He followed Christian, feeling similar to a child hiding behind his mom's skirt at church.

It shouldn't matter what Noah said. At the end of the day, Logan still had Christian's love, and he *had* to believe they could withstand whatever shit was thrown at them. Even if they ended up on the street, they'd survive. But he still burned inside thinking of the humiliation if Noah rejected them—or, worse, only wanted one of them. How would Logan feel, watching Christian and Noah slowly getting to know each other, but with himself on the sidelines? What if that was reversed, and he had to see Christian pushing down every ounce of frustration he felt as he watched them bond?

It's too soon. This is gonna change everything, and we're not fucking prepared for it.

Christian sat on the couch, but Logan sat on the floor in front of him, pulling his legs to his chest. Maybe he could hide behind them, like a fence keeping him safe. It would be better than sitting so close to Noah that their hands might risk brushing, or having to see his expression up close when they finally said what was on their minds.

"Something's wrong, isn't it?" Noah said solemnly, looking between them. "Logan's been acting weird all night. If I did something, I'd really appreciate it if you could just come out with it straight away so we can move on."

"What if you didn't?"

Noah folded his hands in his lap. He seemed to become smaller, tucking a leg under himself and staring at the floor. Logan knew for a fact Noah didn't quite crack six feet, but seeing him shrink—trying to take up less space on the couch, as if he was trying to hide—broke his heart.

Please stop looking so terrified of us, man. I can't take it.

When Noah finally spoke, it was on a whisper. "It had to be me. I've..." He shook his head. "I've been pushing stuff I didn't need to, and sticking my nose in things, and...I don't know. I'm sorry."

"Would you stop?" Christian said. "You didn't do anything. We've had something on our minds, and we wanna talk about it, that's all. Hell, we should be the ones apologizing to you. We shouldn't have held onto it for this long, but Logan—"

"Don't." Logan kicked Christian's shin and scowled at him. The last thing he needed was for Christian to talk about his doting heart or whatever the fuck. He knew he was a big marshmallow—it had gotten him into trouble the whole time he was falling in love with Christian. But he didn't need Noah thinking their entire friendship was built around Logan wanting to fuck him.

Not *just* fuck him either. Hold his hand. Kiss him. Sit in a room with him in dead silence, immersed in his company.

I'm a fucking sap.

Christian grunted, rubbing his leg where Logan had kicked him. "We realized it's important to bring it up right now, that's all. We signed this lease together until next summer, but…"

Noah peeked up at them both. His hazel eyes were wide and pleading, but he didn't say a word.

"…well, we figured things might get a little awkward when you knew we both were…kind of interested in you."

Noah's jaw went slack. "What?"

"Not kind of," Logan muttered. "There's no *kind of* about it. That makes it sound as if we had a choice. Hell, Noah, I don't know how anybody could live with you for long without getting a crush. It's inconvenient for you, and I-I'm sorry it happened, and—"

"Wait, wait." Noah leaned into the arm of the couch, going boneless, and looked between the two of them as though he was watching a tennis match. "I don't understand. When did…why is…*what*?"

Christian leaned over to smack Logan's arm. "I told you I'd do the talking. Now you've confused him. Look."

"Then do it! Don't just beat around the bush!"

Christian rolled his eyes. He might've been trying to look cool and collected, but Logan could see the way his leg was bouncing. He was barely holding himself back from exploding.

When Christian spoke, his voice was tightly restrained. "We like you, man. *Like* like you. I don't know about Logan, really, but there's something about you I can't get my mind off of. You're cool and kind and compassionate, and it's ...it's nice. Could only be a crush, but I can't stop myself from thinking about where it could go."

Logan couldn't let him go on like that. "Except we know you're with Daiki. And that means it doesn't matter what either of us feel, because we respect your relationship with him, okay? We're not propositioning you or asking you to cheat or something. Please understand that."

Noah flew to his feet and began walking away, but before Logan could call for him, he came back. He paced in the living room with his hands over his mouth, still looking shell-shocked. After a few seconds, he looked right at Logan. "Y-you like me?"

Logan hated having to repeat it. It was embarrassing enough having to say it once. "Yeah." His heart thudded, making him dizzy. "I didn't mean to, Noah. But Christian's right. You're something special. I couldn't have avoided noticing you even if I was dense. And...and I'm really sorry."

As quickly as a car running down a hill with no brakes, Logan hurried to fill the silence. "This isn't about us, it's about you—you and Daiki. We can try to forget about what we're feeling, but it could take a while—hell, it might not go away no matter how much we work at it. And that's gonna be really awkward for you two, especially once he's living here. So we're telling you because...if you need to ask us to move out, we will. We just need to know when you want us gone."

Saying the words brought a sense of finality to the situation. He hadn't really let himself think about a life where he didn't get to see Noah every day, but that was exactly what he would have to do if and when they moved out. He'd get a new job, a new place to live, and new classes on campus, and he'd never see that handsome face again.

Goddamn, that hurt. It pierced right through his chest, and it was a puncture he knew would take a good long while to heal.

Noah froze. He dug his hands into his hair and shook his head. "What? No. No, you don't have to go anywhere. I-I don't want that."

"We don't have to," Christian hurried to say. "We're not saying we want to. But you should probably talk about it with Daiki, okay? I don't think he'd want us living here with you, knowing that we both feel something."

"Then you don't know Daiki," Noah blurted. "You don't— Shit, you don't know *anything*, either of you."

Logan whipped his head around and looked at Christian, wordlessly asking if he knew what the hell Noah was talking about, but he only got a blank stare in response.

Noah sank to his knees and leaned forward. "You're sure, though? That you feel something? Both of you. Or is this just a dumb prank?"

It would be easier if he said it was all a joke. The conversation would end, and Logan could go back to licking his wounds privately. But he was too invested in the expression Noah wore. Above all else, Logan didn't want to lie to him. He'd done enough lying to himself all his life. "We're sure."

Noah hung his head so all they could see was his hair. "Seriously, you don't have to do it j-just to make me happy."

What? Logan stiffened. "No." Thrown off-balance by that statement, he rambled as he tried to find his footing again. "We wouldn't prank you about this. I know it's weird to hear, but...no, it's real. All of it." *Happy?*

Noah burst out laughing. When he met Logan's eyes, he was grinning from ear to ear, his freckles hidden beneath a strong blush. "I don't believe it. I can't..." He pointed from Logan to Christian. "Are you both seriously going to sit there and say you don't know I've been attracted to you guys since pretty much the moment I met you both?"

A car coming through the wall would've surprised Logan less than Noah's words. He sank backward, catching himself on the coffee table. "Excuse me?"

"I thought you knew. I thought you knew *everything,* and I-I can't believe he kept his mouth shut. You seriously don't—"

"Can you tell me what the fuck is going on here?" Christian asked, sounding as breathless as Logan felt.

"Daiki. He knew. He's seen it happening the whole time. He used to tease me about it before he and I even got together that first time—when we thought the two of you were still straight. And when you guys came out about dating, God, I thought I'd never hear the end of it."

Noah waved his hands through the air as he spoke, the words pouring out so fast Logan could barely keep up. "The day Daiki left for the summer, he actually offered for us to break up just in case something happened here."

Christian made a wordless sound. "Wait, *happened*?"

"Between us. All of us." As excited as a kid in a candy store, Noah went on. "He thought there might be something there, I guess. And he didn't want me to feel tied down if there was the slightest possibility one of you might want me."

"I don't believe it," Logan murmured.

"I told him no, of course. I love Daiki. I don't want to put him up on a shelf just in case something *might* happen with two guys who are already dating—how ridiculous would that be? If I just threw the guy I adore under the bus for..." Noah looked away. "Well, it's complicated, anyway, relationships with me, and...no. I wasn't going to get rid of him, no matter what he said."

It was a miracle that Logan was already sitting because he didn't think his legs could hold him. Word after word slapped him in the face like a harsh wind, taking his breath away and leaving him dizzy and aimless. He'd come into the room expecting one thing, but this conversation had never been on his list of things to prepare for.

Christian reached out and grabbed his hand, and Logan squeezed it thankfully. It anchored him. At least now he didn't think he'd pass out.

Noah sighed. "I'm sorry. This is a lot. But…I-I just can't believe…I've been holding it all inside this whole time. People like me don't think the three people they want could be attracted to them."

"Stop." Logan looked up at him, not sure where the words were coming from. "You're fucking extraordinary. You're sweet and smart and handsome as hell. I know the world wants you to feel like a piece of shit, but fuck them."

"And find a better world," Christian added. "One with people who actually appreciate you and listen to you…and like you. A lot."

"Yeah. No, yeah, of course." Noah huffed out a quick laugh. "I know that. Sorry. Old wounds come up sometimes when I'm nervous." He rested his warm gaze on Logan. "Thank you."

Logan nodded, because there wasn't anything else he could do. He'd said his quota of words for the month, if not the year, and he was going to spend the rest of it trying to figure out what the hell had just happened here.

"The thing with Daiki is…" Noah chewed on his bottom lip, and Logan watched, captivated, by how it swelled beneath his teeth. "He said that if things happened while he was gone...it was *okay.*"

Things. Heat crackled in Logan's body.

"But I was too much of a coward to do anything about it. I've never done hookups before. I've always been in monogamous relationships, not...not like..."

"Us," Christian murmured.

His voice had a thick, throaty quality that told Logan his mind was going the exact same place. Their relationship together had only started because they kept falling into bed and working their confusion out with their dicks. The temptation to fall into the same pattern by asking Noah into their bedroom right here and now was strong. He'd already heard enough of them fucking—why not ask if he wanted to see it?

Dangerous territory. Logan and Noah's friendship might be strong after a year, but Christian and Noah still seemed to be feeling each other out. Making it complicated by diving straight under the sheets might not be the wisest idea.

But goddamn, he wanted to know how his lips tasted. Anything to keep his mind from flying down the trail to worry and panic.

"We could try it," Christian pointed out. He dropped out of the chair, coming onto his hands and knees. He cocked his head to the side and studied Noah's face as if it held all of the answers he sought. "It wouldn't have to be anything serious right now. Could just...kiss and see how it feels." He reached out and touched Noah's arm, and Logan watched how

Noah shivered. "I mean, we might not know what we're feeling till we have a taste, huh?"

The clear, bubbling heat in Noah's gaze told Logan that, no, they *did* in fact know what they were feeling. Logan scooted closer to the two of them and was immediately sucked into their bubble, where the air was warm and made his mind feel sluggish.

Noah swallowed hard. "...maybe..."

"Maybe what?" Christian's timbre dropped to a rich level.

Noah looked between the two of them. He licked his lips and took a deep breath. "Maybe we...wait a few days and think about it."

Christian immediately collapsed in clear disappointment, his forehead landing on Noah's shoulder as he whined.

"Sorry!" Noah patted Christian's back while Logan grinned and shook his head. Clearly Noah didn't know yet that he should go ahead and punch Christian in the arm and tell him to suck it up. When Noah went on, his voice cracked. "I-I just think that...there's a lot at stake here, right? Our whole friendship is one thing, but I need to talk to Daiki— make sure this is still okay. I mean, life is short and all, but—"

"There's plenty of time to make mistakes." Logan agreed wholeheartedly. God knew he'd done enough shit in his life he wished he could take back—and plenty in his own relationship too. He didn't need anything to move forward right now. Relief that he wasn't being evicted for feelings he couldn't help was enough for tonight. "Don't listen to him. He's being a fucking baby." He aimed another kick at Christian, but his boyfriend rolled out of the foot's path and glared at him while Logan laughed. "He can wait, same as anybody else. His dick doesn't need to get sucked right this second."

Christian growled as he rolled onto his back and shoved his arms under his neck, pouting at the ceiling. "Logan's right. Though it would be nice."

"Buy a fleshlight." Logan patted his foot.

Noah made a small sound, and when they both looked at him, he turned his attention to the floor. "That's another thing. I think we'll need to talk about, um…" He picked at a loose string on his shorts, then huffed. "No, never mind, I'm not going to start talking about my sex life if it's not going to go anywhere. We can cover that later."

Curious though Logan was—he hadn't given it much thought, simply assumed they'd figure it out of they got there—he kept his mouth shut. Noah's privacy was important, and he didn't owe either of them a damn thing. "Sure. We've got time."

The three of them stood up. Noah wordlessly opened his arms as he faced Logan, and Logan walked straight into his embrace. But, for the first time, the hug lingered, with Logan's arms fitting loosely around Noah's trim waist and catching the scent of his shaving soap in the pulse point on his neck. Noah's arms tightened around him, and Logan felt an answering stir in his shorts.

Noah turned his head, his smooth cheek brushing against Logan's. "I've gotta—"

"Yeah," Logan managed in a tone rough with need. "Yeah, Christian and I will just..."

"Are you gonna be mad if you hear us fucking?" Christian asked a little too brightly.

Noah trembled for a moment in Logan's arms, then quickly pulled away. "Do whatever you want; I-I don't care."

"Cool. Then if you'll excuse me..."

"Wh—" Logan found himself heaved over Christian's shoulder in a fireman's carry. "Hey! Son of a bitch!"

The last look he got at Noah before the door shut was of his rosy cheeks, dilated pupils, and lips swollen from biting.

*

Christian dumped Logan on the bed unceremoniously, giddiness ripping through him. "Pants off."

"What the fuck?"

"You heard me." Christian whipped his shirt over his head as he went to the nightstand. "What, you don't wanna fuck?"

"I mean..." The sound of Logan's zipper sliding down was all Christian needed to hear, but his lover went on. "You can't be serious, babe, he's literally right on the other side of the wall—"

"And he can hear what the hell he's missing." Christian found the lube and tossed it over. He couldn't wait another second. "Consider it me reminding him exactly what he could have."

Logan scoffed. "Call it what it is. You're horny as hell, and you've never been able to hold that back."

"Not around you." Christian shoved his pants and boxer briefs down in one fell swoop and wrapped a hand around his cock, giving it a few quick tugs. The pleasure from his own touch wasn't nearly enough to satisfy, and he bit back an impatient groan. He scrambled onto the mattress, watching voraciously as Logan undressed. "Don't tell me that didn't go better than you expected." His gaze flitted over Logan's soft torso. "I can't fucking believe it."

The more Logan stared back at him, the less Christian seemed able to respond intelligently. "Doesn't feel real." Logan angled to scoot toward the pillows, but Christian put a hand on his chest and shoved him down.

Christian was high, really. The adrenaline had shot him straight into the clouds, where he was turning circles as though he might never be able to come down. It made him hungry, and Logan was the only person in arm's reach who could help.

Christian skimmed a line of kisses down Logan's neck, pulling impatiently at his shirt. "Get naked for me."

"I-I'm trying, but you make it pretty hard when you're just—*fuck!*" Logan arched as Christian sank his teeth into his skin.

"Yeah, that's it, be loud for me, sweetheart," Christian whispered, his tone slurred with desire. "Want him to hear. Want him to go get himself off while I'm filling you up with my cock."

Logan whined, his hips pressing against Christian's. Logan's boxers were silky, rubbing their erections together without any pain. As he finally yanked his shirt up to his neck, Christian pulled back to give him room to take it off, settling for nibbling on his collarbone instead.

The only thing missing was Noah in their bed too. Christian considered it only a matter of time at this point; he'd seen the look in Noah's eyes, as if he couldn't wait to eat them both up. Daiki was the only wrench in the plans, and he might be a dick sometimes, but he seemed to be the kind of guy who'd jerk it to stories of his boyfriend getting laid. An exhibitionist through and through, Christian suspected, the kind of guy who'd touch himself with the door half open, hoping somebody might see and come in—

His stomach flip-flopped, and he pushed the idea away, riveted by Logan beneath him and the image of Noah waiting in the living room to hear exactly what they'd do.

"Are you gonna be pissed off if I think about Noah while I'm fucking you?" Christian yanked Logan's boxers down and sent them fluttering to the floor.

Logan breathed a laugh. "Depends— You thinking about me too?"

Christian growled. "If I could get you out of my head for a second, I might actually get shit done."

"Then you can think about him all you want." Logan scraped his nails down Christian's back, lighting up his nerves with an intoxicating rush of pain. "Fuck, Christian..."

"Wonder how pretty you'll look when he fucks you."

Logan gasped, closing his eyes and tipping his head back.

Christian grabbed the lube and squeezed it liberally on his fingers, rubbing them together to try to warm it. "You've waited for it, haven't you? All this time. You just didn't know it." He rubbed his first digit on Logan's hole and chuckled when he felt the muscles there expand, as if trying to suck him inside. "He seems to be a thorough kind of bastard, doesn't he? He'd take his time with you and fuck you until you cry from wanting to come so bad."

"Christian—" Logan moved his hips downward, then seethed when he didn't slip inside him. "Please..."

"Yeah, he'll have you begging just like that." Christian rested his cheek on Logan's chest, breath ghosting over his hard nipple, and watched his stunning face fly through desperate expressions. There was a time and a place for foreplay and taking their time together, but now was a moment for burning alive in each other's company. All Christian wanted was to whisper filth until Logan's cock was leaking. "He'll throw these pretty legs over his shoulders and pound the shit out of you, won't he? Think about those sweet eyes of his admiring you all spread out for him…"

"You're fucking *cruel*."

"You love it." Christian pushed his middle finger inside Logan and smirked when it took his breath away. "You want me to stretch you fast tonight, don't you, slut?"

The word seemed to light Logan up, like it always did. "Do it, *do it*." He pushed down until he took the finger to the hilt, sucking in a breath through gritted teeth, and Christian slapped a hand on his hips to hold him still. "I *need* you, Christian."

"Then you'll let me take charge." As he fucked Logan open with his finger and quickly added a second, urgency rushed over him. He needed to get Logan a plug for those nights where he couldn't keep his hands off him—something he could pull out and replace with his dick instantly, instead of worrying about hurting him if he went too fast.

But Logan was eager, grabbing handfuls of the sheets and crying out with each rough thrust, his hard cock flat on his stomach and leaving a thick glob of slick arousal behind. The beautiful lines of his body curved into a heaving chest and legs spreading as far as they could go. Christian didn't stand a chance of resisting him.

The only way it could've been better was if Noah was right there with them, sprawled on the bed next to Logan, watching and learning exactly how he liked to be touched, what he could take...

"Fuck it," Christian muttered, then scooped Logan up.

"Wh—" Logan locked his legs around Christian's waist on instinct, arms around his neck.

"If a man's gonna spend his whole damn life playing a sport..." Christian carried Logan straight for the door and shoved him against it. "...then he might as well *use* that strength."

They'd never done this before, and even as Christian kept Logan secure with one arm around him and his chest pressing tight against his own, he realized it wasn't going to be nearly as easy as movies made it out to be. But he'd damn well make it good for Logan—no matter if it left Christian aching for days.

"You tell me if you're gonna fall, you understand?" Christian slicked his cock with two quick jerks of his hand, then guided it forward.

"You're not gonna drop me. Do it, c'mon, fuck me." Logan's nails stabbed into Christian's shoulders as he held on tight.

And because Christian was a gentleman, if he did say so himself, he did exactly what his lover asked.

It was rough—far harder than he expected. But there was something achingly visceral about it, not being able to get a steady rhythm as he fucked into Logan. Every few thrusts, his grip would shift, and he'd drive into Logan at a whole new angle just to keep him in place. It took every ounce of Christian's strength to have him, and he wouldn't want it any other way.

"Yeah, yeah, *fuck*..." Logan cried out sharply as Christian's hips drove into him. "Right there, right there, *please!*"

Christian's hands bruised Logan's skin as he held firm, growling through the discomfort in his bones. The door shook—the whole fucking wall did—and when he shut his eyes, he imagined Noah standing outside it with a hand down his pants, getting off with them.

It was too strong of an image. Christian knew then and there that he wasn't going to last.

White flames seared his mind's eye as pleasure wrapped around the pain, tighter and tighter and tighter until he bit Logan's neck and grunted through his orgasm. The sweet sound of Logan begging for his cock took the thoughts out of his head. He mindlessly ground his hips against Logan's plush ass, milking himself dry, until he couldn't do anything but slowly sink to the floor. When they landed, Logan reached for his own cock.

"No." Christian rolled Logan onto his back and crawled between his legs. With his release leaking out of Logan, he took his dick into his mouth and sucked him down hard and fast, taking him far enough that he didn't taste a thing when Logan let go only seconds later.

Christian slid his hands up and down Logan's thighs, trying to soothe him, and pulled off. "Shit," he rasped, throat a bit sore. "They're gonna kill me in rehearsals."

Logan petted Christian's head with a low chuckle. "I didn't ask you to do that."

"Yeah, well, if I'm gonna be a dick and come in three seconds, I might as well let you have the same privilege." Seeing that Logan was relaxed and not needing immediate attention, Christian sat back on his knees. "My hips hurt."

"Also your fault."

"Shut up." He smirked down at Logan. "Keep running your mouth and I won't get you anything to clean up with."

"Hey!"

Christian laughed. He forced himself to stand up, shaky as his legs were, and snagged his boxers. After pulling them on, he opened the door, ignoring Logan's yelp behind him as he scrambled to cover himself.

Noah's bedroom door was wide open. Christian risked a glance down the hall, but when he didn't see Noah in bed, he continued to the bathroom. He wet a washcloth with warm water and grabbed a hand towel for good measure, then paused once he caught sight of Noah on the couch. Noah was sprawled out on his back, eyes closed and breathing uneven, his hips elevated on one of the pillows that came with the couch.

Christian had no idea about the specifics of what Noah had done, but the activity itself was obvious, and Christian's cock ached as it tried in vain to harden again.

"You good?" Christian asked softly.

His attempt to be less surprising didn't help—Noah jolted anyway. He sat up quickly, winced, and shoved the pillow on the floor. "Uh, I-I'm—"

"It's okay if you listened." Now Christian was grinning like a fool. Everything had worked out exactly as he'd wanted. He might walk as awkwardly as an old man for the next two days, but it was damn worth it. "Pretty hot, if you did, to tell you the truth."

"You didn't exactly give me much choice." Noah covered his face. "God, don't look at me."

Christian shook his head. "My bad, man. I'm gonna go put Logan back together. If you need anything, you come find us, huh?"

Noah simply made a weak sound from behind his hands.

As Christian shut the bedroom door behind him, he saw Logan had found his way to the bed. "I think Noah jerked off." He sat next to Logan and brought the damp cloth between his legs to clean him up. "Seemed like it, anyway."

Logan hissed. "Careful. Sore."

"Sorry. Maybe if you weren't such a cockslut—"

"Oh, fuck you," Logan said affectionately as he reached to take the cloth from him. "As if you're gonna complain. Is he okay? Noah?"

Christian slid behind Logan and lifted his head, putting it in his lap. "I think he's fine. Embarrassed that I knew what he was doing. Acting as though I'm gonna make fun of him for it or something."

Logan snorted. "He really doesn't know you, does he?"

"Maybe not." Christian frowned. Logan and Noah seemed pretty well entrenched in each other's lives, but all Christian really had to go on was a strong physical attraction, familiarity with Noah's mannerisms, and a keen curiosity to figure everything else out. "Think he'd let me take him out on a date?"

When Logan didn't respond right away, Christian studied his face. "Would *you* be okay if I took him out on a date?"

Logan opened his mouth, then chuckled and looked away. He balled up the washcloth in the towel after drying himself off and tossed them at the laundry basket. "I guess you could."

"No, no, tell me what you're not saying."

Logan rolled his eyes, but his smile was a bit forced. "I'm trying not to get competitive with you about liking him first and how that means *I* get first date dibs."

Since Logan seemed in no hurry to leave, Christian began rubbing his chest in slow circles. They'd both need a hot bath later, probably with a healthy dose of Epsom salts for their aches and pains, but for now, Christian was content to be together, finally talking honestly like he'd wanted. "You say that as if I'm gonna be surprised by it. We've been competitive since the day we met. Remember? I beat you on a race around the playground, and you went and told the teacher I cheated."

"You did cheat! You got a head start!"

"Wasn't my fault you weren't as fast off the line as me, babe." Christian grinned. "Okay. You can get first date dibs. Might be a while. Who knows how long it'll take before you two decide a little experimenting won't fuck our friendship up?"

Logan shot him a look. "Don't leave yourself out of it."

"No, I can do that. See, I already know I wanna see where this goes. It's y'all who've gotta figure your shit out."

As Logan turned his face toward the wall with a heavy sigh, Christian could practically read his mind. All those years together wouldn't mean anything if he couldn't. But instead of being silent, Logan began to open up.

"It's not easy, okay? It's not just about asking if I *want* him. There's more to it."

Christian thought he might understand. "Looking at somebody and asking yourself if you're doing things the wrong way? If they're gonna get too serious too fast?"

"I'm already chained to your fucking hip, yeah? I know it. I've been trying to do better. I don't wanna get clingy with Noah and scare him and Daiki away—I won't have anybody but you if I do."

Christian shook his head. "No, not true. You're gonna get out there, aren't you? You'll meet a hell of a lot of people. You already started at work."

"One girl isn't enough," Logan muttered. "I don't wanna lose any of you. I'm trying my best."

"That's all I want."

Logan was quiet. He crawled up the bed and rolled his back to Christian, but held a hand out plaintively behind him. Christian got the memo and lay behind him, spooning him and putting an arm around his waist to pull him in close. The sigh he heard spoke of relief, and he pressed kiss after kiss to the back of Logan's neck, delicate and quick.

"You going to sleep?" Christian asked on a whisper.

"Couldn't sleep if I tried with this damn job being what it is. No, I just wanna shut my eyes for a little while."

"Okay."

"You don't have to stay."

Christian smiled as he closed his eyes. "I know." But there wasn't anywhere he'd rather be. Right here, the distance they'd put between them for their own safety finally began to melt away. It evaporated, leaving nothing but the richness of their love behind.

He was damn near spoiled, he knew, but for once he shot a prayer of thanks to whoever the hell might be listening. Christian didn't deserve Logan, but he wasn't going to point that out. He'd stay there and soak it all up until he had a surplus.

Chapter Fifteen

As Logan suspected, he couldn't sleep a wink; his schedule had been fucked over by his night job, and there was no changing it even after a rousing session of sex. He and Christian rested in silence until half an hour later when the air conditioning on his bare skin was more than he could take.

"All right, I can't stand it. Gotta get up." Logan grabbed Christian's hand and kissed the back of it. "You can stay, if you need to sleep."

Christian groaned but let him go. "Mind's racing. If you're not staying in bed, I'm gonna follow you around like a lost puppy."

Logan couldn't help but smile. As much as he knew Christian would be satisfied with just the two of them lying in bed all night, Logan would be miserable. If being sore from his last shift wasn't enough, the ache in his back and bruising around his waist only made it worse. But it was...*nice*, somehow—feeling so vividly alive and knowing to the depths of his soul how much Christian wanted him.

And Noah too. Logan's heart skipped a beat. Going out into the living room meant seeing him again. Knowing that Noah had heard how feverishly they'd fucked brought on a strange combination of adrenaline and worry. What would he think of them? Did it annoy him or was he into it, as Christian had said?

He pulled his clothes on and made a sound of deterrence when Christian headed for the door in nothing but his boxers. "You're just gonna walk out there like that?"

"Ain't nothing he hasn't seen before." Christian smirked. "Might steamroll past the waiting game if he gets a little show, huh?"

"You're the worst." Logan threw a shirt at him, but Christian simply ducked out of the way and left the room.

Can't let him have all *the glory, bastard.*

Logan followed tentatively. The first thing he saw was Christian dropping onto the couch right next to Noah and giving him a bright smile. Subtlety had never been Christian's strong suit. Logan shook his head as he went into the kitchen. He told himself he wanted something to drink, but he knew the truth: he didn't think he was ready to look Noah in the eye. It was possible he'd already changed his mind about everything. Perhaps hearing the force they'd used when they banged against the door was too much—too violent, or something he thought he wouldn't be able to handle. If that was true, Logan didn't think he'd be able to see Noah's face for a full week before he stopped feeling humiliated.

"Good movie?" Christian asked.

Noah cleared his throat. "Yeah, uh...it's okay. I don't know. I picked something random."

"You can find the best gems that way though. Even the shitty ones are funny as hell sometimes."

"Yeah..."

Logan poured himself a glass of sweet tea and forced his legs to take him back into the living room, step by shaky step. Looking at Noah seemed to be the bravest thing he'd ever done.

Christian and Noah were a pretty picture on the couch. Christian's arm draped over the back of it made him look protective, and it was cute that Noah didn't shy away from it. Their legs touched, and Noah looked an inch away from sagging into Christian's side and letting himself be held. But Logan fixated on Noah's restless hand—how he kept drumming his fingers on his thigh, as though he wanted to burn off some energy. *Nervous? Or excited?*

Noah met his gaze and gave him a tentative smile, and Logan was drawn in like a moth to the flame.

As Logan settled in on the other side of Noah, Christian began speaking. "You get a chance to talk to Daiki yet?"

"Oh, um...no. Not really. He's got rehearsals tonight. They're a little behind where they wanted to be with opening the musical, so they're running late most nights to make sure everything's running perfectly. I don't want to bother him."

Christian looked at Noah, who kept his eyes on the TV. "Oh yeah?"

Logan heard the faint impatience in Christian's tone, but before he could speak up Noah answered.

"Yes. I'll probably hear from him tonight before he goes to bed though. He's as much of a night owl as I am these days. I'm not sure how he does it; surviving on caffeine just isn't enough for me. All the energy drinks in all the world can't keep me awake if I don't get a halfway decent amount of sleep."

He's rambling. Logan patted his knee in solidarity. "I feel you, man, but Daiki's a machine. I don't know how the rest of the world manages to keep up with him." It took him a moment to realize his hand was tingling from the contact with Noah's bare leg, then a second longer to realize Noah wasn't moving away. Logan's hand stayed right there above his knee.

He stared. He couldn't help it. He felt as pure as a fucking monk, centered on the feel of Noah's skin, and he almost laughed. *This is what happens to boys who grow up in church, huh?* It wasn't enough if they discovered they weren't straight—they got *too* excited at the thought of somebody's body. It was as if he was going through a second puberty. *Fucking incredible.* Logan's cock didn't care that he'd gotten off half an hour ago. He was stirring up inside all over again, all because Noah showed no desire to leave.

Be patient, idiot. Logan trained his eyes on the movie as if he wasn't holding himself back from dragging his hand slowly up Noah's thigh. His own desire didn't matter right now—Noah's comfort did.

That didn't stop Christian from reaching to tug at Logan's hair, as though he was *trying* to rile him up, but, hell, that was Christian.

Noah's leg tensed under his hand, then released, and Logan glanced at him from the corner of his eye. He didn't look upset. "You okay?" Logan asked.

Noah let out a shaky sigh. "Yeah. Can I ask you both something?"

"Shoot," Christian replied.

"Is this just about the sex to you?"

The question was so preposterous that Logan looked at Christian with a wrinkled brow. "What?"

"Seriously. I need you to tell me."

Noah shifted, and Logan took his hand away, then pushed Christian's arm to make sure he'd do the same. Noah needed space, if this was something he was worrying about.

"There's just...people do that, okay?" Noah continued. "With me, with other trans people. We're just some fetish for them to exploit, a-and I don't *think* you guys are the type, but if you're looking to do some specific sex thing with me just to check it off your bucket list, that's a no-go."

Maybe it was because Noah was the only trans person who'd ever came out to him, but Logan was blindsided. Yet, as he thought about it more, it made sense, and it left a deep disgust in his gut.

"Hey, no, we're not like that," Logan said quietly. "I'd never thought about using you. I told you that you're something special, and I meant it."

"Even that. Some *thing* special." Noah leaned forward, small and vulnerable. "I know it's just language or a turn of phrase, but it gets me nervous. I just need to know you're not trying to get with me only for the sex."

"Man, I think you're hot as hell," Christian interjected, "but you've gotta believe there's so much more about you that I wanna know. I'm wanting to get to know *all* of you."

Noah looked at him. "Even if you don't get to fuck me?"

As Logan watched, Christian paused, giving the idea serious thought. He narrowed his eyes in consideration. "I'll be real with you, I haven't had a partner I didn't sleep with since, fuck, middle school, I think. I almost forgot those kind of people exist."

Noah didn't look away. "Just answer the question."

After a quiet few seconds, Christian sighed. "I...yeah. I still wanna learn what makes you tick, Noah, even if sex never happens."

"And you?" Noah whipped his head around and gave Logan a direct, challenging stare.

Logan didn't hesitate. "I like you for you. I'm never gonna push you for anything you don't wanna give, and that's final." He jerked his head toward Christian. "Listen, at the end of the day, I've still got him. I've got my hand. If I'm ever feeling a little hot and bothered around you, then fuck, I can just get up and leave the room and take care of it, yeah? It's whatever."

Noah flicked his gaze over Logan's face, frowning, before he slowly nodded. "Okay. Glad to hear it." He relaxed, leaning straight into Logan, who lifted an arm in surprise to welcome Noah in. With his cheek resting on Logan's chest, Noah sighed. "I do have sex, for the record, but I don't bottom. Ever."

Logan met Christian's eyes over the top of Noah's head and quirked his brow in question. *That okay with you?*

Christian simply gave him a smile and rested a hand on the nape of Noah's neck. "Well, lucky for you, we both do."

One of Noah's hands found Logan's stomach, where it tugged at the fabric restlessly. "Okay. Well. I'll keep that in mind."

If concentration had been hard with Logan's hand on Noah's leg, having the man pressed flush against his side was complete torture. He didn't know if the way Noah played with his shirt was a nervous tic or an invitation, but it did nothing for his concentration. Within seconds, he was staring blankly into the distance, lips parted and heart pounding.

Noah's ear, he realized, was directly over his fucking heart. The guy could probably hear exactly how keyed up he was. *Fuck.*

The sound of soft scratching told him that Christian was dragging his nails over Noah's scalp. Then the quiet moan came as Noah tilted his head further, burying his face in Logan's chest.

"Sensitive?" Christian whispered.

"Mm..." Noah's arms covered in goose bumps, rising right before Logan's eyes, and heat stirred inside him in response.

If Logan didn't end this now, he never would. He slapped Christian on the back of the head, not quite enough to hurt. "Hey, if he says he wants time to figure out what he wants with us, fucking give it to him. Don't be sitting here trying to seduce him."

Christian chuckled. "Should I stop, Noah?"

Noah made a rough sound and then steadied himself with a hand high on Logan's thigh.

Logan looked down quickly at Noah's thumb an inch away from his cock. "Fuck," Logan whispered, clenching every muscle in his body in an attempt to keep from getting hard. "Noah, I-I really want you to answer that too, if you don't mind."

Noah's hazel eyes met Logan's. Without any hesitation, he spoke in a rough voice. "Can I kiss you?"

"I fucking wish you would."

Noah's mouth met Logan's eagerly. Unlike Christian, who knew the exact way to ease his tongue to meet Logan's and make him melt, Noah kissed with the quick excitement of a puppy, as if he was afraid that if he stopped Logan would leave. It was sweet, in its own way, making happiness bubble up inside Logan's chest like soda.

Logan took Noah's face between his hands to guide the kiss, tilting his head and slowing the movement of his lips until the other man followed his lead. Noah whined against his mouth, and when Logan opened his eyes, he saw Christian buried in Noah's neck, teeth moving gingerly over his skin. Noah's body angled with the press of Christian's until Noah and Logan had their chests flush together.

He'd never imagined his first threesome starting this way—three bodies trying to figure out the best way to fit on a too small couch—but he wasn't going to complain.

Noah broke the kiss with a shivery gasp and tilted his head back to invite Christian in. They traded places, Christian taking Noah's mouth and Logan finding his collarbone. A fog spread through Logan's head.

Roughly one brain cell was left to encourage him to slow down, and it gave up the fight the second Noah reached for his ass to pull him closer.

Logan moaned. He slid his thigh between Noah's legs—and everything stopped. Noah threw one hand against Logan's chest and shoved Christian backward with his elbow, and the world snapped into stark, sudden focus.

"Sorry." Logan began to move away, but Noah tightened his hand around his shirt.

"No, it's fine, y-you just, I feel like I should..." With his face a vibrant pink and his eyes flitting frantically around the room, Noah looked as though he was losing his mind. "I need to say this."

"Well, c'mon, then," Christian growled, sliding both arms around Noah's waist and tugging at his ear with his teeth.

"Christian," Logan said sharply.

Christian met his eyes, then looked at Noah. His expression shifted in recognition as the seriousness of the moment seemed to settle on him. "Sorry." He let him go. "I'm a dick. Go on."

"It's fine, I'm just... I've had top surgery—you both have seen that—but I haven't had anything else done. I don't even know if I want to." Noah looked between them so fast Logan thought he was going to give himself whiplash. "My cock's a lot smaller than yours right now, and it's, like, hypersensitive? So I keep a bottom of some kind on when I fuck around with people—a harness or boxers or something."

"Okay, so, your cock," Logan said slowly, working at memorizing everything he just heard while Noah stared at him with an unidentifiable look. It was a struggle to stay above water, but Logan managed little by little, questions on his mind. "If it's that, uh, hypersensitive, should I not touch it at all? Like..." He gestured to where his thigh was still nudging Noah's knee.

Noah winced. "Going under my boxer briefs to rub it? No, I don't enjoy how that hurts. But this is fine." He threw both arms around Logan's neck. "Full stimulation of the whole area around my cock is fantastic. We're just moving a little fast, a-and I wanted you both to know all of that before one of you tried to take my underwear off or something—I don't want either of you doing that."

Christian blinked. "We can slow down. We've got all the time in the world. I know I've got a one-track mind sometimes, but I'm being serious."

"No, I don't want to slow down," Noah effused. "I'm so fucking turned on right now, and I..." His eyes widened. "Daiki."

Logan's chest sank, his dick practically howling in disappointment, and Christian thudded his head against the wall.

"Fucking Daiki," Christian murmured.

"Hold on, hold on, it'll only take a few seconds." Noah fumbled for his phone. "Seriously, I-I just want to check in and make sure this is still fine before we do anything big."

There was a special, torturous place in hell, Logan thought, for sitting under his possible new lover, feeling the heat of Noah's cock bleeding through a thin layer of fabric, and not being able to move a damn muscle. He closed his eyes and tried to concentrate on anything but how desperate his hands were to learn the shape of Noah's body.

When the quiet sound of Christian tapping his head on the wall became too annoying, Logan reached out for him. "Fucking, stop."

Christian responded by smirking, then sucking one of Logan's fingers into his mouth, and Logan trembled with barely restrained need as he pressed his face into the back of the couch and suffered. It had been a few years since he'd come too fast from anything, but this scenario was setting him up for a hell of a lot of embarrassment.

"H-Hey, Daiki?" Noah was FaceTiming him like he always did.

Daiki's voice lifted. "Hey love! How're you feeling?"

"Good, good, um...quick question, what we talked about earlier—about Christian and Logan—is that still on the table if something happens?"

At that moment Christian chose to kiss his way up Logan's sensitive inner arm, and Logan let out a moan.

"Holy shit." Daiki said the words slowly. "Are you about to dick somebody down in the living room?"

Logan turned his head, catching a glimpse of Daiki. The sheer joy on his face couldn't be hidden.

"No. Not the living room. Not the couch." Noah shook his head. "I'm not getting jizz on the sofa, and, uh—"

"Hey, can you put the boys on for a second?" Daiki teased. "I just need to ask them what the hell took them so long—"

Christian snatched the phone out of Noah's hand and sneered at it. "Hey, bro, shut up so we can fuck your boyfriend."

Instead of getting angry, as Logan expected, Daiki laughed. "That's big talk for a—"

Christian hung up and tossed the phone on one of the couch pillows that had tumbled to the floor. "Son of a bitch."

"He sure is," Noah replied affectionately. He was already getting to his feet and moving quickly toward the hallway, and Christian followed hot on his heels.

Logan stayed behind, still catching up to the feel of Christian's mouth on his skin. His lips continued tingling from Noah's kisses, his cock so hard he swore if he moved even an inch he'd come.

"Logan."

He looked up and met Christian's eyes.

Christian beckoned with two quirking fingers. "C'mere, babe."

Like a puppet on a string, Logan floated to his feet and followed the command.

Christian took his hand and led him along. It was perfect, exactly what Logan wanted. Times like this—when he and Christian fucked after wrestling each other to the ground and when Logan's thoughts ran a little too hot—made him desperate to be walked through whatever was going to happen piece by piece. He trusted Christian. They knew what the other liked or hated. He knew Christian would never do anything that would make him uncomfortable, and he'd stop the second Logan asked him to.

That made giving in to him so much sweeter.

Christian stopped him at Noah's door, and Logan leaned around him to see what was happening. Noah was throwing things off his bed and making a huge mess on the floor. "We can go to our room, if you want."

Noah shook his head. "All my stuff's in here." Then he froze. "Uh, not, not that I'm saying we need to, um..." Noah took a deep breath and faced them. "We can, like, mess around if you guys want? We don't have to do anything...big. I don't have to fuck you or anything."

Christian chuckled. "I am one hundred percent not opposed to the fucking. What about you, Logan?"

Logan blurted before he could think too hard. "Christian only fucked me a little while ago. I'm probably still stretched out." That wasn't what he intended to say, but he couldn't find a reason to be embarrassed, not when both of them looked at him so intensely.

Noah nodded slowly, eyes wide, his expression suggesting he wasn't thinking all that clearly either. "Wh-What do you like being fucked with?"

Logan blinked a few times. "A...cock?"

Christian snorted and threw an arm around his shoulders, hugging him close, while Noah covered his mouth to hide a smile.

Noah went to his closet and pulled out a few small boxes. "No, I mean, like..." He opened two of them and pulled out two dildos, then held them where Logan could see them better. "I've got about...five of them? Do you enjoy something skinny? Something long?"

Logan took them, holding both dildos by the base, cocking his head to the side as he studied them, heart starting to thud erratically again. He'd never been fucked with a toy before, and he'd never thought he would be—not with Christian being his boyfriend. But there was something *satisfying* about these dicks, even just aesthetically. He held in his left hand, a long, slender one, the same pale tone as Noah's flesh, and in his right, a vivid pink cock, shorter but covered in ridges.

Noah held up two more, and Logan gave them a glance, then dropped the ones he was holding on the floor.

"What the fuck?" Logan breathed as he took the largest one out of Noah's hand and cradled it in his own. "This is unusable."

"I mean...not if you go slowly and believe in yourself."

The weapon Logan held in his hands was something his mind could barely comprehend. The dildo was colored with a rich selection of earth tones—browns and yellows bleeding together—with its already large head leading into an even thicker shaft through a number of bumps and ridges that finally ended with a sudden swell he didn't quite understand. It made his hole clench needily on sight.

Christian rested his chin on top of Logan's head. "You want it?"

"I-I'm not *this* stretched, but..."

Noah stepped closer. Even just inches away, he made Logan's body heat up. "I have lube."

"What if I can't take it?" Logan's mouth spit the words out before he was ready to acknowledge those nervous thoughts. *I'll look like an idiot and I'll ruin this and nobody will have a good time—*

Noah cupped his hands under Logan's, silencing his thoughts instantly. He smiled. "Then we try another cock. No big."

Was it that easy? They were both watching him so patiently, neither in a hurry. And, for some reason, the toy looked damn enticing.

For the first time, I'll have pushed my body to do something Christian's hasn't. Logan couldn't stop grinning. "Let's fucking do it."

"Hah!" Christian clapped his hands together once, then scooped Logan into his arms in a bridal carry. "You'll take good care of my boy, won't you, Noah?"

"I'll do whatever he wants," Noah was quick to say, following on their heels.

For once, Logan found he didn't mind being talked about as if he wasn't right there in the room with them. He clung to Christian, arms around his neck, and breathed in his rich scent. He swore he could still pick up the smell of sweat from when Christian had fucked him so vigorously only a short time ago.

Shit, this is the same fucking day. Everything had changed so quickly. A few hours ago, Logan wanted to run far away from the apartment and never come back. Now here he was, Christian lowering him onto Noah's bed with a great sense of care and smiling down at him with love vividly gleaming in his eyes.

"You're staying, right?" Logan asked. Something about Christian's words had him scared he might disappear this first time—as though Noah was the *only* one who'd be taking care of him.

Christian chuckled as he clambered over top of Logan, getting his back to the wall. "Of course I am. You think I'm leaving you alone with this stud?" Christian looked Noah up and down. "He'll rock your world, and then you'll never wanna see me again."

Noah stopped in the middle of opening his nightstand drawer. "Don't say that! That's not what I want!"

"Just joking, man." Before the words were even fully out of Christian's mouth, he reached a hand for Noah. "You look like you're gonna run now. C'mon."

"I-I don't want…" Noah exhaled sharply, then started again. "I've never done spontaneous sex with someone I'm not dating before. I'm nervous. Things could go really wrong if we're not careful, and the last thing I want to do is drive you both away."

Logan closed his eyes, an incredible amount of relief washing over him. He chuckled and covered his face. "I thought you were gonna throw us out the second you found out we wanted you, Noah. Even if I end up giving you shitty sex, it's a hell of a lot more than I ever expected to get."

When he dropped his hands, he saw Noah watching him with hesitance, and he held his hand. "Please come kiss me?"

Noah scrambled onto the bed the very next second. Logan welcomed Noah on top of him, resting his hands on his roommate's thighs as they pressed into his hips. He leaned up, silently begging for that kiss once more, and Noah met him there with a quick peck.

"Can I touch your hair?" Noah asked, a hand resting on Logan's neck.

He grinned. He was feeling magnanimous, and he wanted his scalp to tingle. "Gentle. Don't pull or anything."

Noah cupped the back of his head and kissed him again. Noah found his rhythm more easily this time—nice and slow, tasting Logan in bits and pieces.

Logan's hands crawled up Noah's sides, higher and higher, until he felt him stiffen, and he broke the kiss with a sudden realization. "Sorry. Where can I touch you?"

Noah pressed his forehead against Logan's temple, his breathing rough and ragged. "Anywhere above the belt. Chest is, uh...still feels weird sometimes? So if I tell you to stop, just do it."

"Yeah." He *liked* this—liked knowing he didn't have to guess what Noah wanted, that they could just say what they liked and hated, from Logan's protectiveness about his hair to Noah's care with his chest. Logan spent so damn long in high school trying to figure out what girls wanted in bed without asking.

I was a fucking fool. Now he could give himself over to the rise and wane of the tide. He could ease higher and higher on Noah's body and hear him groan as he leaned into Logan's palms.

Logan didn't know how the hell just kissing Noah could feel so good. It was already incandescent with Christian—how could he be lucky enough to get that with two different people?

Christian. Logan's eyes flew open and searched for his boyfriend.

Still resting his back against the wall at the far side of the bed, Christian watched them with a small smile, eyelashes low. His legs were spread, the swell of his erection on proud display.

As Noah pulled away to tug one of Logan's earlobes between his lips, Logan hitched a breath and managed a few words. "Didn't think you'd be a watcher."

"You're one to talk. We have one amazing night of group sex, and you spend half your time watching me get fucked," Christian drawled back. He rubbed his dick through his boxers and cocked his head to the side. "And who was up all night listening to me fucking someone right under him in the bunk bed?"

"Couldn't...couldn't exactly slee—*fuck*..." The sharp dig of Noah's teeth into his skin seemed experimental, but it took the words right out of Logan's mouth.

Christian chuckled. "Shut up and let me watch you get fucked."

There wasn't much else he *could* do at this point. As desperate as he was to keep some of his connection to Christian—to keep him from thinking Logan didn't want him there at all—the tanginess of Noah's shampoo and the silkiness of his bare shoulders under his hands were pulling him further and further away. He wanted to lose himself in Noah.

For the first time, he realized he had permission to do exactly that.

"Noah..." Logan bucked his hips in a wordless plea.

Noah hummed. "What?"

"Just..." Another roll upward didn't get him anywhere. "I-I want..."

"Just tell me and I'll do it."

Another laugh from Christian warmed Logan's cheeks. Rather than ask, he pulled at the waistband of his own shorts, and Noah lifted his weight enough to let him. His cock was hard enough that it ached, dark and flushed and slick with need, and he looked up at Noah with desire.

Those wide eyes that had always looked innocent to Logan now seemed nothing but eager. Noah swore under his breath as he reached for his nightstand drawer, his chest right above Logan's eyes, and Logan pushed up the hem of his shirt to see pale skin gradually revealed. Noah didn't stop him, simply kept digging through the drawer, and Logan leaned up to press kisses over the freckles he found.

"For now..." As Noah spoke, a few condoms landed next to Logan's head. "We'll use these. Have you guys been tested recently?"

Christian grunted. "Nah. It's been just the two of us, so we really haven't had to."

"Me neither, so we'll just...*fuck*, Logan." Noah finally whipped the shirt off his head.

It wasn't the first time Logan had seen him shirtless, but it was a rare enough occurrence that he took his time to study his physique. As he drew lines up Noah's freckles with his fingers, Logan studied the leanness of his torso and the burgeoning strength of his arms. He traced over one of the long scars, watching Noah's face to see his reaction, then thumbed over one of his nipples. "Not sensitive?"

Noah shrugged, though the smile he gave looked a little sad. "It happens. They weren't really sensitive before, anyway, so..."

Before Logan could think to reply, Noah kissed him again, and his mind drowned in the sweet, soft pleasure of it.

It didn't take long for Logan to learn that Noah had an incredibly talented mouth. Now that he had calmed down significantly rather than taking off faster than a rabbit, Noah showed a level of patience Christian always seemed to lack. Inch by inch, he tasted Logan's skin, descending over his collarbone and nipples and ribcage with a tantalizing slowness that had every cell pulsing a bright red. Logan couldn't survive such intimate torture. He threw a hand out and found Christian's bare calf, then dug his nails in and fed on the sharp hiss he received.

The rip of the condom's wrapper should've been a fanfare of relief, but it only hitched Logan's body a level higher, making it vibrate with extreme anticipation. He wasn't going to last long. He was going to embarrass himself right there with both of the guys he adored.

"You're not allergic to latex or anything, are you?" Noah asked, his voice far rougher now, raspy with desire. "Should've asked before. Gotta be careful what I use with my toy."

Logan shook his head. "Latex, fine. Noah, I'm gonna come the second you put anything on or in me."

Christian burst out laughing. "He's not wrong, man, you've gotta be careful with him. He's got a hair trigger when you've got him this turned on."

"Shut up!" Logan whined.

"Hey, hey, it's okay." Noah rubbed Logan's stomach. "Have you ever used a cock ring?"

Logan shook his head.

"Okay, well..." Noah looked between them. "It's better to put it on when you're not already hard, because it can hurt. We might need to save that for next time."

"No, no." Logan grabbed Noah's arm. "I like when it hurts. Please. I-I wanted to last longer than this."

"He's not lying to you." Christian lifted his hips and tugged his boxers down, then threw them across the room, not an ounce of shyness about being naked. "Loves it. He's a little painslut. Fucking amazing to watch him go wild when you really get him going."

Noah winced, but he began carefully easing the condom down Logan's cock. "I'm not a sadist; I'm not going to know when it's too much. You need to tell me."

"I will, I will," Logan babbled, though Christian snickered with apparent disbelief.

Keeping his body in check as Noah slicked the condom with lube was the hardest thing Logan had ever had to do. Each brush of fingers lit him aflame. Stabbing his palm with his own nails did little to curb the need for release. But Noah slid a loose ring carefully around his cock, and even with his great care, Logan's cock still pulsed painfully with every inch and a half of progress.

"If you don't tell me when it's too tight, we stop," Noah said firmly, and when Logan nodded, he began to cinch in the ring around the base.

"Oh, *oh*, shit, okay..." Logan panted, hands shaking, hyperaware of the slow pressure around his shaft, and only when he found himself picturing it somehow snapping shut and severing his whole dick did he lift a hand. "Stop."

"Okay." Noah trailed a finger over the head of Logan's cock and chuckled when he thrashed with a gasp. "Is this a bad time to tell you you've got a pretty dick?"

Logan had no idea why that tiny bit of praise threw him into the heavens. With wings on his heart, he floated there, one hand still on Christian's leg, the other reaching for Noah's scratchy cheek. *God, please don't let me come down.*

They might be changing everything in this one moment. This might never happen again. He'd already played that game, watching Christian distance himself and missing him so badly he thought his heart might have a permanent crack in it.

There was a healthy fear they'd both turn tail and leave him after today—that maybe he wouldn't be good enough in bed to keep their attention.

Noah kissed his inner thigh, and Logan shot back to the present like a bullet.

A finger, covered by a condom, swirled around his hole, centering him as rapidly as Noah's voice. "Here we go."

Lips wrapped around the head of his cock and sucked gently, an agonizing slowness that made Logan groan. He barely noticed Noah's finger easing inside him, and after a cursory few seconds of circling, a second finger joined it with a more noticeable spread.

"Fuck," Christian whispered beside them, and Noah replied with a moan that shook Logan from the inside out.

Whatever stretch he'd kept from before, Noah had already found. Logan risked a look downward, eyes widening when he got a look at his cock. It looked massive, compared to his normal girth. He figured it had to do with the ring itself, but he found himself intimidated by its appearance—as if it was ready to explode. Noah didn't seem the least bit afraid. His pretty red lips wrapped around it without any appearance of disgust at the taste of lube, and when their eyes met, he winked.

Logan went boneless with a groan, and Noah took him even deeper.

The scissoring fingers worked deftly inside him, opening him up with such skill he could only imagine how many times Noah and Daiki had fucked silently in their dorm room, hiding it from the rest of the world. In seconds, he grazed over Logan's prostate.

As a sweat broke over him, Logan shivered. "Shit, shit…"

Noah pulled off with an audible pop. "Three fingers okay?"

Logan nodded feverishly. If he didn't get something inside him in the next five minutes, he'd die.

Logan had stretched himself once to four fingers as a challenge, but Noah's fingers seemed to be thicker. As soon as the third one eased inside, a pleasant ache made Logan's heart skip a beat. He opened his mouth, but stayed quiet as a rush of endorphins flooded him in sharp pursuit. *Oh.* There was no way in hell he was going to ask Noah to stop, not now.

The slick sound of Christian jerking himself off turned Logan's attention to him, and he drank in his lover's slow work on his own cock. Christian's bottom lip was neatly tucked between his teeth, his legs spread wide, and his abs clenched; he looked as though he was seconds away from letting go. He didn't have the patience for edging—he'd rather drown himself in an orgasm and then float in the aftermath of cuddles and sweet touches.

"Feel good?" Christian asked in a tense voice.

Logan nodded, eyelashes fluttering. He didn't have words anymore. His body was being wrecked little by little, but his mind was floating again, drifting somewhere beyond the limits he thought he had. Noah had some ability to pull him apart as easily as clay and make something new out of him, and all Logan knew was that he'd spend the next three months thanking him profusely.

The fourth finger, he hadn't anticipated, but every muscle in his body clenched, pushed to the limit, at the verge of breaking—

"Logan."

Noah's voice broke through the fog. Sweet. Caramel. Thin as spun sugar, forcing him to zero in.

"I need you to relax, sweetie."

Sweetie. Something about the endearment made him melt.

"Here. Right here. You feel this?"

There was something shifting inside him.

"Just open up right there for me, Logan."

He could do that. He could do anything, as long as Noah asked him so gently. He relaxed his muscles.

"There, look how good you're being."

Was he grinning like a fool? Absolutely. He couldn't keep the blissed-out look off his face. He was only a man melting into the sheets, becoming whatever Noah needed—because it was what *Logan* needed too.

The mattress squeaked when Christian shifted. "Logan?"

Though he heard his name, he couldn't find it in him to reply—only to turn the grin in his direction.

"He's okay," Noah said quickly. "He's a little, uh...hazy right now. Out of himself."

"That's fine?"

"He's safe here, with us. You can read him better than me and say if I'm pushing something too far. Does he look like I need to stop?"

"No, he's fine. Happy as a clam."

They're discussing me. Logan spread his legs until they ached and slid his hands under his head, hoping to put on a pretty show for them. He'd spent years watching Christian strive for new limits, even to the point of hurting himself to reach them, but the glistening pleasure of being the one to push himself now with both of them watching...it was addictive.

He could keep doing this all night.

Seconds passed. Minutes. Hours, days, months. Logan wasn't sure. Just that there was the easing of sensation as he accommodated Noah's fingers and the sparkles tingling in his brain and the buzzing right in the tips of his fingers and toes...

And, out of nowhere, something blunter pressed against his hole. How much time had he lost? Was he ready for Noah already? Logan lifted his head and stared, trying to make sense of what he saw—the black harness Noah wore like boxer briefs, the ring at the base of his shaft holding it in place, and the vibrant colors of the cock dulled by a slick condom over it.

"Are you ready?" Noah asked, massaging Logan's inner thigh with one hand.

He blinked. It didn't matter that he felt as though he could handle anything. In this strange, soft, colorful headspace he'd slipped into, Logan found himself needing to be affirmed. "Am I?"

When no one replied, he looked at Christian and repeated with urgency, "*Am* I?"

"You sure are, babe." Christian shifted his weight so he could hold Logan's hand, sitting on his knees beside him. "You gotta tell us if it's too much, okay? See, you've got my hand right here? Squeeze it."

Logan did.

"Good."

One word shouldn't bring him that much delight.

"Now, if you start really hurting and you can't speak, you just give my hand three little squeezes in a row, and we'll slow down, okay?"

Logan nodded. He watched Christian with utter adoration. How lucky was he? How many boyfriends let their lover be fucked by somebody else that they liked? This whole time, he'd half expected Christian to call everything off—to declare it one big practical joke. But it seemed the main event might actually happen. Noah had put almost his whole damn hand inside Logan's ass. That didn't seem to be a joke to him.

When Logan's eyes wandered back to Noah's fervent face, he smiled as he nuzzled Christian's leg. "Will you fuck me, Noah?" he asked, words slurred.

A look of relief came over Noah. He nodded. He began to push forward.

Logan expected a world of pain, but none came. The head of Noah's cock slipped inside him easily, giving a full stretch that tapered into the drag of the first ridges...and nothing bad. He was perfectly prepared for it. There was nothing awaiting him but the satisfaction of being *good.*

And the shift to exquisite pleasure.

"Oh..." Logan's eyes fell shut as he gasped, head tilting back. "O-Oh, shit..."

"God, you're gorgeous," Noah whispered. The slow pulsing of his hips—in a bit, then out, again and again—set up a dizzying anticipation for more. With each breath Logan took, he didn't know what awaited him: a new stretch, the graze of novel stimulation inside him, or the push against his prostate.

He loved it. Fucking adored every single second. He dug his nails into the back of Christian's hand and whined.

Sounds Logan had never made before bubbled out of him, spreading through the room loud enough for their neighbors to hear. He couldn't stop. Every second ratcheted the exquisite sensations a degree higher, and it wouldn't be long before he rocketed through the ceiling.

"Don't stop, don't stop—" He cut off in a cry when he felt something too big, *far* too big, press against his rim.

"What's wrong?" Christian asked breathlessly.

Noah muttered, "That would be the knot."

"The *what*?"

"Don't ask."

Logan had no idea what they were discussing, only the awareness that Noah was pulling back. "No, I want it, I *want* it."

"Logan."

"I-I can take it, I promise, I..." Suddenly Logan wanted nothing more than to know exactly how far he could go. His cock already throbbed. His hole clenched eagerly around Noah's cock every time he eased out. What was a little more? He *needed* it.

"Goddamn." Noah leaned down and fervently kissed him, and Logan gave himself up to the air.

He had no concept of when Noah began fucking him in earnest, just that he seemed to know Logan could handle it now—that he could take their tongues twisting together, the hands bruising his hips, and the dick trying to split him in two. That impassable swell slapped against Logan's rim with each pass, pushing a millimeter deeper, until he couldn't manage a word. He drifted so close to the edge that, for a long second, he couldn't breathe.

Then, with one slow push forward, Noah filled Logan all the way to the base, and Logan came in a sharp burst.

He saw white. Distantly he thought he might've screamed, but he was too fixated on how *full* he was—not an inch left empty. He didn't feel human anymore. He gradually dropped back to the mattress from where he'd arched, then a hand gradually coaxed the cock ring off as he gradually softened.

When Logan opened his eyes, the first thing he saw was Christian's hard cock in his peripheral vision.

"I think he's a little...high," Noah murmured. "He might need a few minutes to really come back. Touching will help, I think? It always helps with Daiki."

"You fuck Daiki like this?" Christian sounded more in awe than anything.

"Well...not with this cock yet. We're building up to it."

Because he couldn't think of why he shouldn't, Logan ignored the conversation in favor of lifting his neck and taking Christian's erection in his mouth.

His boyfriend's moan instantly filled the air. Fingers found his hair, pulling him into a comfortable rhythm—one of Logan's favorites, one that he couldn't manage on his own with how spent he felt. Happiness spun through him, and he relaxed his head, giving in to Christian in every way.

Noah made a quiet choked sound. "He's...okay with that?"

Christian hummed. "He likes it." He rubbed Logan's chest. "Makes sense, doesn't it? You saw... *fuck*, how...*eager* he was to make you happy."

Noah. Noah couldn't come inside Logan. He couldn't be happy, not like he'd made Logan. Multitasking had never been Logan's strong suit, but it was worth trying. He reached out toward Noah's hips, making a weak sound.

Noah blinked. He was in the middle of removing the condom from his colorful cock. So on the ball. He deserved more than just blowing Logan's whole fucking mind, then being left out in the cold. Noah looked at Christian. "What does he want?"

Logan tried to pull off, but when Christian held him firm he melted again. He didn't want to stop sucking on him anyway. Instead, he jerked his hand up and down in midair, fingers curved, and Christian chuckled. "He wants to get you off. Do you have a way you wanna come?"

Noah stammered, then cleared his throat. "Logan, is...is it all right if I grind on your thigh?"

That made him think of his first sexual experience alone with Christian—Logan on his stomach on the floor, Christian grinding his cock against Logan's ass, Christian so dizzy with pleasure, and Logan so excited to get him off with only his body. He groaned in anticipation and shot him a thumbs-up.

Noah's weight settled on him, straddling his thigh, and the shivering sound he made as he pressed down made Logan wish he could come again. Three times in one night? He hadn't managed that since sophomore year—but, goddamn, what he wouldn't give to go back.

He was a tool being used to drive his lovers higher. The taste of Christian's skin on his tongue made the eyes roll back in his head, and the rhythmic grinding of Noah's hips had him feeling fucked all over again. Logan could stay like this for as long as they wanted. He didn't need to breathe, eat, drink, or sleep. He just needed *them*.

He was almost disappointed when Christian filled his mouth with his release instead of lasting all goddamn night. The flavor was still not his favorite, but he gulped down every drop of it, if only because he knew it would please Christian. Logan's hands found Noah's hips, holding them loosely as Christian crawled away and grabbed Noah by the chin to give him a searing kiss of his own.

They were stunning together. Noah went weak, welcoming a deeper kiss, as his hips began to stutter. A flush spread down his neck, into his chest, until for a moment, his moans went silent—then rose to twice the volume as he came.

As the two of them collapsed, Logan finally found his voice. "Wow."

Christian laughed. He slung a leg over Logan's waist. "There you are, babe. Are you back with us?"

"Always been here." He blinked a few times. "I...think. It was...it was just a *lot*. I'm still a little..."

"Yeah. It's okay. I didn't expect you to go over the edge. A little subspacey." Noah rolled onto his side and smiled. "I didn't think you trusted me that much."

"I trust y'all with my fucking *life*." It was easy to think he might even be in love with *both* of them.

Logan was covered in their fingerprints. He had the taste of them both on his tongue. He couldn't imagine not having it again. But something held him back from saying it. He knew Noah loved Daiki, and Logan didn't want to intrude on that if all they got to do was roll around in the sheets.

But there'd be time to figure that out later. Right now...

"I need to put the toys away," Noah said. "And throw this harness in the washer. Fuck."

Christian grabbed Noah's hand. "What, no cuddles?"

"Look at this." Noah gestured up and down the bed. "It's small. You're both barely fitting in it."

"Ours is bigger." Christian paused. "Don't tell me you're trying to weasel out of the afterglow here, mister."

Noah opened his mouth, closed it, and looked away. "I-I didn't...want to assume you'd both still want me here—"

Logan cut Noah off by wrapping around him like a starfish, making Noah squeal.

A second later, something ticked in Logan's brain, and he pulled back. "Fuck, fuck, sorry, no full-body contact, I-I—"

"It's okay." Noah touched his cheek. "Hey. It's okay."

"But I didn't ask."

"You should've, sure, but...I don't mind, if we're going to be...sleeping together?" Noah shook his head. "What do we call each other? What the heck are we doing?"

Logan already knew what he wanted, but he couldn't be the first one to break the silence. He looked up at Christian.

After a silent exchange, Christian met Noah's gaze. "Wanna go on a date sometime?"

Noah's eyes widened. "Are you serious?"

"Yeah. You, me, Logan. We should date. See if we're all jiving the same way. After that, if Daiki's okay with it, maybe we could try being boyfriends."

Carefully, Logan watched Noah's expression. If there was a moment of hesitation, he'd take it all back. He'd never demand a thing.

But instead, Noah filled with joy, his hazel eyes sparkling as he covered his mouth. When he nodded, Logan pulled him back in, nestling him on his chest, and Christian wrapped an arm around his waist.

For once, everything was perfect. Logan wasn't so broken that people ran away from him. He wasn't being abandoned by anyone. He was *strong*. He was capable of standing on his own two feet, but right now, he didn't have to.

The bed was too small, and Logan could barely breathe, but he wasn't going anywhere.

Chapter Sixteen

The rush to prepare for opening night was somehow more and less hectic than Christian could have imagined. More, because he *embodied* Samyak now without having to think twice about his lines, and less, because every time he thought he couldn't take another hour during their tech rehearsals, he'd go home and find Noah and Logan waiting for him.

A guy didn't deserve that kind of luck. No one did. Not even the greatest peacekeepers the world had ever seen deserved two sweet kisses on the lips and two bodies cuddling on either side of his so he'd finally drop off into a restless sleep.

Christian was pretty damn sure he didn't deserve the sex either—but, fuck, he wasn't gonna complain.

Still, opening night came scarcely before he was ready. Logan and Noah had taken the night off from work. And Christian was terrified.

How could he believe he could do this? That he was a decent enough actor to share a stage with countless others with far more experience than him? How did the director know he wouldn't go out there and ruin the entire show, night after night?

Why was he worth taking a chance on?

But right before he had to change into his costume, there were three texts on his phone. One from Noah, telling him how nice it had been to wake up beside him that morning and how he couldn't wait to buy Christian dinner to celebrate his success that night. One from Daiki—a string of inappropriate emojis surrounding the encouragement for Christian to break a leg. And one from Logan, simply saying how goddamn proud he was of Christian and how he couldn't wait to see him on stage every year for the rest of their lives.

Somehow, it was through their words that he found the strength to go on—yes, including Daiki's, ridiculous and annoying as he could be. The three of them settled him, lifted him, until he was on stage without a single thought toward Christian Daniels.

He floated through every moment of the show. He railed against the world in a monologue, despising those in power who used soldiers like him as their playthings for a war they never saw the effects of. He wept real tears when he embraced his dear sister at her farm while her girlfriend looked on.

And, during the curtain call, he locked eyes with Logan and Noah right in the front row and blew them both a kiss in his ecstatic, tingling bliss.

They made him bold. They made him *brave*. So brave that, while he knew they were waiting for him in the lobby where everyone else was celebrating, Christian ducked into an unused room backstage to make a call.

"Hello?"

Christian took a deep breath. "Hey, Mom."

"Hey there. Do you know how late it is?"

"I do. I'm sorry." He rolled his eyes to the ceiling and kept them there, trying to summon the strength he'd had on the stage. "Just got done with my first performance of my play. Figured I'd give you a call."

There was a long moment of quiet. "How'd it go?"

"Amazing." He exhaled slowly, closing his eyes. "I was amazing, Mom. I've never felt that good in my life."

His mother grunted on the other end of the line. "Well...your dad and I aren't gonna be able to make it down, so—"

"I know." He'd known from the moment he told her about the show that she wouldn't be there—not because she couldn't find the time, but because she wouldn't *want* to find it. Christian was an imposition. He always had been. "That's fine. Hey, Mom?"

"Mm-hmm?"

"I'm changing my major to acting."

"Excuse me?"

"Yeah. I'll switch classes here soon. Probably this weekend. I just wanted you to know."

"That's the dumbest thing I've ever heard." Her voice lifted in familiar outrage that threatened to shake Christian down to the ground. "You can't seriously think you're gonna make a living with that. I, *we* won't support you, we—"

"You don't have to." He forced himself to look in the mirror again. He drank in the sight of himself in his costume. For the first time, Christian Daniels, who had led his soccer team to repeated championships in high school, actually felt important and worthwhile. He'd picked soccer. But acting had picked him. He was more blessed than he knew how to say. "I still have my scholarship. Don't you worry about a thing. This isn't going to change anything."

"Christian Daniels, I swear, if you—"

"It's already happening, Mom. I'm telling you because I want you to know, not because you're gonna change my mind, all right? I've gotta go— Logan and Noah are waiting on me."

"Christian!"

"We'll talk later. Love you." And then he hung up.

Bold was the word he'd decided to use to describe himself. But *stupid* would probably fit better. Yet for some reason, all he could do was cover his eyes and laugh, filling up with bubbles of joy and relief.

He couldn't have done it without them.

*

Christian had never been a huge fan of airports. He could count on one hand the amount of times he'd flown. A tiny high school soccer team like the one in Greenbarrow didn't receive fancy invitations to go to high-profile distant tournaments, and his family never had the funds to travel much. *What kind of airport needs a goddamn train?* The bustling chaos of the Atlanta airport made him draw closer to Logan, his shoulder bumping his.

Logan shot him a look, but took his hand after a moment of consideration. "What's up?"

"Nothing." Admitting weakness in public still wasn't his prerogative. "Just...it's busy here."

"Yep." Logan looked around. "Atlanta's a busy fucking place, man. I've been worse places, but..."

Christian grunted. He didn't have a story of his own to tell about being somewhere crowded and obnoxious. Already, he wondered why he and Logan had come inside to see Noah off. If he'd known he was going to feel this suffocated, Christian would've dropped them off, then circled the airport until Logan was finished saying goodbye to Noah at the ticket area. Now he was stuck, waiting for Noah to check his suitcase, wondering if the airport was so crowded that everyone was running out of oxygen, not just him.

Logan tipped his head back, his hair tickling Christian's neck, and watched him upside down. After a few seconds of silence he smiled. "Hey, when're we running away somewhere together?"

"What?"

"Like Noah's doing today, going to NYC to see Daiki. When're you and me going off on a little adventure of our own?"

Christian opened his mouth and then shut it again. Vivid images assaulted his mind, from spending time with Logan on a beach to hiking with him through mountains. They were blissful thoughts, and ones he hadn't let himself fantasize about too deeply—money didn't seem likely to make them an option any time soon. But now that the seed was planted in his head, he couldn't ignore it. "Yeah, I...I dunno. But I'd like it."

"Mm-hmm?"

I'd love it. He let go of Logan's hand and wrapped his arms around his waist from behind. "Maybe...for our anniversary. Go somewhere for Christmas together."

Logan's eyes twinkled as his grin widened. "Don't make promises you're not gonna keep, now."

"I'm not." Christian chuckled. "No, baby, I want it. I wanna take you somewhere nice and let ourselves relax."

Logan hummed. He closed his eyes, as if he was blissfully lost in a fantasy of his own. "Well, lemme start counting the days, then."

As they continued waiting, swaying slightly in place, Christian realized he was calmer now. Somehow just a few short words from Logan made the raucous noise of the airport fall away, leaving him somewhere safe and contained. Had Logan known that when he pulled him in? Christian wasn't used to having a person be his security blanket, but it was nice. *I'm fucking lucky.*

Christian couldn't keep himself from leaving a quick kiss on Logan's lips. "You know how much I love you?"

Logan sagged against his chest with a content sigh. "Can't be more than I love you. That's impossible."

"Fuck you. I love *you* more."

Logan elbowed him, and Christian poked him in the side, leaving Logan squealing like a baby as he bounced a few inches away with a laugh. He gave Christian a cheeky grin.

"Do I even want to know what you two are doing?" Noah drawled as he came to their side, pulling his rolling carry-on bag behind him.

"Foreplay," Christian leered, lunging to try to grab Logan by the shirt, but his boyfriend whirled away and put Noah between them as a shield. "Hey, no fair!"

"Whoa!" Noah spun in a circle with the force of Logan's pull, and Christian stepped forward, catching Noah by the hips before he could go through a second rotation. Noah looked up, expression stunned.

It was a nice look, having Noah held between the two of them. Protectiveness surged through Christian. He cradled Noah's cheek in one hand, the other still holding a fistful of his shirt at the waist, and slowly smiled.

"You're coming back to us, yeah?" Christian murmured, his voice rough. "You're not just gonna run away and elope with Daiki and never see us again?"

"You think I could stay away from you guys?" Noah was breathless, so quiet that the words seemed to be carried by a whispering breeze. "I spent almost a year wanting you both."

He entwined his fingers with Logan's and moved closer, looping his other arm around Christian's waist in an embrace. "I don't know what's going to happen with us. I don't know where things are going once I get back. But I promise, even though I'm leaving for a week, I'm not going to forget this happened."

Christian didn't know he needed to hear that until he relaxed. He ran a thumb over the dimple in Noah's chin.

Logan kissed the back of Noah's neck. "You'll call us, right? FaceTime?"

"You want me to?"

"Hell yeah! What the fuck?" Logan laughed.

"I-I just didn't know if...if you'd be busy with work and..."

Christian rolled his eyes. "All right, listen. I know you're going there to see your boyfriend's little play *first*. He's top priority. If you're too busy, you don't *have* to call us, but..."

Noah peeked up. "But?"

"...if you miss us...hell, just know we're already gonna be waiting by the phone."

Noah beamed. His dimples deepened in true delight. "I can't wait until summer's over and I can have all three of you in the same apartment with me."

That provided its own set of complications. Christian could come up with ten things that might go wrong, and having the four of them in tight quarters with a guy shared between all three of them would be at the top of the list. But now wasn't the time to talk about that. They needed to get Noah on his plane and head home before traffic got any goddamn worse.

Christian heaved a sigh and held Noah tightly. Noah, so much shorter than him, rested his head on the middle of Christian's chest, and Christian itched to pick him up and take him back home where they could spend another few dizzying hours kissing.

"Be safe, yeah?" Christian whispered, because no words could sum up the weight of his ache for Noah.

"I will." Noah came up onto his tiptoes in a look Christian was starting to find familiar—a silent request for a kiss. He was happy to oblige him. In an airport full of people who just saw him kiss his boyfriend, Christian took Noah's mouth with a certain desperation, cupping the back of his head and trying to pour out everything he couldn't yet say. Noah whimpered and went boneless in his arms.

It would have to do for now. *But when he gets back, all bets are off that night.*

As Noah sank back to his normal height, Logan coaxed him to turn around and gave him a far gentler kiss. Christian drank in the sight of them together— how they fit so beautifully, how Noah leaned into Logan with eagerness, and how Logan smiled when they broke apart. "Text me when you land?"

Noah nodded.

The three of them walked to the ticket area, Logan holding Noah's hand and Christian keeping a loose and affectionate grip on the back of Logan's neck. As Noah broke away from them to join the line, something made Christian linger, watching him.

"You think he'll look back?" Logan asked.

Before Christian could reply, Noah turned to them, grinning as he waved. Christian chuckled. "He's too much of a sap not to. I love that about him."

Logan turned his head quickly at that statement, but Christian wasn't sure he was ready to say anything more. Not yet. Time would tell.

Instead, Christian slung an arm around Logan's shoulders and steered him away. "I'm hungry. You're buying me lunch."

"Hey! I bought lunch last time!"

"Too bad, baby."

Logan melted at that title, like he always did, and he sent Christian a distinct look. *You know what you're doing when you say that,* he might as well have been saying.

Christian winked. *You should've known what you were getting into with me.*

About the Author

Suzanne is an asexual woman with a great love for writing erotic romance and enjoys spending her time confusing people with that fact. She believes there is a need for heightened diversity in fiction and strives to write enough stories so that everyone can see themselves mirrored in a protagonist. She lives with her spouse and cat, and, when not writing, Suzanne enjoys reading, playing video games poorly, and refusing to interact outdoors with other human beings.

Website: https://www.suzanneclay.com

Email: suzanneclaywriting@gmail.com

Facebook: www.facebook.com/suzanneclaywriting

Twitter:@suzanneclay_

Tumblr: www.suzanneclay.tumblr.com

Other books by this author

Chiaroscuro Series
Painting Class
Figure Study
Life Drawing

Rough Play Series
Playing Around

Playing For Keeps

Little by little, Christian dressed the tray. A bowl here. A glass there. Colorful fruit scattered in the bowl, followed by orange juice poured in the cup. He studied the effect, set a second glass on the tray, then swore faintly under his breath and shook his head.

It wasn't that he was particularly artistic—his talents as an actor certainly didn't lend themselves to beautiful arrangements—but he was practical. There was only so much room on the tray, and he had two men to feed breakfast to.

He still wasn't used to that.

Bread popped free of the toaster, and Christian seized it, adding it to the large plate in the middle. He buttered both slices all the way to the edges, a practiced act after the past few months, and followed it with a jar of jelly on the tray. It might not be elegant, but it was passable enough for a nineteen-year-old guy living in an apartment with minimal dishes.

Milk went into the second glass, but when he placed it next to the other and lifted the tray, it was unbalanced, and he set the tray down.

Jesus Christ, I can't even figure out how to feed my boyfriends?

Boyfriends. Two. Sweetness filled Christian's sleepy chest.

He wished he could give them the world. But sloppy fruit, overcooked toast, and soggy eggs would have to do the job.

It was only fair. This was their last day together, just the three of them. And he wanted to do something nice for the tousled boys still sleeping in his bed.

Christian rebalanced the tray, picked it up, and carried it down the hallway. He paused at the open bedroom door and leaned into the doorframe, studying the two heads poking out from under the covers. Logan, his wild curls tousled on his pillow, slept as peacefully as a baby, so deeply that a direct explosion might not even wake him. Noah, however, was a bit more restless, rolling over to curl up behind Logan and spoon him. The faint sunlight peeking in through the curtains made his freckles stick out on his pale skin.

They were both so damn beautiful. And he was looking forward to the opportunity to spoiling them a little more today.

Christian entered the room and set the tray on his nightstand. He sank onto the mattress and smirked when Noah groaned and peeked up at him.

"Morning, sleepyhead," Christian murmured.

Noah huffed and rubbed his eyes. "Does it have to be?"

"Yep. I can't put the sun away."

"I'm sure you could if you tried." Noah's lips quirked in a faint smile as he reached up and touched Christian's cheek. "You're dang talented."

Noah's fingers slid behind the base of Christian's head, tugging him down little by little until their mouths met in a soft kiss. Christian sucked in a slow, hungry breath and cupped Noah's face until he cradled it in both hands. The nervous, awkward kisses from June were gone now, replaced with a sleek ease and confidence as they parted their lips, welcomed each other in that much deeper.

It was absolutely exquisite—and completely unfair that Christian got to have this kind of rightness with *two* people, much less one.

"Pretty picture." Logan's rough voice suddenly lifted from the other side of Noah. "Should wake up to this more often."

Christian chuckled and pressed his lips to Noah's cheek affectionately before leaning over him to greet Logan as well. "You're supposed to still be asleep, baby."

"Am I?" Logan grinned and greedily pulled Christian in for one, two, three more kisses. "Maybe I sensed a nice way to begin the day, huh? You, between me and Noah..."

There was a knock at the door, as if specifically designed to torture Christian before Logan could finish seducing him.

"Leave it," Noah whispered, his hands running down Christian's bare sides to the thin pair of boxers he wore.

Christian laughed and pulled away. "You know, Logan, I think we might've finally corrupted this boy." He slapped away Noah's fingers, shooting him a cheeky look as he headed toward the hallway.

Interruptions were few and far between in this apartment complex. With how close it was to campus and how affordable the rates were, it was mostly populated by Fulton State college students, and since classes wouldn't start for another few days, not everyone had moved in yet. Christian wracked his brain to remember if he'd ordered a package or something as he padded on bare feet to the door and then opened it without checking through the peephole to see who it might be.

Daiki stood on the other side, three thick suitcases piled up on the ground behind him, and Christian's mind went completely blank.

"Whoa!" Daiki laughed, his dark eyes twinkling as he flicked them up and down Christian's body. "This the show you give all your visitors, Daniels? Goddamn."

"What the hell are you doing here?" Christian furrowed his brow and crossed his arms, instinctively trying to draw up another inch even though he already towered over Daiki. "Y-You're not supposed to be here until tomo—"

"Daiki!" Noah's voice cracked shrilly from behind Christian. Knowing better, Christian drew aside just before Noah raced through the space he previously occupied and flung himself at Daiki. "Oh my God!"

"Sweetie, hey, hold on!" Daiki's amusement echoed through the complex as he stumbled backward, then finally caught himself before he could topple his suitcases open. He clung to Noah without shame and welcomed him into a kiss so hungry it made Christian turn his eyes away. Noah groaned against Daiki, the force of his enthusiasm driving Noah's back against the doorframe.

In front of the whole damn world? Really? His thoughts filling with sourness, Christian stepped back into the apartment, where he caught Logan's startled gaze from the bedroom door. They made eye contact for a long moment after which Christian shrugged helplessly.

Logan stepped in, touching Christian's arm lightly and comfortingly when he passed him. "You two coming up for air any time soon?"

Both Daiki and Noah chuckled, and when Christian glanced their way once more, he saw with relief that they'd finally broken a little more apart. He understood it. He really did. Even before he and Logan realized they'd been in love with each other since they were children, a week without seeing him could drive Christian to acting completely ridiculous the next time they met. And Noah and Daiki, who'd been dating for a whole half year longer than Noah, Christian, and Logan had been in a relationship? Who'd been apart for the whole damn summer? They clearly ached for each other.

Christian just selfishly wished it hadn't gotten in the way of his own plans.

"What's up, Logan?" Daiki chirped happily, reaching out to shake his hand.

"That's all you're giving me?" Logan snorted and came in for a hug, wrapping his arms around *both* Daiki and Noah.

Christian recognized what he was doing—breaking through any lingering awkwardness about their connection to each other. It was downright necessary, wasn't it? Daiki had been kind enough to give both Logan and Christian permission to pursue Noah while Daiki was gone for the summer, but the four of them had never really *talked* about what it would look like or if Daiki had any lingering reservations. The relationship between the three of them was still developing, still fragile.

It wouldn't take much for Daiki to destroy it if he wanted to.

Stop it. Christian maintained his distance, arms still crossed. While Logan was being a welcoming red carpet, Christian was a wall Daiki was going to have to fight to get through. He knew it was childish, but he couldn't help it.

"What happened to flying in tomorrow, dude?" Logan asked. "We were all set to pick you up and everything."

Daiki shrugged. He petted through Noah's hair, finally managing to bring them both inside. "I've never seen a plan I didn't wanna change. You should know that by now."

His gaze wandered to Christian's, and they watched each other. Irritation swelled up within Christian's chest, pressing against his ribs until they threatened to crack. Daiki's eyes glimmered in clear amusement as he stepped away from Noah and tipped his head back.

"Still ugly as ever, I see, Christian."

More than aware of his boyfriends studying this exchange, Christian didn't say anything at all. His lips thinned as he moved past all of them to grab Daiki's suitcases and bring them inside.

"Good to see you too." The comment was quiet, barely whispered at all, but it pricked at Christian's ears, and he forced himself to keep moving forward and set the bags in Noah's room. He took a certain degree of pleasure in how one of Logan's shirts was balled up on the floor, in how many condom wrappers filled the trash can by Noah's bedside. The unfamiliar territorial nature raked through him, head to toe, and left a strange tingling delight in his scalp.

Half of him wanted to drag Daiki in there, so he could see exactly how much of Noah belonged to the both of them.

The other half was terrified by the impulse.

He made himself emerge, even kept his arms by his side rather than locking them over his chest once more. Daiki had his phone out, his temple touching Noah's in a tender way as the two of them studied the screen.

"That's amazing," Noah breathed. "Look at you go!"

"It's not a big deal." Daiki pushed his sleek black bangs away from his eyes. "It's, you know, everybody's working their ass off out there, not just me."

Noah scoffed, and he shook his head. "Yeah, okay, I see them, they're awesome, but it doesn't change the fact that you were blowing up the stage. I've never seen you dance so well before."

Christian's responses came like flashes of lightning from the sky, searing his bones and rattling his heart. The competitiveness was desperately familiar. Yes, Christian had spent the summer performing in a play of his own—the first he'd auditioned for in years, the first he was *proud* of given how hard he'd fought to be in it—but Daiki had been practically begged to return home to his local playhouse to lead their musical. Christian knew the rich, painful desire to bare his teeth and puff his shoulders and reclaim his place as someone *exceptional*, rather than a person Daiki could stand above.

What Christian wasn't used to was the utter *fear* coursing through his veins.

He let himself leave, finally, going to the bedroom to pick up the forgotten tray of breakfast. It might be eaten, and it might not, but it was cold as hell now, and he figured he might as well rewarm it. But as he carried it past the other three, Daiki reached out and stole a piece of toast, and Christian froze, staring at him.

Daiki quirked a brow. "What?" He grinned. "Is this only for guys you're sleeping with?"

He saw red, a bull preparing to charge—and Logan scooped the food right out of his hands. "You've gotta be hungry after that flight, Daiki," Logan went on, light and breezy, blowing some of the flames out in Christian's head.

"Oh!" Noah grabbed Daiki by the hand and dragged him toward the kitchen. "Come on, I'll make you something so you can eat with us!"

But there would be no peaceful breakfast scene, and Christian knew that well enough. Not when he was about to burst out of his skin with frustration. His plans had fallen away. His dreams of whisking Logan and Noah out of the apartment, maybe to the park or to get ice cream in the sweltering heat of Georgia summer, evaporated into steam. He locked a hand around Logan's elbow, cupping it, and tilted his head toward the bedroom. "Hell, listen. Let Logan and me get out of your hair, all right? Y'all go ahead and catch up with each other."

Both Daiki and Noah paused, and Daiki wrinkled his brow. "What?"

"It's better that way." Christian waved over his shoulder as he guided Logan away. "It's been a while. I know y'all missed each other."

"But I—" Whatever Daiki had to say was cut off the moment Christian shut the bedroom door behind him and Logan.

Christian leaned against the door and took deep, slow, cleansing breaths.

Logan snorted. "Nice." His cool palm found Christian's heated face. "About a year ago you would've kicked the shit out of him."

Christian rolled his eyes. "I pretty much *did* do that last year. Surprised you don't remember. At least this time, he learned how to knock."

Logan laughed as he pulled away and went to get dressed. Christian took a little longer.

The first time he'd ever seen Daiki, Logan was pinned under Christian. Daiki had opened their dorm door, and the scene had given him quite the wrong idea—Christian and Logan had only been *friends* then. But now the idea was *right*, and Daiki still had the shittiest timing in the world.

By the time Christian made his way to the closet and pulled a shirt on, Logan was waiting to wrap his arms around him from behind.

"Be cool. If I didn't know any better, I'd say the guy missed us."

"The hell are you smoking?" Christian lightly elbowed Logan away, playful, but gave him a kiss on the forehead as he passed him to grab jeans off the floor. "He spent all summer being an asshole about shit."

"Teasing you, you mean? About Noah? About me?"

"Yeah?" Christian shot him a look.

Logan's expression wasn't one he expected—but they'd been friends for thirteen years now, before they even started dating a half a year ago. Logan's faces were chronicled in Christian's memory. This one was exasperation. "*Teasing* ain't picking a fight, baby. You should know. We've been teasing each other since we were six."

"It's different with us." Christian hugged Logan tight and nuzzled his hair. "Things have *always* been different with us."

Logan hugged him back with a sigh. "Yeah. Yeah, they have."

"There's something you're not saying. I can hear it."

Logan patted his back. "Yeah, well, you ain't ready to. C'mon. Let's go out, get some breakfast. Give them some alone time."

The way Logan took Christian's hand and interlaced their fingers did wonders for his thudding, confused heart. Logan didn't play his cards close to his chest very often, but when he did, neither hell nor high water would make him break his silence until he was ready. But at least he wasn't pulling away and forcing Christian to deal with his shit alone.

Hand in hand, they walked down the hall. Christian spared a glance toward the kitchen, already opening his mouth to say goodbye to Noah—to see if whatever Logan had been hinting at was written on Daiki's face—but it became clear he shouldn't even bother.

Noah and Daiki were buried in each other's arms, Noah's spine pressed into the counter, Daiki's shirt gathered in passionate and needy fistfuls as they kissed the life out of each other.

For just a moment too long, Christian stared. And then he let it go and followed Logan straight out the door without a word.

Also Available from NineStar Press

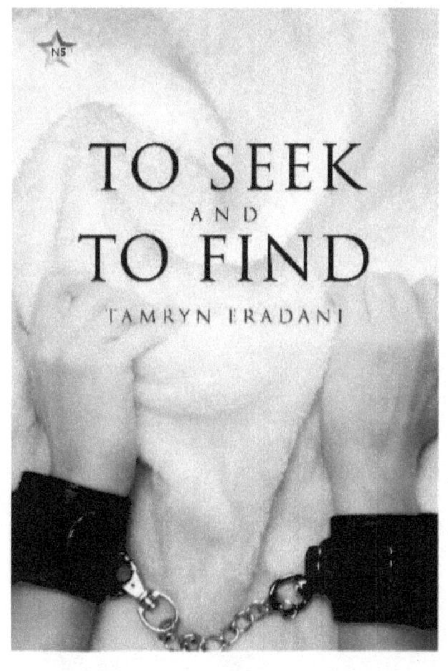

Connect with NineStar Press

www.ninestarpress.com

www.facebook.com/ninestarpress

www.facebook.com/groups/NineStarNiche

www.twitter.com/ninestarpress

www.tumblr.com/blog/ninestarpress

www.ingramcontent.com/pod-product-compliance
Lightning Source LLC
Chambersburg PA
CBHW032208180726

48284CB00001B/238